PINEHURST

BOOK THREE

HADES' CURSE

A NOVEL BY: NICOLE GRANE

Nicole Grane

PINEHURST BOOK 3

HADES' CURSE

Redwood House Books

Printed in the United States of America
Charleston, South Carolina

ISBN-13: 9798834585268

Nicole Grane

OTHER BOOKS BY NICOLE GRANE

Immortal Wounds

Pinehurst

Tokens from Juliet

Pinehurst Book 2: The Search for the Oracle

Immortal Bound

UPCOMING

Pinehurst Book 4: The Fight for Mount Olympus

Nicole Grane

DEDICATION

This book is a personal triumph for me and a testament of my children's love and support. Without them, this book would still not be written.

First and foremost, this book is dedicated to all of my beloved readers who have waited longer than anyone should have to wait for a sequel. You have understood and stuck with me these many years. I will never forget the kindness, support, and continual encouragement that I was given. I truly love each and every one of you!

Secondly, to my dear cousin Marie, who has waited these many years for me to finish because she had to know what Havoc was up to. Happy 96th Birthday! Hang in there . . . Book 4 is just around the corner!

Nicole Grane

LIST OF SPELLS

Aperto: open
Acqua: water
Aeras: air
Anemos: wind
Chioni: snow
Elafry: light
Floga: flame
Fotio: freeze
Imobla: immobilize
Inabilitara: to incapacitate
Megalonoun: grow
Pagoma: petrify
Pagos: ice
Petra: stone
Proothó: propel

Nicole Grane

x

TABLE OF CONTENTS

Chapter 1

Antonio had already made the long climb to Mount Olympus. He hadn't wanted to leave Iris on her own to figure out the cure for Evie's father, but it was necessary. Evie had been gone for nearly three hours—something that had never happened before. Time had always seemed to stop when she was whisked into Hell; for him to actually experience the passing of it, with no sign of her, he didn't want to consider the reasons why. His heart constricted every time she disappeared. If minutes were seconds, then hours surely were days for her. Days that were most likely filled with fear and pain.

Hades had taken Evie at a most inopportune moment—like there was ever a good moment. They had been so close to making love that his body still ached from the touch of her. He'd wanted to . . . oh how he'd wanted to . . . but she wasn't ready, and deep down he'd known that. With her world crumbling around her, Evie managed to think of others. Her father, sick and dying, was counting on her to cure him; and she'd rather condemn herself to a lifetime of literal hell than fail him.

Never had Antonio met such a shining soul. Evie had sacrificed so much of herself for him as well, and *he* would not fail *her*. Somehow, he would get her back. Even if it meant challenging the Lord of the Underworld himself.

Antonio pushed his legs to move faster, running at a speed that would surely rival a wild horse. Where he got the strength, he did not know. His feet, although he could not see them, moved seamlessly through the cloud-like terrain.

He slowed to a stop as his eyes scanned his surroundings, searching for any signs of life. "Father!" he yelled out to the heavens. "It is Antonio, Son of Amara, I beg an audience with you!" His request, less forceful than before, was meant to appear humble. He needed Zeus' help and he'd grovel to get it.

The sky echoed with thunder. Zeus appeared, inches away from him—already opening his arms. "My son."

"Father, help me." The words came out sounding as defeated as Antonio looked.

"You need not beg my son. Ask it, and it shall be yours." Zeus held Antonio to his chest, his strong body giving him the support he needed to remain standing.

"My Evie. She has not returned from Hell. I fear Hades is keeping her."

Zeus pulled back and looked at him. His hands still rested on Antonio's shoulders, as if stealing him for what he was about to say: "Hades does not have your Evie, he announced. "I do."

Relief washed over Antonio like a giant wave. He crumpled to his knees, thanking God in silent prayer. "Where is she," he asked, tears of joy filling his eyes.

Zeus was not smiling. "She is in my temple . . . awaiting death."

"Damn that Antonio . . . summoning the stairs to Mount Olympus. Freaks me out every time!" Havoc paced back and forth beside Iris. "No one should be that close to Heaven—yuck!"

Chaos shuddered from his chair. He didn't like the fact that he and Havoc were associating with such angelic beings. Mageians, as a rule, were to heavenly for a demon like himself to consort with. Why Havoc continued to help these creatures—without what he deemed acceptable trades—was beyond him; but, he would say nothing.

Chaos loved Havoc. An emotion he was not familiar with. He hadn't told her yet, and he didn't plan to. Havoc was a free spirit—more so than any other pixie he had ever known. It was what pulled him to her, like a moth to a flame. He couldn't imagine she'd like being bound to anyone for all eternity . . . and that is exactly what would happen if they ever made, what the Mageians referred to, as love. Pixies mated for life.

"Chaos, did you hear what I said?!" Havoc, in all her glorious beauty, was standing before him. Her hands were clenched into tight fists and were perched on her delicate hips. She wore a fitted mini-skirt, hot pink—his new favorite color, and a black shirt that was cropped just above the cutest belly button he'd ever seen. Her legs, long and slender, were supported by black stiletto heels—bless the one Havoc referred to as "*Barbie*", for generously clothing his woman.

"Yes, My Lady?" A harmless endearment, but nonetheless sweet. By the look on Havoc's face, she'd forgotten for a moment what she'd been clearly mad about and Chaos couldn't help but smile inwardly at that.

"*Iris* needs water from a bubbling spring of all places . . . where in the world are we supposed to get that?"

Chaos smiled confidently. "My Sweet. Are we not surrounded by mountains? Surely if we follow a stream upward, we will find its beginning. Hence, the spring."

"Brilliant!" Iris exclaimed, causing Chaos to cringe. The girl's excitement at times was more than he could stand. "The two of you go. I'll head into the kitchen and begin assembling the ingredients. Oh, I'll need a pomegranate too," she added as she rose to her feet. "The book here says that the juice, blended with the spring water, heated to boiling, will create the steam needed before I place the Manna-Ash blossom into the pot. Only *then* will the petals secrete the oils that are needed for Mr. Hollyander's cure."

Chaos noted how in awe, Iris looked as she observed the purple and white flower Antonio had placed into her hands hours ago. The delicate blossom needed constant contact with something living in order to remain alive—she hadn't dared to put it down. He didn't know how she remained so calm. Not only had she accepted Antonio's parentage as if this sort of thing was common in her world, but she pressed on with her task of saving the Guardian's life with controlled determination. He almost admired her. Almost.

Havoc stared at Iris wide-eyed. "A pomegranate?" she questioned dryly. "Really?"

"Yes, please."

Havoc scoffed dramatically, but Chaos knew his woman would not tell Iris no. For some reason she liked the girl, and Chaos would not ever take away a "friend" from his love, she had so few. And truth be told, it was his fault.

"Fine. But, I sure hope the Child of Light appreciates what we do for her!" Havoc pointed her tiny manicured finger at Iris. "And she better be prepared to part with that sapphire ring of hers. This errand running isn't cheap, you know!" She grabbed hold of Chaos's hand abruptly and the two of them disappeared.

"Death?" Surely Antonio had misheard.

"I warned her," Zeus spoke from above him. His words, cold as ice, rained down upon Antonio like sharp knives chipping at his skin.

"What do you mean, you 'warned her?'" Antonio rose from the ground, his shoulders, squared with Zeus'.

"While she slept at your side, I visited her. I gave her the same choice that I had explained to you: if she did not bed you before Hades, I would come for her."

"You threatened her? I told you she is innocent. She is not ready for physical love!"

"*You* seemed to think she was ready," Zeus countered. His knowing expression made his son blush.

"You will not watch us! I will not have you look upon her when she is indisposed." Antonio could feel his blood boil at the thought.

"I have already seen her naked body . . . a sight to behold I must say. I can see why you wish to bed her."

Antonio gnashed his teeth together. His staff was in his hand, the blades extended and ready for battle. "Are you saying you would take her as your bride?"

Zeus laughed without humor. "If only it were that simple. Come with me now." He extended his arm to his son. "I will take you to her."

With eyebrows drawn together, Antonio took the offered arm and was transported to what could be none other than Zeus' private temple. He stared in awe at the massive white marble pillars that stretched high to a vaulted ceiling. Its brilliant mosaics depicted heavenly beings that Antonio had only dreamed about. Statues of gods he did not know existed, were staggered throughout, giving a far more celestial feel than he'd expected.

His heart stopped. There, in the center of the room, was an altar. His Evie lay upon it, her red curls falling down around her.

Antonio ran to her without hesitation. Only then, when he'd reached her, did he notice she was asleep. He touched her neck to be sure . . . there was still a heartbeat, her pulse fluttering strong beneath his fingertips.

"Why is she covered in this cloth?" Antonio moved to lift the sheet then paused. He closed his eyes a moment, shaking the thought away. No, surely she was not—

"I believed you would prefer that I had her covered," Zeus said. "Or would you rather I remove it, so that all may look upon her naked body?"

Antonio spun on his heel, his eyes tight with fury. "Why . . . is . . . she . . . naked?" The words came snarled.

"Do not falsely accuse me!" Zeus thundered. "This is how I found her when I snatched her from Hades' bed. He lay atop her in his own skin, no clothing between them. He meant to sway her then. Had I not stolen her . . ."

Zeus didn't need to finish. Antonio took in a deep breath, trying to assemble what patience he had left. "Did he . . .?" Antonio wanted to vomit. The idea of his Evie . . . his sweet, innocent Evie, being taken by such a beast was unthinkable. Hades would die by his hand if he touched her in that way.

"I do not believe so," Zeus answered. "Although, I cannot be sure."

The grimness of the implication twisted the sword-like thought into Antonio's heart all the tighter. He could hardly breathe.

"The Child of Light must willingly give herself to Hades. That was the bargain. Only then will he have the power he craves to take Mount Olympus. I have not sensed he possesses that power." The word *yet* hung heavy in the air. "That does not mean, my son, that he has not taken her by force, simply to have her. He is a man with needs, and he grows tired of waiting for her."

Antonio's hands were clenched into tight fists at his side. He looked back at his sleeping Evie. "Wake her. I need answers."

"Her answers are moot," Zeus declared. "You did not see the way she responded to his touch. You did not see the compassion in her eyes. She was naked in his bed, my son . . . clearly she has made her choice."

Antonio was covering his ears, trying to block the words from entering his head. He wouldn't listen. He would not believe Evie had chosen Hades. He roared out in frustration: "Wake her!"

"So be it." Zeus waved a hand in Evie's direction. She gasped, choking on her last breath—as if the very life had been strangled from her lungs—which Antonio believed that it had. Zeus would pay for that. Evie was *his* and no one would harm her.

I sucked in air, desperately gasping as it forced its way into my lungs.

"Evie!"

My eyes shot open. Antonio . . . in Hell . . .? No, he couldn't be here. I jumped upright, trying to see through my fog, glimpsing faint shapes and a silhouette. "Antonio?"

I was suddenly wrapped—enveloped from shoulder to toe in a silken cloth; covering my—

"I'm naked!" I snatched at the offered sheet, pulling it tight as I clumsily stumbled off some sort of table. "Why am I naked?!"

"Evie, I—"

My other hand involuntarily sought my neck, my attention diverted from a panicked Antonio to a scowling Zeus, not five feet away; and I remembered. I staggered back, pointing a shaky finger. "Y . . . you attacked me."

Zeus' voice boomed with unrepentant clarity, "You had been warned."

"Warned?" How dare he! "You *choked* me for no reason . . . there was no warning!" At least I was pretty sure he had. I hadn't technically *seen* him. But, no one else could have plucked me out of Hades' domain like that and brought me—where in the hell . . .?

My eyes darted around my surroundings, all-the-while keeping Zeus in my peripheral. I was standing in a room, brilliant in gold and pearl—adorned with angelic stone figures and intricate mosaics of what looked to be heavenly beings; unlike any I could have ever imagined.

"You are in my temple," Zeus answered my unspoken question as I stared up in awe at marble pillars, stretching up like giants into a swirling cloud-like sky; that emanated bright oranges and yellow hues touched by pink. I half expected angels to fly by at any moment—though this was clearly not Heaven—Zeus was here. His hard, unfeeling eyes had not stopped boring into me.

I found myself slowly moving away from the altar. Altar . . .? I looked back and forth from Zeus to the "table" I'd been laying on. There was no mistaking what it was: white and marbled, and set higher than any ordinary table. I freaked and blurted the first thing that came to mind: "You were going to sacrifice me!"

The creep didn't even blink at his admission. "You have grown far too close to Hades."

"What?" I couldn't believe it.

I looked Antonio's way for help. He was staring at his father, moisture glistening in his eyes. He said nothing.

"So it's true then?"

No wonder Antonio looked so anguished—and guilty! His father had been about to off me and he'd known it.

"And you were going to just let him?"

"No!"

"How could you?" I jerked away as he reached for me, my hand outstretched, demanding he stay where he was. "I thought you loved me."

"I do!"

"You have no right to do this!" I yelled at the both of them. Mentally stammering for a zinger of a spell to come to mind that would cause Zeus' lightning bolt to spontaneously begin zapping the hell out of the both of them. "I didn't do anything wrong. Why am I being punished?"

Before I could react, Antonio had gathered me up in his arms and began kissing my face and lips repeatedly, joyously. "I knew you hadn't given yourself to Hades."

"What?"

His kisses continued like a relentless rain upon my face. "I knew you were still mine."

"What are you talking about?" I pulled back with all my strength—just missing the next barrage of his excitement.

He froze mid-pucker.

I stared at him in disbelief. "You thought Hades and me . . .?"

Instant shame coated his face.

"*Un-believable.*"

He released his hold, slowly.

I glared over at Zeus. The God had absolutely no boundaries—or qualms when it came to spreading rumors he knew nothing about. No wonder Antonio had been so grief stricken . . . he'd thought I'd chosen his uncle over him. An idea no doubt planted by his loving father.

I shook my head in disgust. Zeus, was every bit the jerk I'd thought he was; yet Antonio was no "angel" in this . . . he'd been all too accepting of my quote unquote guilt!

"Evie, I'm sorry. I should have known. I should have—"

"Yes, you should have," I interrupted sharply, causing him to halt.

There was so much more I felt like saying: like how could he think I'd do that to him, for one? But, I didn't. If there was anything I'd learned since all this mess began, was that time was precious. I wasn't going to waste what little of it I had arguing with Antonio about where my heart was. I thought he'd known, but apparently he needed a reminder.

"Antonio . . . I love *you* . . . *you're* the one I want."

And just like that, his smile lit up his entire being. That was all he'd needed to hear. He pulled me into his arms once again and crushed his lips to mine, kissing me with all that he had—igniting the little bit of my soul that was left.

"I knew the Heavens would not be so cruel as to take you from me." His beautiful words whispered across my ear like a song and touched my heart, making me forget how angry I had been with him; and I loved him all the more for it.

I could feel the blood rushing to my cheeks, turning them scarlet, as he took in a long ragged breath to steady himself. The hot heat of his exhale against my neck was enough to make my legs actually wobble.

Evie . . .

I closed my eyes, daring to imagine what sweet nothings Antonio, would utter next.

He cleared his throat . . . *we're not alone.*

The silent reminder made my eyes pop open, my blood still, and my cheeks go from warm to flaming in a millisecond.

Zeus's eyes were on me. Watching with cold calculation. He wasn't at all touched by his son's loving show of affection, or my self-proclaimed "innocence." He was clearly not buying any of this.

I managed to shrink behind Antonio slightly, using him as a shield. I didn't want his *dad* anywhere near me.

Antonio's grip on my hand tightened. He could feel Zeus' distaste as much as I could, and although he would never admit it, it frightened him. "I'll be taking Evie home now."

Zeus stepped closer, his focus solely on me—as if Antonio weren't even there. And for all intents and purposes, it didn't matter that he was. Zeus' body towered over us like a mountainous threat. He could crush me in an instant if he wanted . . . and the creep basked in the knowledge that I knew it.

"I will permit you the time I gave Child of Light, but know this: If after the Guardian is cured and Hades still has the means to keep you, I *will* make good on my promise."

"Father!"

"I will not allow you to aid Hades in taking what is mine, nor will I allow you to destroy all of this world and the Heavens!"

I jumped as the sky cracked and echoed ominous thunder overhead, as if cementing his words.

"There will be no need," Antonio growled, though his voice was a little less confident than before. "Hades, will not be taking Evie."

Yeah right. There was no way Hades was giving me up—not after my father was cured—not ever. I was as good as dead now and Zeus knew I knew it.

The god grinned. "We shall see."

Zeus waved his hand, transporting Antonio and I back to his room—to his bed to be exact—the both of us, naked.

Chapter 2

Sweet Deity! Antonio shrieked mentally. He was just as taken aback. His eyes grew wide as he realized he was naked too—he was also on top of me; apparently Zeus felt we needed a little push.

"Antonio, I . . ."

He was shaking his head at me, mercifully halting whatever words I was grasping at to say. I was at a total loss. This was the second time that I'd been placed unwittingly in a man's bed, and I couldn't help but feel the flush of embarrassment consuming me all over.

"Evie, I'm so sorry. I didn't mean for him to—I had no idea! I would never . . . please believe me!"

"Of course I do!" I assured; although my "assurance" didn't alleviate the awkwardness of the situation.

I knew Antonio wasn't responsible for our current predicament. He didn't have to say it, but that was how he was. Above all else, my sense of security mattered most to him. It was one of the reasons I fell in love with him; and it was the main reason he made me feel so safe. I couldn't ask for anyone more thoughtful.

"Evie."

I smiled up at him adoringly. "Yes?"

"There is no gingerly way for me to move without . . . um . . . *bumping* . . . something of yours."

I could have just died. Would it have killed him this one time to *not* be so thoughtful? To *not* point out the obvious? Like he was doing me a favor by warning me? I was already acutely aware of the dilemma—who wouldn't be?! We couldn't be any closer, well, perhaps a little more closer, but we certainly couldn't be any more naked then we were. Of course things were going to be bumped. He didn't need to highlight it! Voicing it aloud only made it that much more mentally uncomfortable then it already was. I didn't see a delicate way out of this close embrace either. The moment either one of us made a move, body parts being bumped would be the least of our worries. Body parts would be exposed!

"I'm sorry, I'm sorry!" Antonio's face was turning redder by the minute. He'd been no doubt listening to my inner panic.

We'd had some close moments before, but we had never been *this* close. It clearly surprised the both of us.

"Look, don't worry. Nothing has to get bumped. I'll jump up real fast . . . we could close our eyes and on the count of three—"

"Oh *please*, Son of Zeus."

"Havoc!" If Antonio hadn't still been on top of me I'd have bolted out of my skin.

"That is the singular most stupidest thing I have ever heard of. Like you're really going to keep your eyes shut. Please." The tiny pixie was sitting on the pillow beside us, scoffing dramatically. Actually, she was reclined, leaning her back against the headboard with her legs outstretched in front of her, crisscrossed at the ankles— the picture of relaxation. She even had a small sack of popcorn! She noisily crunched on a piece. "Bite?"

"No!" Antonio and I both snapped in unison.

" . . . And I too would have kept my eyes shut." Antonio pulled the sheet tighter around us.

Havoc raised a skeptical brow. "Seriously? You're sticking with that story?"

"Yes!"

This was so embarrassing. Havoc had a way of making everything sordid. Not that this wasn't sordid, but it wasn't our fault.

"You know," she went on, completely unaffected—munching away—as if the two of us weren't laying there naked beside her— embarrassed beyond belief. " . . . If you two were just a tad less uptight and grouchy, these tender moments might be a *little more* exciting, if you know what I mean?" Her eyebrows wiggled up and down. "This is the root of your whole problem you know."

"Havoc." I'd been wrong before. So wrong. *Now* was the point where I could just die. Sex advice from Havoc—in front of Antonio? This wasn't happening.

This is not happening . . . Antonio was silently pleading. He too was wishing for the universe to swallow him whole.

"What?" Havoc popped in another bite. "I'm just making an observation. Why do the two of you look as if you've just seen Medusa? You should be thanking me for pointing this out. I'm saving you years of anguish. Humans pay big money for this sort of advice." She leaned in closer. "According to an article I was reading in one of

Iris's magazines last week on *Sure Fire Ways to Obliterate Your Love Life*, you two are clearly on the fast track to relationship destruction. We're talking a four-alarm emergency. You need to spice it up, and quick. I recommend—"

"This *isn't* a 'spicy' moment!" Antonio snapped. He'd had enough.

Havoc narrowed her sights from disapproving to utter disdain in a fraction of a millisecond. She did not like being shouted at. Ever. "Not with *that* tone of voice it isn't."

Antonio, hung his head in defeat. The pixie was a head trip of a force to be reckoned with on a good day. Today was not that day. Not even a god would have the strength to logically combat her. How Havoc hadn't managed to have taken over kingdoms by now, simply talking the rulers to death, I'd never know. Antonio was wise to give up.

"You might want to dump this one Evie," She was still glaring at Antonio. "He's crabby. Very unattractive. It's no wonder you two haven't been intimate. Although, what else would you expect from a sky god. They're notorious for being unsatisfying lovers you know. After all, his father—"

"Havoc, just go!" Now was not the time for one of her bashing on Antonio sessions. And my "tender moment" as she referred to it, was not a public event. " . . . You're spilling popcorn all over!"

"Fine." She got up reluctantly, scoffing, acting all put out— like I was the one being rude! *"I'll go.* I'm not one to stay where I'm not wanted."

"Since when?"

If looks could kill I'd have been incinerated on the spot; and then something caught her eye. She grinned. That wicked smirk that brought instant panic to anyone that remotely knew her. She tilted her head slightly, smiling a smile that would rival the *Cheshire Cat's*.

I followed her stare. Oh no.

She winked. "Scrumptious backside Antonio." Then smacked him on the ass and disappeared.

"Please tell me that didn't just happen." Antonio hadn't even looked up. I think if he could have vanished into nothingness right then and there he would have.

I was too mortified to answer. I too was waiting for the sweet kiss of death to take me. Really? She had to comment on his butt? His *naked* butt, that she could clearly define through the bedsheet. And not just comment, she had to slap it?! I was boiling. I swear Havoc did crap like this to torture me. Her goal in life had to be either pissing me off or utterly humiliating me. There was no in between. I half expected her to pop back in with a soda and *dippin-dots* to finish the "show." I could never begin to apologize to Antonio for this.

"Hey," Antonio nudged his nose to mine, forcing me to meet his stare. He smiled sympathetically. "No one, and I mean no one, is responsible for *that*." He gestured to where Havoc had been; only a pile of buttery crumbs remained in her wake. "Besides, I'm the one being sorry here, remember? We wouldn't be in this situation if my father hadn't tucked us in bed together in the first place. You don't need to apologize to me for anything Evie, especially Havoc."

Antonio knew that I had about as much control over the pixie-menace as he did Zeus, and he wasn't about to let me beat myself up over her.

Still, I wasn't comforted. For some reason, I felt totally responsible for Havoc's behavior at all times. It was so unfair. Iris was the one who took her in, yet I was forever stuck with her—and her insults. And her bad timing. *And* her unbelievably tacky comments that constantly made me look like a boob! The list went on and on.

"You're right," I finally agreed. "Let's focus on your sorrow."

Antonio couldn't hold back his laugh. He knew me all too well. He knew I wanted the subject changed or better, forgotten. After all, we had a slightly more pressing matter to attend to.

"Agreed." And just like that he whisked himself up and out of the bed—no bumping; taking the sheet with him and leaving me the comforter.

"How did you—?"

"Demigod magic." He bragged like he'd just been voted *Mr. Universe* for the umpteenth time. I'd swear he was flexing his chest on purpose. ". . . Sorry, it's a gift. It can't be taught."

I chucked a pillow at his smug face, nailing it spot on; he hadn't even seen it coming. "That's also a gift."

His laughter touched his eyes before fading into one of those thoughtful smiles that caught my breath. It was moments like these, when he looked at me like this, that reminded me that he was truly angelic. Yet, there was something so uncharacteristically wild about Antonio just then. His hair was disheveled, hanging loosely around his face, softening his features. But, it did little to hide the desire that sparked in his eyes when he looked at me. Nothing could quite mask that.

"You are truly beautiful."

Now it was my turn to blush. He had said those very words to me right before Hades had whisked me to his world last. When he and I had just agreed to wait until my father was cured before entering into a physical relationship. We'd decided that our lives didn't need another complication. We needed to stay focused. We weren't going to be rushed into anything for fear of Zeus' wrath or Hades' curse. Antonio had understood that I didn't want our first time together to be determined by others—or any time for that matter. The decision was ours; and Antonio hadn't hesitated for a moment to tell me that he wouldn't have it any other way.

And I still wouldn't.

That something in his eyes . . . that something that made my heart jolt sideways as though it were going to explode was back. Could he be any more perfect?

"For you . . ." he leaned over and gently placed his lips to mine. ". . . I shall always strive."

And that ladies and gentlemen, topped any sappy romance line I had ever heard—or could ever hope to hear.

Antonio pulled on his pants and shirt in record time. My guess, the sooner he was clothed the better.

"You guessed correctly," he winked, then glanced around the floor a moment, appearing confused. "Uh, wait here. I'll go to your room and bring you back some clothes . . . yours seem to have disappeared?"

"What? They were right beside the bed," last I remembered before Hades summoned me. I frowned as I looked over to the floor as well, searching. I'd bet my life *Zeus* had something to do with this too!

Antonio was already shaking his head, but he said nothing as he slipped out the door. He knew his father had no shame.

I snuggled into the bedding, smiling like a loon. Replaying every beautiful word Antonio had just said to me, over and over again—wishing I could freeze this moment forever.

"Not so *betrothed* after all?"

I bolted upright—propelled from my blissful state. It took only a fraction of a second for the icy air to engulf me, causing goosebumps to break out cold and hard all over my body. I pulled the blanket tighter, but it did nothing to warm my skin. I scanned the room. I couldn't see him, but I knew he was there.

Nightmares' chilling laugh came from beside me.

I jumped.

"Hades would find this information *most* valuable."

My blood stilled. He was going to tell Hades about Antonio and me. I couldn't let him. I couldn't stop him either. The demon remained invisible.

"What do you want?" I tried to appear indifferent. Like I was some hoity-toity queen and this tawdry subject wasn't worth anyone's time or concern—especially Hades'. Being naked and hiding under a blanket didn't give me the confident persona I was aiming for. The fact that I could feel him through the material as though it were paper thin, wasn't very reassuring either. I only hoped he couldn't see through it.

"You." And just like that, the demon materialized, capturing my wrists above my head as he straddled me. I could hardly move.

"Get off!" I grunted from under his weight, struggling with all my might. "Haven't you ever heard of personal space?"

Why was he so stinking heavy . . . wasn't he like a ghost or something? . . . And what the hell happened to him? His looks had done a total 180.

"I see you've noticed my . . . *transformation*." The jerk was smirking. The kind of smirk totally hot guys gave when they knew that they were totally hot.

Of course I noticed his *"transformation,"* I wasn't dead! Up close and personal like this, who wouldn't? I could only hope that I wasn't gawking too much; though judging by the shit-eating grin plastered to his face, I knew that I was.

He was oddly cherub-like now. His glacier-blue eyes were no longer demon-red. His white skin—no doubt from the lack of sun—accented his slightly shaggy, dirty-blond, run-way model-like hair impeccably; highlighting the streaks of brown that ran through it. As for his body . . . when in the hell did demons have time to work out? He was just, if not more buff, than Antonio. He looked like a freaking movie star/bodybuilder/minor god who could almost give Hades a run for his money. Almost. I had to remind myself that dream boy here was a demon, through and through. The Kewpie-doll expression he wore didn't fool me. This makeover he was now rockin' made him a hundred times more dangerous in my book.

"If you are done admiring . . .?"

My mouth gaped open. "Yuck, disgusting. I am so not admiring you." A total lie, but how dare he!

His hands gripped my wrists, clutching them all the tighter as he let his body press fully to mine; the instant pain from his icy weight was crushing. "As I said," he gritted huskily, ". . . you have something I desperately need." He was looking down on me, his eyes unexpectedly lingering at my lips. Then out of nowhere: "You truly are the closest thing to Heaven I have ever beheld." His eyes locked with mine.

Oh hell no! I knew that creepy look. Roland and Chad had sported it on more than one unpleasant occasion when I caught them ogling me—clearly having one of their cringy male fantasies that I had no desire in ever being a part of; and Nightmares was last on my list of possible lovers . . . or any other weird association he was attempting to orchestrate.

"Get off me, now!" I snapped at him with as much authority as I could muster. I couldn't budge him in the slightest. My feeble attempts to throw him only managed to annoy him all the more.

He'd lowered his face closer to mine, his icy breath assaulting my eyes, drying and freezing them as though I were outside in a blizzard. I could hardly blink let alone look away.

"As I have said," he repeated with a little less patience, " . . . you have something that I desperately need." He looked like a cat that had just pinned his mouse. This "dance" we were playing was sheer amusement for him.

My heart pounded wildly. He had me at check-mate and he knew it. Hell, he could probably taste my fear in the air.

"This isn't a very nice way to ask for a favor," I growled through my teeth, trying to sound brave.

The bastard actually chuckled. "*You* are the key to the gates of Hell."

I froze. I could feel all the color drain from my face. His words blew across my soul, chilling me through to the bone—as if I wasn't already cold enough. How could he possibly know that? Then: *Oh God. Please tell me this guy doesn't want to use me to open the gates of Hell for him too.*

It was as if he'd heard my inner thoughts. Something in his eyes told me that I had just nailed it.

The pain I was feeling from uttering the deity's name, even in thought, was nothing compared to what I knew would happen to me if Nightmares used me the way I feared he was planning. My body would never be able to survive it, and neither would the Outer World. He probably had some freaky friends he wanted to unleash. Friends that would surely make Hades' demons seem like frolicking angles; of that I was certain.

This guy had an undertone of evil unlike anything I had ever felt. If he believed I was the key, my days were numbered.

The vision of my dad's nearly-dead body at Hades' feet flashed in my mind. That would not be me.

All I could think to do was to play dumb. At this point, it was all I had. I managed to grit out: "Do I look like a key?"

In a flash, Nightmares slammed my body into the headboard behind me, causing it to smash into the wall, shattering it beyond repair. I cried out in pain. I couldn't help it. My skin began to blister from his icy grip.

"Do not take me for a fool!" Then, as quickly as his anger had appeared, it vanished, replaced with a dreadful expression I could only describe as ecstasy. "If a key has the power to open a door," he pretended to ponder, ". . . it must also have the power to lock it."

I couldn't concentrate on his words, I'd even lost focus on my frostbitten and burned wrists. My attention was on the blanket between us. Nightmares' sudden attack left it in a precarious position—it barely covered me; and without question, he was considering using me for more than opening the gates of Hell.

He grinned wickedly at my discomfort, adjusting himself all the closer. "Now," his lips just a breath away from my collarbone. " . . . How *does* this key work?"

I blanched at the suggestion, but thankfully I didn't have time to dwell on what he planned to do. In that instant, Antonio crashed through the bedroom door, and to my joy, a vital George Hollyander . . . as tall and robust as ever, stood beside him. The both of them aiming staffs at my attacker.

Nightmares snarled and in a cloud of mist, disappeared.

Chapter 3

"Evelyn!" My dad dropped his staff and brought me into the safety of his arms. "Sweetheart, are you alright?"

Relieved, I held on to him and cried—I was overjoyed. I had never been so happy to see my father. "You're all better," I half laughed, wiping at the tears on my face.

"Yes, sweetheart," he smiled back at me, his own eyes watering. "I'm all better."

"I'm so glad." I hugged him again, tighter. Thankful that my friends had been wise enough to save him, and that he had been quick enough to save *me*.

"Honey, you're hurt." George had taken one of my injured arms in his hands and was inspecting it carefully.

I looked at the frostbitten marks Nightmares had left. How could something from Hell be so cold? Physically, I mean.

"Who was that?"

"His name is Nightmares." I shuddered at the memory, all-the-while noting that my father hadn't asked *what* that was. Like it was totally normal for some guy to snarl then vanish into thin air? Translation: he knew exactly *what* that was, and he didn't seem at all thrown over its disappearing act.

He drew me close once again, mindful not to graze my wounds. "It will pay dearly for harming you. I will see to it."

I smiled and closed my eyes, breathing in the spiced scent of my dad. Choosing to believe that he would fix everything; and for just a moment, a little bit of peace washed over me.

"Sir, if I may?" Before I could even protest, Antonio had reached past my father and took both of my wrists into his hands, encircling them with his fingers.

I winced.

The visible pain on Antonio's face had to be a reflection of my own. "Oh, Evie . . ."

Tears of relief fell from my eyes as my skin began to light up from within, warming— mending itself from the inside out. I looked up at my angel and smiled.

"You are most welcome." He bent down and kissed each one of my wrists softly, sealing his magic.

"How did you . . .?" My father was at a loss for words, shaking his head in disbelief. "No, it's not possible." He looked from Antonio to me, still in his arms, and subconsciously tightened his hold, or maybe it wasn't so subconscious at all.

Antonio kept his expression calm, and his mental wall firmly in place. I had no idea what he was thinking as he watched my father become more uneasy.

"You possess the healing powers of the angels . . ." I could literally see my father fitting the pieces together, and he didn't look happy about it. "You couldn't have healed her like that unless—" His eyes had grown wide. "No . . ."

"Dad?"

"You're the lost son of Amara?" How my dad knew this was beyond me. Then: *"You're Zeus' son?!"* George was on his feet, quickly dumping me like a sack of potatoes as he became an impenetrable barrier, protectively blocking Antonio's view of me.

"Dad!" I scrambled to move alongside him, but his arm came out, holding me back.

"You don't understand Evelyn, he's dangerous."

"Not to me he isn't."

"He is!"

"Dad!"

"My parentage is of no consequence," Antonio seemed unphased by the towering figure in front of him. "You needn't fear me. I'm the same as I've always been. Sir, I love—"

"No!" The word was absolute. "I will not allow this. Not ever!"

"Dad, please!" If George was reacting this way to the news about Zeus being Antonio's father, I hated to think how Hades would take it. "I'm seventeen."

"Exactly." He hadn't taken his eyes off of Antonio. His staff had somehow appeared back in his hand, as if he was anticipating Antonio to shed his skin and transform into some heinous monster and attack. "You don't know what he's capable of, Evelyn."

"I would *never* hurt Evie," Antonio defended.

"She's *already* been hurt because of you."

The proverbial "truth" that my father had just slapped Antonio's face with, cut him to the quick and it showed. It was something he feared to be true. My father pointing it out only validated those fears all the more—but none of this was Antonio's doing!

"Dad, that's not fair. Nightmares is Hades' demon, not Antonio's." I wasn't going to let him blame Antonio, for something that wasn't his fault. And I wasn't going to let Antonio think for a minute that I was unsafe with him.

"And just how would you know that?" My father's question was more of an implication. His attention seemed to be solely on me now.

I stammered, pathetically. I wasn't exactly sure how to lower the boom on George with this one. It almost seemed cruel to come clean. I mean, what was I going to say? That I've been letting demons out of hell for Hades since I rescued you from the Underworld . . . Nightmares was the latest? How could I say that? He'd just recovered from almost dying! Knowing that I'd been forced to take his place would be like plaguing him all over again. I couldn't do it. I wouldn't.

Antonio mentally rolled his eyes at me. He figured at this point, I may as well come clean and get on with it.

As for me, I was just fine with evading this question for as long as possible—forever even. The less my father knew about my involvement with Hades or my ties to the underworld, the better.

George, had other plans: "We'll deal with your knowledge of Hades' consorts later, young lady. As for this," he gestured to Antonio and me. "This ends now."

"Dad!"

"Sir, I understand how you must feel, but separating Evie and I—"

"Is necessary," George interjected sharply. He looked upon Antonio as if he were nothing more than a mere acquaintance that he now had the displeasure of conversing with. A mere acquaintance that had betrayed and deceived him to the very core that is, or so he felt; I could hear it in his thoughts. "How could I not have seen this?"

"Dad," This was ridiculous. " . . . I can't believe you're acting this way. You like Antonio." I cupped my father's hand and brought it to me, hoping that he would look into my eyes and see that he was worrying for no reason. "He hasn't changed. He's the same guy. It doesn't matter who his dad is."

My father looked at me as though I had suddenly gone insane.

I knew what he was thinking: Zeus was not just any "*dad*." I totally agreed. But Antonio was nothing like him. My father had to know that.

George dropped my hand, dismissing my plea.

We apparently weren't going to be seeing eye to eye.

"You will continue to come to harm if you remain with him, Evelyn, it's as simple as that. I was a fool to have entrusted you in the care of another. *I* will look after you from now on."

"I have only ever protected your daughter with my life," Antonio defended. He knew my father's mind—obviously better than I did. Antonio had slipped. From what I'd just gathered from his thoughts, George was ready to kick him not only out the door, but out of my world forever, and Antonio wasn't going to stand for it. "I will continue to do so."

"She is no longer your responsibility," George thundered. "You saw what came for her tonight. Do not deny it. She is not meant for the dangers of your world, or the philandering lifestyle of the gods."

"George!" My father had gone too far.

"I would never expose Evie to such a life!" Antonio was outraged—and who could blame him? My dad had basically just called him a womanizer.

I was beyond mortified. I shrunk away. Desperate for a hole to open and blessedly swallow me into its depths. I'd even welcome Hades whisking me off to Hell right about now—never to return. There wasn't a synonym that could adequately describe my embarrassment, and that was saying something, considering my life as of late has been a series of continual embarrassments.

"You should have known better than to get involved with my daughter romantically." There was no mistaking the lethal warning in my father's eyes as he narrowed his sights on Antonio once more. If I had thought his tone was deadly before, it had nothing on the next statement: "You should have known better than to lie to me."

"Commander . . ." Antonio was treading carefully. He'd never addressed my father this way—at least not in front of me. It scared me that he did so now. "I did not intend to mislead you."

George was already shaking his head. "I may have been ill, Antonio, but I was not unconscious. I am not blind to your feelings for Evie, nor am I ignorant to Hades' plan for her. I will die before I let that beast make it so; and I will die before I allow you to lure her to Olympus."

"Dad." I couldn't stand it any longer. The two men I cared most about in this whole world, looked as if they were going to attack one another if the other one so much as made a twitch in the other's direction. "I'm not being lured anywhere."

"You don't know the beings you're dealing with, Evie. I can't expect you to understand."

"Sir, you approved—"

"That was before I knew what you were!" George thundered. "She is *my* daughter Antonio, mine! No man, demon, God, or heavenly being will have her without my consent." My dad was a fierce protector—I'd known that, but I'd never seen this side of him. He radiated pure power. My dad was the leader of the Divine Army . . . I knew I didn't fully grasp what that was yet, but in this instant, he appeared every bit as formidable as Hades or Zeus.

"Daddy," I'd linked my arm with his, attempting to pull him toward me, trying to break the tension that loomed between him and Antonio. They were nearly nose to nose. "I love Antonio." In that simple statement I sounded so much like a little girl, my voice coming out soft and gentle, I wasn't sure he'd even heard me, not to mention taken me seriously.

His expression softened to anguish. "I'm sorry Evie." He reached out with one hand and cupped my chin, his eyes churning with turmoil—unlike I had never seen in him before. " . . . But you are only allowed to choose once and I . . . I will not let your choice tie you to one of the gods in any way. Their world is not for you."

My eyebrows furrowed as I sifted through his contradictions. I was about to ask him how he can stand there and say that when he himself mingled with the gods—*the* God to be exact—but George suddenly brought me to him, hugging me tightly. The way he did when I was younger and I had hurt myself. My dad was trying to hug away the "hurt" now. The question was: what *"hurt"* was he trying to hug away; and what did he mean that I could "only choose once?"

"She will only have to choose once." Antonio's voice came from behind. "My love for Evie will never waiver. I will protect her from the gods and anything else that means her harm. With all that I am, she *will* be safe with me. I swear it."

I couldn't help but feel touched by his promise. It was . . . romantic.

My dad, however, looked torn. As if wanting to believe in his words for my sake, but resigned to the fact that they were impossible to hold any truth.

"You are not an ordinary man, Antonio. You will bring hardship to Evie's life, and with that, immeasurable danger. Danger more pronounced than what she faces already."

How was that even possible?

"You know there isn't a foe I wouldn't battle," Antonio challenged. "It's why you entrusted Evie to me in the first place." He was insistent on having my dad's approval, and reminding him of the man he is. "You know I would give my life to protect her."

George nodded his head grudgingly in agreement. "I would not have sent you to look after Evelyn, if I had thought otherwise. Your skills as a warrior have never been in question. But Antonio, it is your capability to maintain that strength and endure unfathomable opposition that I confute. You cannot keep them from her—especially now. They will continue to come. They will seek Evie out simply for being dear to you. They will come by the droves once they realize who she is, and god forbid her powers. You will not be able to protect her against the many. She needs protection now that only I can give."

"Wait a minute. Who will seek me out?" I already had two Olympian gods and a crazed wrath on my tail, who else could there possibly be?

"You needn't worry yourself, Evie." My father had hushed me, his attention back to the conversation at hand—as if his statement alone should put to rest any of my newfound concerns.

George was shaking his head in pity. "You should have told me the truth about who you are. This . . ." he motioned between Antonio and me once again, as if we were a sad state of affairs, ". . . could have been prevented. This changes everything, *Son* of Zeus."

That statement alone verbally kicked Antonio in the gut, but he wasn't going down without a fight. "It doesn't have to."

"You're a fool if you believe that."

"Hello . . .!" I was waving my arm in the air, attempting to claim their attention. "I'm still here. I'm not totally helpless, you know."

"Evelyn—"

"No." It was my time to be heard. I was done with this back and forth of them deciding my fate. "Obviously Antonio can keep me safe. He's been doing just fine warding off Hell's creatures for months; and I'm not such a bad fighter myself you know. I can do magic. I can get myself out of a jam."

"Evelyn . . ."

"Dad . . ." I mimicked his exasperated tone. "Quit acting all offended that Antonio didn't confide in you. He had his reasons. I mean, would you tell anyone you were Zeus' son? You can't blame him for keeping that to himself. Besides, he only just found out. He was as surprised as you are."

George was shaking his head again as I no doubt in his mind, prattled on. I could tell he was becoming exasperated to his very core, thinking that I was clueless in all this, and that I was behaving like nothing more than a teenage girl who was headstrong on defending her boyfriend as being date worthy. If only it were just that. I should have stopped there.

" . . . And as for Nightmares attacking me," I added matter-of-factly, ". . . that is hardly Antonio's fault. He doesn't even know who Antonio is."

"So the beast is provoked by another purpose?" George's sharp counter caused me to jump. "And when he *does* realize who Antonio is, do you think the demon would not take the first opportunity to use you as leverage in order to get what it wants? Would the price not be high for a son of Zeus' female?"

My smugness had evaporated. I knew my mouth was gaping. I couldn't help it. I hadn't considered that—any of it. He was right. I looked to Antonio.

He stood squarely with my father. "*As* a son of *Zeus*, I am more capable of protecting Evie. I am much stronger than I was."

That statement surprised me. Never had Antonio pulled the: I'm an all-powerful son of Zeus card. I didn't realize he'd actually gotten any special powers with the title. I don't know why this shocked me, but it did.

His next words were meant to soothe George's mind as much as they were meant to soothe mine: "You don't ever have to worry Evie, not ever. You *will be* safe with me, always, I swear it; and you will have my father's protection as well."

"She will not!" George's patience had maxed out.

"Dad—"

"No. Enough!" The word rumbled around us as if thunder had literally rolled in. "You will not be indebted to Zeus, not ever!"

"Okay!" I stepped back, putting my hand up in surrender. Who would dare argue that command? Besides, we were getting nowhere. The last thing I wanted to do was to fight with my dad—I'd just got him back! I took in a deep, calming breath. "Antonio, wasn't trying to upset you. He just wants—"

"Your blessing."

Wait. *"What?!"* I looked at Antonio, with complete bewilderment. "Blessing?" I felt like I was suddenly five steps behind and three steps sideways—tripping over my feet. It sounded like he was asking my dad for my hand in marriage.

I am.

"You want to marry me?!" I gasped, nearly choking on the air as I breathed in. "You can't be serious?"

"No." My father shielded me behind him once more. "I will not consent to this. Not ever."

"You cannot dispute that she would be wholly protected. As my wife—"

"She is meant for the heavens, not Olympus!" George roared.

"Have you lost your mind?!" I exclaimed, ignoring my father's statement and cutting Antonio off before he could utter another insane idea. This was not helping our cause. I thought we were trying to build my dad's confidence in Antonio, not shatter it! He had to think Antonio was mentally unhinged at this point. Hell, I was entertaining the thought. "Dad, he's not serious. Tell him, Antonio . . . you're joking. You're not really serious."

I was nervously laughing, my eyes looking from one to the other, waiting for them to recognize the ill-timed gag and start laughing too; and then we'd never speak of this again.

"Your father knows I'm not joking, Evie."

"Well I don't!"

Neither one of them were smiling.

I stared at Antonio. My mouth, gaping once again. I couldn't explain away this insanity to my dad if I tried. Antonio had gone rogue on this one.

"You said you were ill, but not unconscious . . .?" Antonio addressed my father, reiterating his words from earlier. ". . . That you know Hades' plan for Evie . . .?" His eyes flickered briefly from George to me, still not liking my father keeping us apart—like Antonio was some sort of dangerous monster that I mustn't get too close to.

George nodded.

"Then you know if Hades takes her, he will use her to fully open the gates of Hell."

"I do."

"Antonio . . .?" I wasn't sure where he was going with this, but I didn't like his tone.

" . . . And, you are aware that if he succeeds in that, he will bring an army of demons into the Outer World to battle for Olympus?"

"I am aware of this as well," George admitted calmly. His eyes, still fixed with Antonio's.

"Zeus will wage war," Antonio insisted. "The human world would learn of our existence. We couldn't possibly hide such a battle."

George looked entirely unphased.

"There would be no stopping Hades in coming for The Heavens!" Antonio wasn't liking my father's casual reactions to what he deemed as catastrophic events.

"His plan is folly," George dismissed, half-turning away. "The Heavens and Olympus are safe. He will never get close enough to Evie again to execute any of this."

"He already has."

That got George's attention.

"Antonio."

I tried to step around George while giving Antonio the *shut up or die look*. I didn't need him filling my dad in on any of the gory details or worse: telling him that some guy stripped me and took me to bed—and not just any guy—Hades!

My father wasn't having any of it. He wanted information and he wanted it yesterday. He kept me effectively behind him. "Explain."

Antonio didn't even blink. "Zeus took Evie from Hades' bed not three hours ago."

And there it was: Antonio had officially thrown me under the bus. No—*kicked* me under the bus—with zero hesitation.

I was frozen, my heart actually stilling. I changed my mind: *This* was the most mortifying moment of my existence; and Antonio was going to pay for it, dearly.

Evie . . . he needed to know.

You asshole! I was shaking my head at him—betrayed.

George looked back at me, obviously truly taking me in for the first time since he'd rushed into the bedroom. I was still wrapped in the quilt Antonio had left me with. And yes . . . I was still *naked* under that quilt.

"You were in *Hades'* bed?!" The question came out in a snarled knot of booming words.

I found myself stepping back—way back. I couldn't answer. I didn't have to. My dad had a visual painting of the whole awful picture—thank you very much, Antonio! I could literally hear him weaving the rest of the tale together—embellishing outlandishly with an assortment of scenarios that might enter a dad's head. I was so dead . . .

"Did the two of you—?"

"No!" I screeched out, horrified that he even asked me that. I mean, I knew he was thinking it, but did he have to ask?

A flash of relief crossed George's face.

"I have staked my claim on Evie, before Zeus himself." Antonio announced this as if his declaration would fix all—sealing my doom with my father even further in my opinion. " . . . And I will do so before Hades."

George suddenly went pale. It was either still from the implications of me wrapped naked in a bed blanket, or Antonio advertising to the world that I was his—either way, a proverbial target had just been painted onto me.

"I'm reluctant to add that Hades too has staked a claim on Evie."

I stared at Antonio, deadpan. "Really? You're reluctant to add that?" *Asshat!*

Antonio was careful not to look at me as I continued to shoot him death-like glares. Not to mention I was *screaming at him mentally to "shut the hell up!"* If it wasn't so painful to use Hades' dark magic I'd . . . oh hell, at this point: *"Proothó."*

With a slight flick of my hand, Antonio flew back, hard. His body involuntarily propelling across the room at warp speed into the wall behind him, smashing into an obscenely large rock mural.

I couldn't help but cringe . . . that had to hurt.

"Damn it, Evie!" He dropped to the floor with a hard thud.

George turned slowly toward me, his eyebrow cocked. He was literally glowering. "I'm not even going to ask where you learned how to do that sort of magic."

I'd lowered my gaze quickly, attempting to hide my demon eyes that were no doubt glowing red before my father could see them.

George resumed the interrogation: *"What claim* can Hades possibly have on Evie?"

I silently begged Antonio not to go on. Couldn't he see how furious he was making my dad? Not to mention me! This wasn't helping.

He rubbed at the back of his head. *It's better he knows.*
No it isn't!

Antonio couldn't be more wrong. My father did not need to know this. I could see my dad's hands clenched at his sides, the one holding the staff looked as if it might snap the weapon at any moment. I had never seen George Hollyander look more unpredictable than at this very instant, and it terrified me.

"She has bargained with him."

"No." George dismissed the accusation entirely. "She would not."

"For the cure to your ailment and to save my life . . ." Antonio didn't need to finish, but he did. " . . . "Evie has given her word that she would return to Hell upon the eve of your treatment and remain with Hades, forever in his debt."

George rounded on me, fury in his eyes. One look at me and he knew the answer, though he demanded I say that it wasn't so. "Tell me this isn't true. Evelyn!"

My mouth popped open, yet no words came out. A cold sweat had formed over me instantaneously. I would have thought my dad could have envisioned for just a moment, understood—at least a little, before condemning. Sure I knew he would be upset. I expected the: "You never should have put yourself in danger for me," speech that any parent would give. Then grudgingly: "but I would have done the same thing if I were in your shoes," bit. And then we'd hug and he would tell me how much he loved me and how brave and selfless I was. Now, he just looked livid—beyond livid! As if there were no argument on the planet that would make him understand what I had done. As if my actions were insane and unforgivable!

Something in me snapped. "I had to! You would still be dying or dead right now, and Antonio would have long since bleed out— Cerberus tore off his arm!" I stood tall with determination. Ignoring the startled looks on their faces. "I begged Hades to help you both, no matter the cost—and I would do it again."

I glared them both down, daring either one to challenge me. I would not let anyone make me feel guilty for what I had done. Giving up my freedom—my *life,* would not go unappreciated!

"Evie, it's not that we don't appreciate what you've done—"

I turned the full weight of my glare on Antonio, and for once, he wisely shut his mouth. Now was not the time for *his* "gratitude."

My father had closed his eyes in what could be none other than anguish. He actually looked pained. He'd sat on the end of the bed, his posture slumping. All his anger, deflated. The weight of *my world* on his shoulders.

It tortured me to know that I was the cause of it. But I could not back down. He had to see that what I had done was necessary. He had to know that I understood full well what this meant. He had to know that to me, it was worth it. That *they* were worth it. I had no regrets.

"I've not been wholly honest with you, Evie."

"Dad?"

"That's a gross understatement, really," he went on, a faraway look in his eyes. "You know very little about your father . . . about the man you believe I am. I should have prepared you more. I should have told you the truth. I was trying to protect you! You couldn't possibly fathom that I am—"

"The leader of the Divine Army?" To his surprise, I finished his thought.

He nodded, his expression wary, but he did not ask how I came by this information.

" . . . And as my daughter, God has granted you a gift, or curse depending on how you look at it; and you must guard it."

My back was already pressed against the wall, but somehow I managed to put more distance between me and my father. "What do you mean?"

I spared Antonio a quick glance . . . he looked just as panic-stricken as I was.

"Whomever you choose to physically love, will share a part of you forever—entwined and bound for all time."

"That's it?" I sighed in relief, half-laughing. That didn't sound bad. In fact, it sounded romantic, the way love should be. Damn, I thought he was going to tell me something awful, like that I was going to sprout three heads and grow wings!

Antonio was smiling too, visibly relieved as well.

"You don't understand," George shook his head. "Either of you."

He shot Antonio an uneasy look. As if he wasn't sure he wanted him to have whatever information he was about to divulge, and that made me more nervous than ever.

"You must be certain, Evelyn. If you give yourself to any man in that way, they will share your burden."

"Okay . . ." normal . . . I understood that. Couples were supposed to share each other's burdens. I still didn't see what the problem was. I was waiting for the bottom to fall out; I would not be disappointed.

"They will share the part of you that controls the power to open the gates of Hell."

" . . . What?!"

Chapter 4

Hades roared! Zeus had snatched Evie from his arms—from his bed. This was unacceptable!

He stormed through the tunnels of Hell, all manner of wretched life fleeing at the sight of him. Those foolish enough to linger were disposed of quickly, their blood spattered the walls and floor. Evie had been taken, and everyone would suffer for it.

The earth rumbled. In his rage, Hades sparked geological disasters all over the world. Earthquakes, volcanoes that once were dormant, erupted and spewed his anger with a vengeance; but it was not enough. Until he had Evie back with him, safe and in his arms, *Hell* would be unleashed upon all.

He threw open the doors and strode into his throne room, approaching its fiery middle; catching a glimpse in a mirror of the monster with whom he was more familiar: his stature had more than doubled, muscles were bulging, fingers and nails elongated. He had thought this version of himself had been lost. Ever since Evie came into his world, bringing the light of the heavens with her, Hades had felt more and more like the man he used to be in the days before he was sent to the Underworld—back when his days and nights were spent care free, and he dared to dream of the possibilities of finding love. Zeus had taken that from him yet again.

Hades snarled the god's name. "Zeus, I command you to appear before me!"

Flames shot up from the floor, licking the ceiling. Zeus' smiling face appeared in the blaze. "You bellowed?"

Hades would give anything to wrap his fingers around his brother's neck. To squeeze the life from him with his bare hands would feel . . . *heavenly*. He grinned at the thought—soon. "You have taken my betrothed."

Zeus chuckled. "Ah yes, the Child of Light. So I did."

The fact that the bastard didn't even bother to deny it, made Hades all the angrier.

"Imagine my pleasure when I found her naked," Zeus continued excitedly. "You pick them well, brother. She is a bit younger than I prefer, but I believe I have already grown fond of her youthful skin, her fiery hair, and the abyss of blue that is her eyes." He mused wickedly. "The Guardian's daughter is a fine trophy."

Hades growled and the earth, mimicking him, rumbled angrily. "She is *mine*! Bound to me and no other—return her!"

Zeus laughed outright.

"Return her to me, renounce your intent on her death, and I will stop the devastation that attacks your precious Outer World."

Zeus' laughter grated at Hades' nerves. "Not good enough brother. I've held her in my arms. Felt her body against mine. It will not be easy to give up such a treasure."

It was a lie. He knew Zeus had not touched the girl . . . or perhaps that was what he needed to believe.

Hades gnashed his teeth. He knew his brother's mind, and it sickened him. The very words would taste like bile in his mouth, but Hades suddenly felt desperate. A feeling so foreign to him, he hardly recognized it. "What would you have me do?"

Zeus' eyes twinkled with amusement. "Allow her to remain in the Outer World until her eighteenth birthday as you initially bargained . . . *untouched* . . . and she may still return to you at every midnight. That bargain, as you know I cannot break; for the two of you willingly agreed to it.

Hades could feel the fury rise-up within him, but he said nothing. He regarded Zeus carefully for several moments. "That is all? Allow Evie to remain in the Outer World until her eighteenth birthday . . . ?"

"*Untouched*," Zeus reiterated. "But, yes. That is all."

"And she will still return to me on every midnight?"

"Yes, yes," Zeus assured as if bored now with the conversation. "You may have her continue to release your monsters for me to kill."

There had to be a catch? Some sort of trick, but what? Hades narrowed his eyes. "What have you to gain from this?"

Zeus grinned. "What I've always wanted of course. The Child of Light's father has been healed brother. He will return to his place at the helm of the Divine Army—an army I hope to one day control. If the Guardian is consumed with freeing his daughter from your clutches, there is no doubt in my mind that he will lead that army straight to you. He may even trade its services for her freedom—an outcome I cannot afford."

Hades thought about that. The Divine Army at his disposal would be a valuable asset . . . but as quickly as the thought entered his mind, it flittered away. Commanding George Hollyander's soul would thwart Zeus and his ultimate desire to govern not only Mount Olympus, but all of creation—destroying the one true deity! A lofty plan . . . but it would wound Evie, beyond repair. Hades had seen firsthand her devotion to her father. She would forfeit her own life for him—she already had. He would not put her through the pain of watching her father wither to nothing ever again. He would not force her to watch her father become a slave to the Underworld. To do *his* bidding. No. He wanted Evie . . . and he would not hurt those dear to her to win her.

What in the name of creation was happening to him? When had he grown, dare he think it, a conscience?

"I will have your word that you will not touch my betrothed or harm her in any way from this moment forward. Agree to this and I will concede to our original bargain. I will not claim her . . . yet." The last part was perhaps the hardest concession he had ever made—or would ever make! Not making love to Evie, as he wished, could very well be his undoing.

Zeus nodded. "So we have bargained . . . so it shall be."

"Have any of you been bothering to watch what's on the television?" Iris asked. She was sitting on the sofa directly in front of the TV, her eyes wide with disbelief.

I got up from the table where Antonio and my parents sat. We'd been eating pizza of all things, attempting to act like normal people. Pretending that I wasn't about to be whisked away to Hell at the stroke of midnight, and that we somehow could formulate a plan that would free me from Hades' curse.

My father however, had been trying to not glare at Antonio for the close proximity in which his chair had sat beside mine, but failed miserably. It was obvious that he hadn't changed his mind on the matter: Antonio was not, and would never be, boyfriend material—like anyone could ever be!

My head had been spinning ever since George dropped the mother of all bombs that I will hereafter refer to as: "G's Curse!" Divine gift my ass . . . who else in all of existence has the "gift" of plaguing the first one they choose to make love to with guarding the gates of Hell? And bonus: not only am I losing a piece of my soul each time I let some creep out, but the lucky one saddled to me will too! Talk about a relationship killer. Antonio had hardly said a word since. He was probably glad my dad shut down his marriage proposal—as absurd as that was—and was thinking of a way to dump me without it seeming too obvious. Hell, I wanted to dump me! I was more than happy for the excuse to get away.

I plopped down beside Iris. "What's going on?"

"Your boyfriend's mad, that's what's going on," Havoc snapped before Iris could answer. She and Chaos were perched on the edge of the coffee table, their little heads making nice "windows" for anyone else trying to see.

Iris was attempting to peer around her to get a better look, but Havoc was either oblivious or didn't care that she was being rude, and wouldn't move aside.

I narrowed my eyes at the little pest in warning. If she meant to cause a situation in front of my parents or Antonio again, she was going to get it. Her earlier stunt in the bedroom was not forgotten.

After hearing how these pixies helped me out with the search for the Oracle, my parents had agreed to let them stay—provided that they behaved themselves. Pixies as a rule were not welcomed house guests. Havoc was currently treading on thin ice in my book. *Very* thin ice. I didn't like the look in her eyes; not *one* bit. It was obvious Antonio was upset. She didn't need to call attention to it.

"In case you're confused," she spoke as if I were four years old and an idiot, ". . . I'm referring to boyfriend number three."

"Evelyn Hollyander!" George's face had turned an unflattering shade of red; my mouth was gaping.

My mother sat beside him, shaking her head in disapproval.

"I don't have three boyfriends!" I defended.

How dare Havoc say that—especially in front of my parents! I didn't need them thinking I was some kind of tart who had multiple guys on the side.

Antonio looked livid.

"Now, Havoc . . ." Iris scolded the mini-menace while patting my hand sympathetically. Her voice was soft and sweet. "That wasn't very nice."

Havoc sat there sputtering, pretending to look mildly remorseful.

Iris was forever playing the referee: "You know Evie only likes Antonio." She offered Antonio and my parents a reassuring smile—as if that would erase the preposterous outburst from their minds—if only. The television caught her attention once more. "Look!" she pointed.

I reluctantly broke my death-glare from Havoc to see a 'breaking news' broadcast.

"This is bad . . . Mount St. Helen is threatening to erupt as we speak." Iris was pointing at the message crawling across the bottom of the screen, concern written on her face. "That hasn't erupted in decades."

I frowned, struggling to look past Havoc and her *big head*. Yellowstone was also beginning to rumble. I stared open-mouthed as they showed a short clip of a buffalo stampede; plumes of dirt being kicked up behind them as they hurried past a news crew. The camera guy must have dropped his camera because we were now getting a close-up of someone's sneakers.

"George . . .?" There was a small hint of worry in my mother's voice.

My father was holding her hand, his eyes and ears, intently gathering as much information as he could.

I looked back at the television. "Why would you think Hades is responsible for that?" As soon as the words left my mouth, I realized that I had just inadvertently acknowledged Hades, as boyfriend number three. Damn that Havoc! Damn, damn, damn her!

She turned and flashed me one of her exasperated looks. This one screamed: are you for real? Thankfully she didn't take this opportunity to gloat about my faux pas.

"*Hello* . . .! Zeus, took you didn't he? Right out of Hades'—" she paused and had the good sense to glance toward a very alert George Hollyander. His eyes were still on the television—but his ears were on us. "Hades is furious." She motioned to the screen. "A geological disaster like this . . . only he could do that."

They were now covering Mount Bromo in Indonesia, and reports from South Asia stated activity on the Barren Island . . . some sort of underwater volcano—who knew?

"That's not my fault," I protested, pointing at the television. "I mean, even if Hades, *is* doing all that . . . it can't have anything to do with *me*."

Even I'd heard the doubt in my own voice. Every eye in the room was on me.

Havoc's impeccably manicured brow was raised.

"Fine," I conceded. She was probably right. Hades had to be in a rage by the way I'd left him—not that that was my fault either! "So what am I supposed to do about it?" I asked the little know-it-all who was already rolling her eyes at me.

"The only thing you can do stupid . . . get back to your man and pronto or the entire world will pay for it."

A collective: "No!" was expressed by all—including me.

" . . . And he is *not* my man!"

Havoc shook her tiny finger. "You're making a big mistake, Child of Light, denying Hades like this. And don't you dare say I didn't tell you so when the entire planet goes up in volcanic flames! You do realize how close we are to Yellowstone, don't you? Can you say: *super volcano*?"

"On that note . . ." Chaos interjected, effectively halting my rebuttal. "I think Havoc and I would be safer in Hell."

"My daughter has spent enough time in the company of that beast!" George thundered. He'd slammed his carefully folded paper against the table like a gavel and was on his feet. "She will not return to him or Hades will find an army at his door."

My mother was nodding her head in agreement.

Hey!" Havoc shouted angrily. "Don't shoot the pixie! I'm just saying . . . Hades is pissed. If Evie doesn't return to him at midnight like bargained, there *will* be Hell on Earth—literally; and I just got this outfit," she added with a dramatic huff as she admired her attire. "Ash doesn't wash out of cashmere you know." She pretended to dust herself off, like the conversation itself had somehow soiled her precious garment.

I scoffed in exasperation. I could just strangle Havoc sometimes. Worrying about her dumb dress instead of me: her supposed "friend!" Some "friend" she was. Her temperament changed like a tropical wind. One minute she was being "nice" and helping me, the next, raiding my jewelry and kicking me repeatedly for being solely responsible for any hardship that came her way—like getting mud on her shoes while retrieving water from some bubbling spring. I still didn't know how the hell that was my fault.

My father's voice became low and lethal. He narrowed his eyes at Havoc. "If Hades, dares summon my daughter, ash on your cashmere will be the last thing on your mind."

"Now let's *all* just settle down," Chaos had risen and was attempting to deflate the scene. Somehow he looked ten feet taller.

Havoc crossed her arms dramatically. She was silently fuming. She didn't like being scolded by anyone.

"Evie, is not going anywhere," George reiterated.

I recognized the deadly look on Chaos' face. The house would come down in an instant if someone so much as flinched in Havoc's direction. My father didn't intimidate him in the slightest. "That would be up to Hades, now wouldn't it?"

"Alright!" I interrupted before George could rebut. "Arguing isn't getting us anywhere. Chaos is right." Hades was in total control and everyone knew it.

"Evie . . ." Iris' soft worried voice came from beside me. "It's 11:45."

I looked at the clock.

Don't even consider it. Antonio's warning came through loud and clear. It was the first time he'd "spoken" to me in hours.

Do I have a choice? I shot back, incredulous. We both knew the answer: a big fat *no*! As far as I knew I was Hell-bound in fifteen minutes—and with George healed . . . this could very well be my last moments here.

"We need to talk."

Four words I would have feared months ago when I first crushed on Antonio. Now, they terrified me. With fifteen minutes till midnight and Hades chomping at the bit, Antonio wanted to "talk?" This couldn't be good.

I sighed heavily as I got up and motioned for him to follow. "Come on . . . I need to get my bag ready for school tomorrow anyway."

School—ridiculous. The world was on the brink of disaster and I was heading back to school. You think George might have said we were on an extended vacation or at the very least called in a few sick days for me or something? No such luck. 8:00 a.m. I'd be back at Pinehurst, textbook in hand; and Leech, eyeing me relentlessly like her vulture. I wasn't sure what was worse . . . looking at Ms. Leech's bird-like beak daily or my impending view from my new residence in the underworld. It was a toss-up.

My dad had somehow beat me to the stairs. He was standing there, like a giant ogre daring me to pass. "You're not going to see Hades tonight Evelyn, I forbid it."

I stared up at him in disbelief. "You forbid it? Are you kidding me? Do you know how to break the bargain I made with him, because I don't. Hades has lived up to his end and I have to live up to mine. I don't have a choice."

"Your father's only looking out for you, Evie." My mother had chimed in. She'd been unusually quiet tonight, letting everyone else talk and offer suggestions on how I might gain my freedom— though she herself didn't look at all that worried about it. As if this was just some unfortunate affair that she would toss some cash at and clear up in the morning.

I didn't know why her united front with my dad bothered me so much, but it did. Maybe it was because she stood beside him, arm in arm—as if they hadn't spent a day apart. Or maybe it was because my impending doom was coming off as part of yet another unfair universal plan in her mind that made the life of a teen parent beyond trying—as if the catastrophic events I faced were "normal" parental complaints.

"You don't owe Hades anything, darling."

I was dumbfounded. "How can you say that?" For anyone to dispute it was absurd. "Hades freed my friends and he gave me the information I needed to save dad. I owe him everything. We all do!"

"Evelyn—"

"No!" I cut my father off, but I couldn't help the small smile that crept onto my face when I looked into his eyes. It was worth the price I paid to see him standing before me, healthy and alive; even though he was clearly pissed and ready to battle. I stood on my tiptoes and kissed his cheek. "Don't worry George, I'm never gone for more than a few minutes."

He frowned. He didn't like it, but deep down he knew I really had no choice. None of us did.

"At least give me ten before you send in the army, okay?"

"Five!" George warned grudgingly. " . . . And not a minute more, Evelyn. And *you . . .*" he pointed over my shoulder to Antonio, ". . . Better mind what I said." His icy stare communicated his threat: I was hands off as far as Antonio was concerned.

I smiled flatly. "Thanks, dad." . . . For embarrassing me yet again. I patted him on the shoulder as I moved past him and up the stairs. I knew he was just being a dad, but did he have to be so . . . *my dad* about it? I mean, not everything had to be stated as a military command. His words practically had their own accompanying ominous echo that lingered in the air around him.

I didn't even want to know what Antonio was thinking . . . I could only imagine. He followed a few steps behind, careful not to look my dad in the eye as he passed; his thoughts were once again guarded.

My mother had taken my father by the hand and was leading him toward the kitchen, muttering something about ". . . If it comes to that, I will."

I tried to shake off the weird feeling. The feeling that told me things were not as they seemed with Gwendolyn—but what else was new? My parent's newfound romance was mind boggling to me. All I could do was to chalk it up as her latest cryptic behavior and hope she was back to "normal" by the end of the week. She probably just needed a new hat or something . . .

Antonio passed me up suddenly, catching me by the arm and practically yanking me the rest of the way up the stairs and into my room in less than a millisecond; he shut the door just as quickly behind him.

"Okay, you obviously *really* wanted to talk, so talk." I rubbed at my shoulder, surprised it was still attached. "We don't have much time before—"

Antonio closed the distance between us and crushed his mouth against mine. His soft lips moved hard and rhythmically—I couldn't catch my breath.

"Antonio . . ."

His hands had swept up my arms to the nape of my neck where he held me still. That fire I'd felt from him days ago was back.

"I meant what I said, Evie." His kisses were relentless. "My love for you will never waiver." His beautiful words drifted past my ear like an enchanted melody, trickling down to my heart, and then his arms were around me.

My mind and body were betraying all rational thoughts. Enveloped in a blissful fog, I let everything fade away as he drew me closer, his kiss nearly devouring me.

"I can save you."

If this was saving, I wanted to be saved. My back was against the door—literally. I could feel the wild beating of his heart or maybe it was mine, there was no way of telling. Not a speck of air separated us.

A small moan escaped him as my fingertips traveled along the length of his back, tracing their way blindly, it was just as muscled as his chest that pressed against me. How I had ever thought Antonio was a Mageian was beyond me. He was so much more than that. His body alone screamed god, and that was exactly what he was. Well, a demigod anyway.

He lifted me up. My legs, having nowhere to go, wrapped themselves around him for support. Antonio may have agreed to wait for us to make love, but that didn't seem to be the case anymore. I couldn't help but meet every kiss just as eagerly.

"I want you Evie, always."

I couldn't remember how to speak. I tried to form the words, but my mouth wouldn't cooperate. I was overcome. I wanted to say that I wanted him too, that I always would. That we would always be together; and then an overwhelming feeling took hold of me: we didn't have forever. We didn't have *always*. If I was ever going to be with Antonio, it had to be now. It was literally now or never.

I don't know why I hadn't realized this before . . . Zeus had been right. If he hadn't have brought me to his temple when he did—although I will argue to my death he could have done it in a gentler manner—Hades would have claimed me as promised and I wouldn't be here in Antonio's arms, able to love him. I'd be in the Underworld—lost—forever!

I couldn't bear the thought. I held onto Antonio all the tighter. Desperate that not even a sliver of air should separate us again.

My fingers had twined themselves through his hair, holding his kiss to mine. I didn't have to say the words . . . Antonio knew that I was ready to make love to him, as he was to me.

And then his tortured thought came out in a ragged, shaky plea: . . . *Is there truly no other way?*

It was like an electric pulse had run through me, shocking me back into consciousness. I jerked away, startled by his inner words; they weren't to me.

The passion that had shrouded his face a moment ago had flickered to uncertainty, but only for a moment; and in that moment, his walls were down.

"Evie . . .?"

I didn't feel so love-struck any longer. My wits were slowly coming back to me, weaving themselves over me like a tapestry of dread. I released myself from him, ever so slowly.

He knew he'd opened himself up. He began to tread carefully.

"Don't over think this Evie, please." He gripped my shoulders as he brought his forehead to mine, attempting to reconnect with me, but it did little good. "I can free you."

I think I stopped breathing. I stood there like a statue, in shock.

"We can break this curse, Evie . . . together."

No, no, no . . . this wasn't happening. He did not just try to do what I thought he did. He wouldn't!

"You won't ever have to return to Hell again." Antonio stood in front of me, his head seeming to sway this way and that, as if trying to catch my attention, though he had it entirely. "Evie, did you hear me?"

Now it was Antonio's turn to look confused. His eyebrows were drawn as I continued to resemble a piece of petrified wood—unmoving. "Don't you want that?"

The question was loaded, and he knew it.

He held my face gently between his hands, his eyes becoming hopeful. "The solution to our problem is right here. It's so simple. We don't even have to think about it."

And that was the catalyst . . .

I sucked in a breath of air, like it had been my first. "'We don't even have to think about it?' Are you freaking kidding me?" I was outraged. I shoved away from him with
newfound strength. "Who the hell says that?" I couldn't believe he'd actually uttered those words.

"Evie, that's not what I meant. Look, you know this will work."

"No, it won't . . . and I can't believe you tried to coerce me! What kind of sadistic ass are you?"

"Evie please, hear me out."

"No! Us being intimate is not a business arrangement, Antonio. And asking me to end your life to save my own, by the way, *isn't* saving me." I kicked him in the shin—hard.

"Ow! Evie, please." He hopped up and down on one leg, rubbing at what I hoped would be a nice fat nasty bruise. "I'm sorry. I was trying—"

"Oh, I know what you were trying. And to think, I almost— errr!" I kicked him in the other leg.

"Damn it, Evie!" He was bent over, clutching both legs. He didn't know which one to rub more.

"I can't believe you did that to me, Antonio. You ruined it!" I wanted to cry, but I was so mad. "We agreed that we weren't going to let anyone, or anything push us into this."

"Evie, it's not like that."

I batted his hand away as he reached for me. This was not something the man I loved would do; this had Zeus written all over it.

"Evie, I'm trying to save you! My father's right. If he hadn't taken you when he did . . . you thought so yourself!"

My mouth was gaping. "How dare you use my—*his*—tampered thoughts against me."

"No, no, no, I'm sorry!" Antonio limped out of reach, putting a hand up in surrender; he knew my mind.

My eyes were narrowed. I didn't believe him.

"Evie, you know that I love you. This is the next step for us anyway. It's not like we haven't talked about it, or nearly . . . Look, I know I shouldn't have pushed this way. I know you're not entirely ready. I only—"

"Just stop." This conversation was over. I turned away from him. I didn't want to think about what Antonio had just done—or that he was conversing with his father while doing it! Our nearly intimate life was clearly not intimate. It was a mental three-some!

"Evie." Antonio turned me back toward him, his sad thoughtful eyes beseeching mine. "Forgive me. I beg you. I didn't know any other way. I . . . I'm desperate. I can't lose you. Not to him. Not like this. Not when I can take your place."

"Antonio . . ." There wasn't any more I could say. My heart was breaking along with his. I couldn't stand to see the failure in his eyes. As if he alone were responsible for my impending doom. As if he alone should shoulder my fate. This was all so messed up . . .

On some level I understood why he did what he did. He was a wreck trying to save his love from a life in the Underworld. A life that would no longer include him. But it was still wrong. He'd tampered with my mind. Nothing he could say would ever change that; and I would never forgive Zeus for influencing him in this way.

I stood there, hopeless. "There's nothing we can do." There was nothing anyone could do. The minutes were fleeting away from us and we both knew it. Time was no longer on my side. We had to say our goodbyes. My father was cured. Our time together was over.

"Evie, don't do this." His eyes churned with despair. "Don't give up."

He was asking the impossible. I knew my tears were already spilling over. I could not imagine ever giving up on loving him, but that was exactly what I had to do.

Damn! Why couldn't I be like any other girl on the planet? Find a boy, fall in love, and spend the rest of my life in their arms . . . dancing on hilltops and receiving bouquets of wildflowers. Okay, that last part might be a stretch, but dang! Was it too much to ask for some normalcy? Giving your body and soul was a big enough step as it is . . . knowing that the result would encumber the one you love with the responsibility of tending the gates of Hell for the rest of their existence was . . . well, anything but normal. I wouldn't do it. I couldn't.

I reached up and gently pushed the hair that had fallen across his face aside. How many times had I done that? How many times had I uncovered the endless surprise of emotions that always stared back at me when I looked into his eyes. Yet, he had never appeared so desperate then in this one moment. What an impossible story we were . . .

"Evie . . ." he clutched my hands in his. Hope, daring to linger in his eyes once more.

"I'm sorry Antonio, I can't." I released his grip and stepped back, needing some distance. "I won't give myself to you wholly as a means to secure my safety. The cost is too high."

"Damn it Evie!" He was angry. "You won't ever have to see Hades again!"

Never see Hades again . . .? That had never even entered my mind—in any of this. Sure I didn't want to spend my life in the Underworld, and I would do whatever I could to thwart it, but to never see Hades again . . .? I couldn't fathom it. I didn't want to; something inside me had started to ache.

"He doesn't have a hold on you yet."

But he did. I could feel him, even from afar, Hades called to me. His image, always a blink away: I would never forget the devastation in his eyes as I was ripped away from him—torn from his very grasp and world. It would be forever etched into my memory. Hades had never been more broken in that very moment, and it was because of *me*. He was changing somehow and my heart was listening. His hold was stronger than ever.

Antonio couldn't hide his anguish if he tried; he'd read my thoughts. "My father was right . . . he has gotten into your head!"

"No." I was attempting to downplay what we both knew to be true. Suddenly, I was filled with a combination of guilt and a need to protect the bond I had with Hades. I would never be able to rationalize my feelings for him to Antonio.

"Evie—"

I put my hands up, silencing him. I could never give him the life he wanted with me. I would never be able to make love to him—or to anyone for that matter; their life would be forfeit. They would be in constant danger, not to mention their soul would inevitably turn dark and be lost forever. I could never inflict that torment upon anyone, especially Antonio. The awareness of my own soul blackening was unbearable—a torture I kept hidden within myself. It was a price I had agreed to pay for the safety of my loved ones, and I did not regret my choices. But to openly inflict them upon someone else, upon the man I loved . . . what was left of my soul wouldn't allow it.

"I can't place this burden on you, Antonio. I won't. Don't ask me again."

The clock in the hall began to chime.

Antonio turned frantically toward the noise and back. He grabbed onto my arms, desperate—wild with panic.

"Evie, you're not placing any burden on me. *I'm* choosing to take your place! I'm stronger. I can shoulder this. I can keep you safe!"

I knew he spoke the truth, but my safety wasn't a concern anymore. I knew Antonio would carry any hardship I took on. That was who he was: an angel. My angel. But the guilt I would have for inflicting this life upon him far outweighed the fear for what it would do to me in the end. Not even a demi-god could survive what he was begging to free me of. I was already darkening . . . however *his* soul was as bright as the sun; and it would stay that way if I had anything to say about it.

"Evie, please. I'm begging you."

I brushed my thumb across his lips as the twelfth chime tolled. "You'll always have my heart . . ."

Chapter 5

I looked up into a radiant sun, letting it hit my face and warm my body. I was standing on the beach again, my beach, the beach that Hades had created for me.

My bare feet dug into the hot sand. The sensation was calming. I needed calm. My heart was heavy. The look on Antonio's face as I had faded from him was excruciating. His eyes had spoken of determination. He was not about to let me get away with my current form of thinking. He was dead-set on freeing me from my ties to Hell . . . and I was terrified as to what lengths he would go to achieve his goal.

I took in a deep breath before looking around. I was alone as far as I could tell. A flock of gulls landing in the wet sand near the water's edge was the only sign of life; aside from the rolling sea that crept up behind them, causing them to scatter back into the sky, squawking.

The last time I was here seemed like ages ago. Hades had carried me out into the water. He'd held me protectively in his arms when he learned that I couldn't swim.

I didn't have to close my eyes to remember those strong arms around me, the gentle words of comfort he whispered, and the promise that he would never let me go. I recalled the overwhelming sense of safety I'd felt in his embrace. It frightened me then . . . and it frightened me now. Hades was not the same man he once was. He was softer . . . caring . . . and my mind didn't quite know how to comprehend what to make of it.

The quiet here was almost deafening. A million thoughts and images pulled at me—screamed even, but one filled me with immeasurable guilt: how was I ever going to look Hades in the eyes, or myself for that matter, once he learned that I had played with his emotions? That I had never intended to stay with him. That it had all been a lie. I would never be able to keep that from him forever. Eventually he would learn the truth: that I loved another.

The realization of that would destroy his heart, of that I was sure. He was taking an enormous risk sharing the most minute piece of it with me. A piece that he had been afraid to share for over a millennia with anyone; and I was abusing that love and trampling on it with no regard to how it would affect him in the end—as if he was incapable of emotion! As if he didn't deserve to be loved in kind. *I* was going to break his heart quite literally, and that was perhaps the most cruel and calculated act I could ever do.

I kicked at the sand. What a colossal jerk I was. Leaving a line of collateral damage in my wake—from heaven to Hell! And it would forever be this way because I was a doomed mess.

Damn, it was hot! Normally my clothing changed when Hades brought me into his world. I "somehow" always seemed to appear scantily clad. Currently, I still wore the white t-shirt and jeans I'd had on when I was whisked from my dad's house a few minutes ago. The shirt was fine, but the long pants were definitely out of place here.

I sat down and began rolling my pant leg up. I had to get my head on straight. Antonio had me all flustered . . . trying to convince me that making love to him and condemning him for all of eternity would end my dilemma—and that he'd be okay with that! He'd *clearly* lost his mind. If he actually believed that Hades would just let me trade places with him and skip off into the sunset, without recourse—after burning him . . . no way. We'd be lucky if he let either of us live.

I rolled the other pant leg up with more vigor. None of that mattered now anyway. I had to push the last fifteen minutes from my mind. I had to put that life behind me. My father was cured and now it was time for Hades to collect on our bargain.

I would always love Antonio of course—regardless that he and I could never really be together. Like, physically. But you don't have to be physically physical or physically beside someone to love them or even be in a relationship with them. People lived without it for craps sake. There *were* long-distance relationships . . . there were mental relationships!

I paused mid rant. Had I just actually reasoned out a mental relationship in my head? Like a guy with a pulse could live with that for any length of real time?! For all that was holy, *I* was mental; and clearly needed to stop having entire conversations with myself since I gave crap advice!

I stood up, dusting the sand from me, glad that no one else had the displeasure of hearing my inner stupidity.

. . . And speaking of stupidity, why did men overreact 24/7?

Antonio had read way too much into my private reminiscing. Insinuating that I had romantic feelings for Hades—ridiculous. I mean, what was he even thinking? Just because I had recognized Hades' anguish with me being taken from him . . . that he seemed to care deeply for me—which I had no control of, didn't mean I cared for him back. I mean, just because I have a conscience and feel guilty for playing him—which incidentally he deserved for putting me in this position in the first place—didn't mean I *liked* him, like, romantically. It didn't! It just meant that I was a caring and perceptive individual who happened to notice that he was insanely attractive.

I rolled my eyes at the ridiculousness of it all. Honestly, a guy holds you tenderly and keeps you from drowning, and you're not expected to feel a little enamored of him . . .? I'd be made of stone if I didn't. It's not like I was swooning or fan-girling.

A shadow caught my eye along the water's edge. *Hades* . . . no other looked like that: tall . . . muscled . . . golden . . . I could spot him a mile away blind; he radiated pure man.

"Bad Evie!" I scolded myself, though I couldn't help it. Hades was one of the most handsome men I had ever seen—or would ever see. More so than his ass of a brother, Zeus. As for Poseidon . . . I could only hope that he looked like a troll and was blissfully married. All I needed was for what Havoc would call: "boyfriend number five" to show up and be hell-bent on obtaining *"the key"* for himself as well.

I trotted down to the shore line, surprisingly excited to see him.

"Hi!"

Hades didn't even look at me. It was like I wasn't even there. He stood there, staring blankly out to sea.

I couldn't believe I was saying this: maybe Havoc was right . . . he must still be pissed about Zeus snatching me away from him. But that wasn't my fault! I hadn't gone willingly. Why would he be snubbing *me*?

The silence was becoming uncomfortable. I was about to turn and leave when—

"Are you alright?" His tone was even, too even. He was tense. I could see his hands in tight fists at his sides, awaiting my answer.

"If you mean am I hurt . . . no, but I'm not alright." I stepped in front of him, forcing him to look at me. His dark eyes were fathomless; I could get lost in them forever. I looked away. "I don't know if I will ever be alright." With the spiral that my life had taken, '*alright*' seemed like a fanciful unattainable dream.

Hades took in a breath, exhaling slowly. He continued to stare at me, as if trying to assess "the damage" for himself.

"Did Zeus . . . *touch* you?"

I blanched at the idea. "That's what you're upset about?"

"Do not make me repeat the question."

Yep. Nailed it. . . . And by the look on his face, I did not want to make him repeat the question. It was clear that he'd thought about nothing else since my departure and was teetering on the fine line of control and utter chaos.

I prayed I was answering truthfully. "I don't think so, but I wouldn't know. I was in some sort of coma." My time on Mount Olympus had been a complete blank—until I was awakened that is.

I subconsciously began rubbing at my neck. I swear I'd never be able to shake the feeling that Zeus's fingers were never really far away.

A low growl escaped him. "If I find that he has violated you in any way . . ." He didn't finish. He didn't need to. The promise was unmistakable. He diverted his attention once more, pretending to be interested in a flock of birds in flight. "They are beautiful, aren't they?"

Beautiful? What the . . .? My eyebrows drew together. I watched the birds skimming the water—ordinary seagulls. Yes, they were beautiful, but I would have never expected Hades to note it.

"You didn't bring me here to watch birds, did you?" I couldn't hide the irritation in my voice. I'd been excited to see him, why is beyond me, and I thought he'd be genuinely excited to see me. Instead he was acting as if he could care less.

He turned, and the full weight of his violet stare settled on me, causing my legs to quiver and my heart to quicken. *He* was beautiful; and there was pure passion in his eyes. Absolute, unquestionable, passion . . . and . . . no. It couldn't be . . .

"I have made a bargain with my brother," he announced. "One that will allow you to remain in the Outer World until your eighteenth birthday, as you and I initially agreed upon."

I gasped. I had more time!?

"You look pleased." Hades turned away from me again. As if he couldn't stand to see my newfound happiness.

"I am pleased." Why lie. "I just got my dad back. I'm not ready to leave him. I . . . I'm not ready to be here."

"Of course." He gave a quick nod in understanding before waving me off, not sparing me another glance. "You may go now, Evie."

Wait. "What?" I just got here and he was dismissing me? "What do you mean 'I may go now'? I thought I was supposed to be releasing demons to torment your brother in your plight to take over Mount Olympus or something? I thought you'd be mad that he took me away from you. I thought you wanted me—"

"No!" He rounded on me, the harshness of his frustration striking me where I stood. "I do not *want* you," the word caught in his throat, and it made my heart nearly stop. "I do not want you . . . *yet*," he amended before turning away from me altogether, leaving his muscled back expanding and tightening with each controlled breath, for me to face. He began walking out into the water. A path which he knew I could not follow.

I scoffed in disbelief. What in the hell was going on? He'd asked if I was alright, he was allowing me to stay in the Outer World until I was eighteen, and *now* he was excusing me from opening his stupid gates and releasing demons—not that I was complaining on the latter, but had it finally snowed on the equator? This was *not* the Hades I knew. Something was wrong. Very wrong.

"Hades, wait!" I ran after him, ignoring the water that sloshed over my feet and ankles.

But, he didn't wait. He walked on, leaving me behind. Each wave that washed over him seemed to draw him further out into the water and further from me . . .

I needed answers. Did I still have to return to him every midnight, or was he releasing me from that part of the bargain as well? And what about Nightmares . . .? I hadn't been able to tell him about the demon visiting me again. Was he still planning on capturing the creep and sending him back to Hell or was I on my own?

My world had become more upside down and uncertain by the minute, and it scared me. So much so, that I could hardly consider the most important questions of all: why had Hades bargained with Zeus? What could he possibly have to gain that would justify my time in the Outer World to continue longer than he'd already deemed necessary? What treasure was worth more than "the key?" What was worth letting *me* go?

I was waist deep before I realized how far out I was. The waves crashed against my chest. Twice now I'd lost my footing, struggling to remain upright. I squinted my eyes in a futile attempt to keep the salt-waters spray from blurring my vision. I looked back over my shoulder toward the beach, it seemed so far away, like a mirage that drifted in and out of focus.

My eyes sought Hades again. He was sitting on a rock a little ways away, looking out to sea—blissfully ignoring my attempts to reach him—the jerk!

I was mad now. How could he just leave me without explanation? Casting me aside until he decided to '*want me*?' I was *not* an object to be acquired when it struck his fancy. He couldn't possibly be that delusional to expect me to be at his beck and call— waiting for him to suddenly '*want me;*' as if I'd let any guy have that kind of control over me—ever!

The more I thought about it the angrier I got. I could feel myself glowering. He wasn't much closer to me than the beach, but I wouldn't find answers on the beach, and I was going to *get* answers.

I waded out a little further, deciding to take my chances. Too bad I didn't know a "dry up the ocean" spell—I wasn't even sure there was one. Though this was Hades' world, and as I'd discovered long ago, my magic had limits here—unless it was *his* spells I was casting, and the price for using those were high. My hands tingled even now at the very thought of using his dark magic. Besides, this wasn't a *real* ocean anyway, so the water couldn't be that deep . . . or dangerous . . .?

I held my head up and pushed on, careful to keep my arms out for balance. Jumping up and clumsily hopping every time the sea swelled and threatened to wash over me.

I was close to him, maybe twenty feet or so when an enormous wave rose up high from behind another. My eyes widened.

Oh . . . my . . . God . . . "Hade—!" My scream was washed away with the thunder of the wave, taking me under and tumbling me along the ocean's floor.

A moment later I felt a hand grip my arm, yanking me up toward the surface.

My body struggled against the current, relentlessly shoving me back to colder depths. I needed air. I was desperate for it. Panicking, I kicked and thrashed to reach the top.

Another wave came down with driving force; the hand never let go. It lifted me against the pressure of the water, above the foaming sea, above the next approaching wave.

I was suddenly in Hades' arms. I clung onto him like the life preserver that he was, gasping and choking for air. I had never been so thankful to see him.

"What were you thinking coming out here?" he shouted. "You could have drowned!"

True. If I was going to continue to visit Hades' island paradise, I really needed to learn how to swim.

I leaned heavily against his shoulder, sputtering, as the water divided. Literally parting ways and cutting a path that led back toward the beach. I watched in awe at the liquid walls to either side holding their form. Not even the slightest hint of the ocean's spray dare touch us.

"You walked away from me," I rasped. "I wasn't done talking to you." I glanced up at the hard expression on his face and shrunk back, wishing I'd said nothing.

Hades drew me closer to him, tucking my head in the crook of his neck as he carried me along, his grip tightening.

I was completely worn out. My body ached as though it had been beaten repeatedly—which it had.

"Foolish girl," he scolded again, though I could tell he wasn't all that upset with me any longer.

My nerves were calming. The rhythmic sound of his heartbeat as I breathed in the smell of his salty skin, soothed me. I was alive. Once again, Hades had come to my rescue.

"Thank you."

He said nothing as he carried me across the golden sand, carefully laying me down under a giant palm tree that had suddenly materialized. Large feather-like leaves blocked the bright light from my face, letting only slivers of the warm rays shine through with each movement.

"Are you alright?" He seemed more like the old Hades than the cold man who'd turned his back on me a few minutes ago.

I had rolled to my side, still sputtering between coughs. "I wanted . . . to ask . . ." but then I stopped. All the answers to the questions I thought so important a few minutes ago, faded away. I turned back toward him. He looked worried. He was rubbing small circles with his hand on my back attempting to comfort me. I'd frightened him . . . truly frightened him. Suddenly, there was only one question I needed the answer to: "Why don't you want me anymore?"

Hades looked as if I'd sucker-punched him in the gut, and to tell the truth, the question took the breath from me as well. Although I needed to know, I found myself dreading the answer.

I'd reached up with one hand and pushed his wet hair aside, giving me full view of the man, I thought I knew.

"I never said that I didn't want you," he defended quietly. "I only said that I don't want you now; or rather, I cannot have you now."

I could feel my eyebrows draw in confusion. "Oh," I breathed out before looking away from him again, feeling deflated. I was still confused. I didn't know how to respond to that.

"Isn't that what you wanted to hear?" He smoothed a hand down the side of my face, his fingers gently guiding my chin back toward him. "Why do you look so distraught?"

I shook my head, unable to answer. My fears had come full-circle: I could hardly look him in the eyes. The reasons for my distraught look were too many—and none of them I wanted to admit aloud—each one worse than the other. Deep down I felt guilty for tricking him all this time. I made him think that I was planning to come to him willingly when I actually had no intention of staying with him at all. I made him think that I cared for him. . . . But perhaps the cruelest and most twisted reason for the distraught look that clung to my face: was because deep down I knew, I'd always known, that he had fallen in love with me, wholly, and I had been using that knowledge against him so that I could have more time to break this horrid curse and free myself of him forever. No matter how I had tried to rationalize or downplay Hades actions and feelings toward me, no matter how hard I had tried to dismiss them as impossible, I'd known.

The million dollar question was: why should I care?! He started this whole mess. He was King of the Underworld . . . he wasn't supposed to be capable of love; not the kind of love Antonio could have given me anyway. He'd robbed me of that. So why should I care if he wanted me or not? Why should I care what he thought of me? Why shouldn't I hold my head up and look him in the eyes? If I gave myself to him fully, he'd use my power to control the gates of Hell. He'd destroy the Outer World—I could never trust him— especially with my heart!

I stiffened. I had absolutely no idea where that last thought had come from. The realization that Hades meant a whole lot more to me than I had been allowing myself to admit, struck me hard. Especially because maybe, just maybe, Antonio had been right. Maybe Hades *had* gotten into my head. Maybe the thought of him not wanting me hurt more than I was willing to admit. Because maybe, just maybe, *I* was falling a little bit in love with him too?

I hadn't realized he'd captured my hand in his until he'd given it a slight squeeze.

I looked up at him timidly.

"Do not ever put yourself in danger for me again." Although it was a command, the gentleness of his voice was beseeching. "It would destroy me to lose you." He turned my hand slowly and pressed the softest of kisses to my wrist, all-the-while his dark eyes never leaving mine. "I do not believe I could go on."

Who was this man? I found myself mindlessly tracing the outline of his jaw. My fingers, lightly stroking the stylish shadow of stubble that grew.

"Do not caress me like that," he warned, leaning into my touch. "I want you desperately, Evie. You will make it impossible for me to let you go. Heaven itself could not promise the sweet song your touch gives."

Such romantic words had never been uttered in the history of the universe, or in any of the sappiest of romance movies, and Hades was *not* sappy. Nor did he say such things—or so I thought.

I swallowed loudly, afraid, but like a train wreck I couldn't help but watch. No matter the destruction. I had to know: "How much do you care for me?"

I visually startled him. He couldn't have possibly fathomed I'd ever ask that question, and neither could I.

He regarded me carefully. I knew he would not say the words. I wasn't even sure he was capable of saying them. As far as I knew, Hades had never *loved* anyone. Yet, the way he looked at me, the way he held me, the sweet words he crooned . . . if this wasn't love, I didn't know what was.

"Enough to let you go, for now." And there it was: Hades was being selfless. For me.

I took in a shaky breath, summoning the strength to stay strong. To not let my heart ache for him. To not fall further under his spell. I didn't know what to say but I had to say something.

My lips parted when he crushed his mouth to mine, taking me by surprise. Pouring every ounce of emotion he possessed into this one kiss.

I kissed him back—matching his intensity. I couldn't help it. Never had I felt such an overwhelming engulfment of utter devotion. Never had I felt as though I were the beginning, middle, and end to someone's world. I never wanted this feeling of elation to end. I held him to me as long as I could, my fingers gripping his hair as his kiss became harder, more rough.

Hot tears fell from my eyes. I was more than a mess of a girl—I was a nightmare. No wonder *Nightmares* was drawn to me! How could I say I wanted to be with Antonio when I was so torn? And yes, I was officially torn!

Hades was nothing to sneeze at. He was strong, powerful, beautiful, and he was in love with me—desperately! But was he capable of *truly* loving me for all time, and could I return that love? Could we ever have a real future together that wasn't doomed by the confines of Hell?

Hades had come to my aid whenever I needed him, saving my friends and battling Megera when she had attacked me. Yes, there had

been prices to pay, but there were times when he simply helped me
. . . like healing me without asking for anything in return. Times when
I felt his strength weaken because of it. Times that he had willingly
harmed himself so that I would not suffer.

Antonio was beautiful too. He offered truth, light, and love.
The fact that he was a demigod and an angel had nothing to do with
his appeal. Antonio had helped me rescue my dad. He had traveled to
Olympus to obtain the cure for my father when I could not. He had
battled monsters—both Mageian and mythological—all to keep me
safe. He had proclaimed his love for me to Zeus and to my father . . .
he wanted to spend forever with me! So why was I suddenly doubting
the measure of that love?

Hades pulled back ever so slightly, his kisses becoming softer
until he grazed my mouth one last time, a whisper of a touch. A
promise that it would not be the last; and I found myself praying that
it wasn't.

"I know you are troubled," he began, cupping my face
between his palms and drawing my face close to his again. "I know
you fear you cannot trust me." His eyes were deep and endless, like
windows to his soul. . . . And it was in this moment, I knew that he
had one.

There was a tenderness about Hades that I believed that no one
knew, no one but me that is, and it was this tenderness that touched
my heart and detached him from the beast I once saw him as.

"I will earn your trust Evie, I swear it."

I could feel myself smiling. I couldn't help it. I didn't doubt
his words.

He reached up, smiling himself as he captured one of my stray
curls between his fingers, admiring it a moment, before letting it
spring free.

"I shall always strive to make you smile."

Now that was an empty promise. There was no way Hades
could ensure a lifetime of smiles—especially living in the
Underworld! Though, I couldn't help but grin at the thought of him
trying.

"You must still return to me at midnight . . ."

And there it went.

" . . . Not because I want you to release a demon!" he added quickly, sensing my dismay. "But, because I cannot bear to go more than a day without seeing you and knowing for myself that you are safe and well."

Ok, the smile was back. That statement alone would quicken any girl's heartbeat.

"Because," he added, taking my hands in his once more and bringing them to his heart. "I cannot *be,* unless I bask in your light."

. . . And that stilled it. My heart had officially stopped. I found myself grinning up at him like a love-sick schoolgirl. Who says this stuff—and means it? Certainly not the God of the Underworld. This had quickly become an unexpected and complicated turn of events . . .

Hades loved me. He wasn't pushing me away. He wanted me—more than anything! He was just being kind and giving me more time with my family.

He cleared his throat softly, pulling me from my musings. His eyes slightly evaded mine as he scooted back a little, attempting to regain composure with a bit of distance.

I smiled wider. The big bad King of the Underworld had allowed himself to look smitten and was now blushing. I'd never seen anything more adorable in my entire life.

"Are you well enough to stand?" he asked, changing the focus off of him as he offered his hands for support.

I nodded, but I was grateful for the help as he lifted me up.

We stood there, face to face, staring into one another's eyes for several heartbeats before Hades stepped back entirely, severing all contact.

My skin felt cold without his touch, and my mood dampened. What power did this man wield over me?

"I'm sure you wish to be on your way. You must want to spend some time with your father before you resume your schooling."

My posture slumped entirely. School . . .? Even *Hades* was pushing school? Honestly . . . with all else that was happening, school seemed unimaginable and entirely unimportant. I'd have thought Hades of all beings would be on board with that frame of thinking.

"An education is a highly sought after. I remember—"

"Yeah, yeah," I cut him off. I didn't need the after school lecture on "*be cool, stay in school,*" from him too. I'd nearly forgotten: "Nightmares came to me last night."

And just like that, my sunny day turned gray. Literally. A cloud bank had rolled in and had darkened the sky. "Tell me everything," he demanded. "Leave nothing out!"

I nodded, quickly gathering my thoughts, though my words came out stuttered. Hades was pissed, and that always made me nervous. "He, he knows you used me to open the gates of Hell," I began shakily. "He knows I'm the key. He, he says I have something he needs."

Hades' eyes shifted to red and I instinctively moved back, the demon part of me was cowering inside.

"He isn't the same though," I blurted, knowing I had to go on. "He's changed. He looks my age now. He looks . . . Mageian."

"What?!" Hades snarled in utter disbelief. "That cannot be."

I shook my head, unable to comprehend it myself. Though my knowledge of what I thought demons could and couldn't do, was extremely lacking.

"It's true. He's not wrath-like anymore. He felt like a regular guy."

I blanched, realizing that I should have kept that last bit of info to myself. The little distance I'd put between Hades and me was non-existent now. We were toe to toe.

"What do you mean: 'he *felt* like'?"

I couldn't believe I was debating whether I should tell him that Nightmares had been up close and personal with me. Of course, I shouldn't! But my stupid brain couldn't formulate a believable lie.

"Your hesitation is painting images in my mind," he growled, ". . . images I do not like."

"They're probably not too far off," I'd muttered without thinking, then slapped my hands over my mouth.

The sky above instantly blackened as a shadow of darkness wrapped around us. Lightning flashed.

I instinctively reached out, my body seeking the shelter of Hades' frame. The ominous surroundings seeming more eerie than the angry god in front of me. I leaned against him. Forgetting that in doing so I could hear his inner thoughts.

"No, no," I jumped back, " . . . he was clothed!"

"*You,* were naked with him?!"

Thunder crashed. Exploding and reverberated at ear-splitting octaves.

"No!" I yelled over the storm. "Well . . . yes. I mean—you're the one who took my clothes in the first place, and Zeus only gave me a sheet! It's not my fault Nightmares showed up before I had a chance to get dressed."

I had my hands over my ears attempting to block the fury of Hades' sudden typhoon. I was practically screaming my defense when piercing water droplets struck me.

"Hades, stop!" I was not going to be blamed for this. "

His anger continued to rage. He stood there, frozen like a statue in a coma-like state.

The ocean now mimicked the sky. The once blue and inviting water had turned dark and tumultuous, crashing against the shore.

I jumped back, not wanting the water to hit me.

"He didn't touch me like that!" I assured, knowing his thoughts had to have gone there. "My father came in and scared him away. He didn't hurt me. Hades, I'm fine!"

I threw my arms around him, hugging him tight. Hoping the feel of my body safe against his, would jolt him out of his destructive mood. Either way, the closer I was to him, the less likely I'd be washed out to sea by one of his angry waves.

"Hades please, stop!"

I did the only thing I could think of to draw him from his demon. I kissed him. Harder than I had ever kissed anyone.

It took a millisecond before his lips caught up. His strong arms wound around me, pulling me tighter to him, his body melding with mine.

I became slowly aware that the storm was dissipating around us. The rain was no longer driving, and the darkness had turned to an inviting summer day.

"I should have been there," he breathed out sorrowfully, his arms still holding me close. "I swore to protect you. He would not have been so bold if I were there."

I shuddered. Had he been there, he'd know that Antonio had been in that bed with me only minutes before—something I still feared Nightmares would divulge.

"I'm fine, really." I half-smiled up at him, grateful that he was consolable once more.

" . . . And the demon breathes another day because of it." He kissed my forehead and drew me close again, needing the contact.

"Hades," I began cautiously, a little afraid to ask. "How come you haven't caught him yet?"

His body tensed. "Nightmares is of the spirit world. He does not belong to me . . . but to Satan; and it is he who has helped him to elude me."

"What?!" I staggered out of his embrace, utterly shocked. Havoc had suggested it, but until now I never truly dreamed there was a being Hades couldn't catch. Sure I'd had my doubts, but at the end of the day, Hades was the *king* of punishment. He was unbeatable! He was a god! The fact that Nightmares has "eluded" him, didn't bode well for me. Not at all.

"That does not mean that I will not capture him," he assured darkly. "Fear not!"

But, my confidence in Hades ability to protect me, where Nightmares was concerned, had wavered—considerably.

I'd wrapped my arms around myself, suppressing a shiver. Trying to understand how all of this could happen.

"Why would you release something that belongs to Satan . . . something you have absolutely no control over?" The question was rhetorical. The answer: "I'm an idiot," would be the only accepted response.

Knowing that a creature whose master is the darkest being ever known to have touched the Earth was after me, freaked me out to say the least. Knowing I'd have to deal with said creature *myself* apparently, freaked me out even more. I'd had no idea that Hades was chummy enough with Satan to borrow the family pet; and Nightmares was far from house broken in my opinion.

"I didn't know you two were on the same team?"

Hades looked insulted at the suggestion. "We *are not* on the 'same team.'"

I raised a skeptic brow.

"I was repaying an old debt, and in doing so, *I* gained an advantage."

"Well," I smiled flatly. "I sure hope I'm worth it."

"A war is about to break out, Evie. A war that I plan to win. If Nightmares takes over the dreams of the gods, one god in particular, they will be too weak, too disoriented, too *easy*, to conquer. My brother *will* fall, by my hand."

"And so will I."

"You will not be harmed."

Yeah, I'd heard that before. . . Hades could be like a dog with a bone sometimes. Now more than ever he seemed hell-bent on destroying Zeus. I was willing to bet my little abduction from his bed was the trigger to his newfound determination. Nightmares was the vessel for his newest strategy of attack. And I . . . I was not going to suffer for it.

"Perhaps someone should clue Nightmares in on the details of your little plan," I interjected sarcastically. "He seems to have his own agenda for world domination, and he's focused his sights on me."

Damn Hades, for getting me in the middle of this war of the gods! If he couldn't handle his demon assassins, then he had no business letting them run around fancy free! There were so many things wrong with the normality of that statement, I didn't know where to begin. The reality of my world was truly distorted.

Hades' jaw was clenched. "He will not 'focus' on you again."

Like he could honestly promise me that. But I would have to force myself to believe him if I was ever going to be alone again. Nightmares scared the crap out of me. I had to trust that Hades would find a way to capture and destroy him. I had to. My sanity depended on it.

"Evie." He took my hands in his once more. His strong fingers, tenderly twining with mine.

I looked up into his determined eyes. They were once again violet, beautiful.

"Have faith in what I say."

"Faith?" I didn't know he knew the word.

Then I heard the full threat of his thoughts: *If I must follow her every moment of every day, I swear with all that I am, that beast will not harm what is mine.*

Lovely. Now I had two stalkers!

Chapter 6

"Can you believe that only yesterday I was mixing the cure to save your father's life?" Iris had been prattling on for the last forty minutes, her excitement palpable. "I mean, how can they expect me to sit here and grow sweet potatoes of all things after something like that?"

I rested my elbows on the table, slouching forward, and pressed my fingers into my throbbing forehead. We were smack in the middle of third period Biology, cramming for the final exam, and Iris was nowhere near done complaining.

Havoc had long since left, having "popped out" under the guise that Chaos was expecting her—the traitor—how could she just abandon the friendship train and leave me to fend for myself on this one? Why should I have to endure Iris's mood alone?

". . . I mean honestly, Evie."

"The rest of the world has no idea that you cured my father, Iris. If they did, I'm sure you'd be in line for the Nobel Prize."

Iris giggled and waved me off, her cheeks flushing a brilliant shade of pink. "Oh Evie, you know I don't like to be made a fuss about."

Was she kidding?

"I'm just pleased I was able to help. I mean, I'm sure *anyone* would have had that incredibly ancient and otherwise unknown spell lying around their house *somewhere*. No need to present me with an *award*; silly idea."

"You're too modest," I replied dryly.

"Oh," she waved me off again, still giggling. Though she had a slight far off look in her eyes. No doubt she was envisioning the very moment of acknowledgement. Knowing Iris, she probably had her acceptance speech written out in her head.

When was that damn bell going to ring? I didn't know how much more I could take of this. Iris had been this way since we got back from my parent's house early this morning—not that I blamed her. I didn't want to be here either. With midnight trips to Hell, surprise pop-in visits from Nightmares, and Zeus pushing Antonio and I together at his discretion, I was exhausted; and quite frankly, I needed a vacation! The very idea of attending school was ridiculous. I didn't care that my parents thought I was safer here. That there was some magical ward around Pinehurst that was supposed to keep me hidden—like that helped when Gargoyle Roland tried to kill me, or prevent whatever it was that took over Ms. Leech's body like *Invasion of the Body Snatchers*. As far as I was concerned, Pinehurst was a magnet for trouble. . . . And as for Nightmares . . . well, I half expected him to slither through the door at any moment.

But for Iris, it was much more than that. She had been on the outside. And when I say the outside, I mean *outside* the gates of Pinehurst. She had never really experienced that before—except for the occasional trip to The Islands with her parents—but that didn't count, and that had been years ago. Sure they came to see her, and she went home on holidays . . . but Iris's parents kept her far from the human world. They were afraid and didn't want humans to learn what they were.

Living with the Hollyander's for two days had opened a door for her that would never again—according to Iris—be closed. We had given her a taste of freedom and she liked it.

The staff at the local pizza parlor had been gracious, right up to the point that Iris threw a surprise fit and refused to leave until she'd mastered the *Ms. Pac-Man* game in the arcade room. The flying slices of pepperoni pizza she angrily lobbed, had magically hit the manager in the head when he "hinted" it was nearly time to close. The entire ordeal would have cost my dad a pretty penny to keep quiet, however, after mentioning that Iris had been "locked up" for most of her life and didn't know any better, the guys waning tolerance softened. He'd been ready to call the cops and throw Iris in the slammer. Instead he only charged my dad for a "modest house cleaning fee."

". . . Honestly, Evie, could you imagine the cures I could invent if I could only get more of that flower? How can I just sit here when I could be saving the world from disease, or even death?"

Yes, she had already written her Nobel acceptance speech and was currently working on her sainthood.

I looked at the clock on the wall and sighed. I swear it was moving backward, thirty minutes to go! The longer I sat here listening to Iris, the more I realized she was right. I mean, what *were we* doing? How was growing sweet potatoes going to help me—or fourth period English for that matter? We should be holed up in my room this very moment, devising a plan of attack on Nightmares; not to mention a solution to my mid-night excursions to Hell. As much as I'd softened toward Hades, I didn't want anyone but me controlling my whereabouts.

"Excellent girls!" Mr. Meyer was standing over us, looking down on our potato starts. "And look how healthy the leaves are."

I glanced at my project, surprised that tiny leaves had begun to grow already; considering I hadn't done anything but give it water.

My eyes flickered to Iris. The barest hint of a smirk flashed across her face. That sneaky little . . . she'd used magic and I hadn't even seen her do it! There was more to Iris than met the eye.

"Well now," Mr. Meyer began as he puffed out his chest, as if he alone was responsible for our brilliance. "This is the sort of effort I like to see." His eyes, gazed around the room, no doubt taking in the baffled looks of the other students—myself included. "Clearly Miss Hollyander, and Miss Matson, have embraced the significance of this assignment."

We all waited with bated breath . . . If Mr. Meyer was going to divulge the 'significance of this assignment,' or any assignment, no one wanted to miss it. The abundance of useless information dealt out in this class was staggering. The prospect of anything actually being beneficial was too much of a temptation to miss.

"I apologize for the interruption, Mr. Meyer."

That voice . . . it was like the sound of nails on a chalkboard, grating through the room. But that's not what caused me to cringe. The blanket of ice that had wrapped itself around me was suffocating. My skin felt as if I were literally being pricked with tiny needles.

I winced as I spun around in my chair. Ms. Leech was standing next to a boy with blond hair and black eyes: Nightmares! I nearly fell out of my chair.

The old bat gave me a quizzical look before turning her attention back to Mr. Meyer. "This is Mr. Epiales," she announced. "He's just transferred from Hoffmyer."

An instant muttering of whispers began amongst the other students.

Hoffmyer was the Mageian school that housed the trouble makers of our world. And as much as I believed "*Mr. Epiales*" was a troublemaker, he certainly hadn't come from Hoffmyer. No, this kid had come straight from Hell, and his eyes were fixed solely on me. He grinned, and the blanket of ice tightened.

The classroom door flung open once more. Antonio and all his stunning glory rushed in. His hair was tussled, and he appeared slightly out of breath. He surveyed the room, detecting the threat without any explanation from me. His eyes locked on Nightmares—they'd met before. Antonio had already moved to my side, placing himself between me and the demon—an impenetrable wall that warned the creep: severe bodily harm would come to him if he dared to cross it.

Nightmares curiously cocked his head to the side, his eyes squinting ever so slightly as they narrowed in on Antonio. It was as if he was pondering something heavily but couldn't quite come to a conclusion.

It was in that instant that I knew Nightmares knew Antonio was not a Mageian. He didn't know what he was yet, but my gut told me that it wouldn't be long. We were on borrowed time. All hell was about to break loose.

"Excuse me Mr. Meyer, but Miss Hollyander is needed in the gym right away."

The perplexed expression plastered to Nightmares' face dissolved into a glowering sneer. He didn't like Antonio separating us, and he certainly didn't like him screwing with the torturous attack he was currently implementing. A look of sheer self-control keeping him where he stood was evident. Had the room not been filled with witnesses—who oddly looked transfixed like Nightmares was the coolest dude to ever stroll into class—I had no doubt that a battle royale would have broken out here and now.

"Very well Mr. Vasques, you may take Miss Hollyander." Mr. Meyer waved us off, his attention fully on the new student whom, along with the rest of the class, found entirely captivating. "You may sit there, Mr. Epiales." He pointed to the only vacant chair in the room—that thankfully happened to be far from mine. "Epiales . . . what nationality is that?"

As I took up my book bag and joined Antonio at the door, I was surprised to hear Nightmares speak.

"It is Greek." His voice was clear and even. Tinged with the accent of his *claimed* homeland.

"It also means nightmares," Antonio offered as he rushed me out the door; but not before I caught the look of pure hatred, Nightmares flashed our way."

We were so dead.

Antonio had me by the hand and was leading me across the lawn toward my dorm at an almost impossible speed.

"Aren't we supposed to be going to the gym?"

He yanked me along, faster.

"Okay . . . no gym."

"How did that bastard get past the safety wards?"

The fact that he hadn't asked *why* Nightmares would bother to be here in the first place, confirmed my own belief: he was here for me.

"He'll never have you," Antonio promised, hearing my unspoken thoughts as he continued to hurry us along.

I was freaking out. How did he even know I was here? Then: "How did you know *he* was here?"

Antonio glanced my way briefly, not missing a step. "I heard your thoughts."

Normally I would have been mad that he'd been eavesdropping in on my mind again. Today however, I couldn't have been more relieved.

"Iris!" I nearly halted in my tracks, yanking Antonio back in the process. "We just can't leave—"

Antonio had snaked an arm around my waist before I'd finished my sentence and was ushering me onward. "He won't touch her. As you said, he's here for you."

"But . . ."

"He won't risk his cover."

I managed to look over Antonio's shoulder toward the classrooms, expecting Iris to come running out, screaming for help. "How can you be sure?"

We had just trampled through Ms. Leech's manicured tulip border—an offense practically punishable by death. Antonio was clearly trying to put as much distance between me and Nightmares, and he didn't care whose flowers he'd decimated to do it.

"He had the opportunity to attack but didn't. I challenged him, but he did not engage. I can only assume the demon doesn't wish to be recognized, and that worries me far worse than if he had struck."

We rounded the corner of the boy's dorm rooms, just missing what would have been an unfortunate collision with a bronze statue of Herman, a strikingly freaky replica of the bird from hell. When had Leech put that up?

Antonio quickened our speed. We were at a full sprint now.

"Why don't we just blow his cover and tell the whole school what he is?"

Antonio was already shaking his head. "Who would believe us? We don't have any proof that he's a demon. And in case you didn't notice, Nightmares doesn't give off the same aura as other demons do. He appears Magian."

I hadn't realized that until Antonio had said it. No wonder Ms. Leech acted "normal" with him . . . as if he were just any other annoying student that she had the displeasure of sharing the same air space with; I truly had no idea why she would choose to spend her days in a school when she detested children so much.

"But, they would believe *you*, you're a Slayer!" More like a slayer-god as far as everyone else was concerned. Every teacher and student in this place thought Antonio walked on water. Even Ms. Leech gave him the respect due. "Since when have you ever needed proof?"

A slight smile crossed his lips. "I may be a Slayer, Evie, but my standing isn't good—at least around here."

"Since when?" I nearly tripped over one of Leech's stupid, *"No running on the grass!"* signs, followed by a close call with a: *"Don't lean on the oak tree!"* sign.

We'd reached the dorm stairs and took them two at a time. Antonio was only slightly out of breath. Me—I was gasping and on the brink of a total collapse.

"With no tangible proof, Ms. Leech will dismiss my accusations entirely."

I stared at him blankly.

"She's still mad that I was partly responsible for the destruction of *The Kitchen* before spring break."

"What?" I was leaning over, clutching my knees. I could just smack Antonio . . . making me sprint a marathon like that on the fly . . .

I recalled the wrestling/kick-boxing match Antonio and Roland had over me a few weeks ago—*The Kitchen* had been nearly destroyed, with Chaos' help of course. But why would she hold a grudge about that? My dad had more than paid for the repairs—and last I heard, we were even getting an outdoor patio with bistro tables this spring as part of the remodel. My dad had basically given the old crone a blank check: "George Hollyander's generous contribution to the continual beautification of his alma mater." Emphasis on the "continual," as Leech had explained it during the welcome back assembly this morning.

Antonio frowned. "She thinks I'm a hot-head and the only reason I haven't been kicked out, is due to my affiliation with your father." His hand paused on the door, his cheeks flushing ever so slightly. " . . . And my time should be spent focusing on the business of being a slayer, not showing off like a neanderthal." And with that, he pushed through the front doors, leaving me standing there and totally speechless in his wake.

I entered the common room a few moments later, Antonio was directly ahead, quietly observing Ms. Spencer who was once again glued to the TV—*Days of Our Lives* was in full swing on the big screen. The characters were engaged in some sort or romantic love triangle, she hadn't noticed either of us come in.

I pulled my sweatshirt over my mouth, trying to muffle my still abnormal breathing. I really needed to re-think my cardio plan.

You need one first.

Hey!

Yeah, yeah, come on.

I half-grudgingly took his offered hand as we tiptoed past Ms. Spencer, trying not to dwell too much over Antonio's ill-timed wise-crack.

There was no need for him to charm her this time, immobilizing her as he'd done once before when we'd needed to sneak into my room undetected—being a demigod had its privileges apparently: Antonio could become invisible at will.

He had come into his powers the moment he'd summoned his father Zeus, when he needed to enter Mount Olympus to retrieve the Manna-Ash blossom for me in-order to save my father's life; a debt I would never be able to repay. One of Antonio's powers had been the gift of invisibility. Antonio simply had to think he was invisible and he became such. Lucky little—

You're invisible too you know!

Yeah, as long as I'm holding your hand . . .

Then don't let go.

His smugness was tangible.

I am not being smug. It's a fact. It's not my fault my father's a god.

'*It's not my fault my father's a god.*' I mimicked, proving my point further.

Says the girl whose dad is the Leader of the Divine Army!

Please. Like anyone cares about that.

Oh yeah, no big deal at all.

And why again didn't you feel the need to tell me that you've become all-powerful? There was no way that was an accidental slip of the mind.

I am not 'all-powerful.' . . . And I've already told you . . . I'm only just discovering my abilities. It's not like I was given a handbook you know! You make it sound like I'm keeping things from you.

Wasn't he? *. . . And way to turn that around*—typical guy-move.

Now it was Antonio's turn to roll his eyes.

We took the stairs to the second floor. The both of us knowing that if Ms. Spencer saw the elevator doors suddenly open and no one appeared to get on or off, she would have the building labeled as "haunted" before we reached my room—with an anti-ghost task force consisting of one insanely good looking human whose muscles have muscles, assembling for an overly exaggerated search and destroy mission. *The Wrath Watcher,* was an all-time favorite of hers.

I had my key out and my door open in the next instant. Once inside, Antonio let go of my hand, the both of us visible again to the naked eye.

"Quick, lock it." He moved past me to the window, yanking the curtains shut. Only small slivers of light peaked out from the edges.

I turned the lock.

"We have to get you out of here."

"What?" I spun around. "We just got here!"

"Evie, please." He had his fingers pressed against his temples. He was already pacing the small path of carpet—the only bit that wasn't littered with clothing—thank you Havoc for tossing every *Barbie* outfit ever known to man onto the floor! "We have to get you out of Pinehurst," he clarified.

I bent down and began mindlessly picking up the debris. "Where do you suggest I go, Hell?"

Antonio stopped in his tracks. He looked down at me, scowling. "That *isn't* funny."

"It wasn't meant to be. It's literally the only place Nightmares can't get to me." At least I didn't think so.

"I'm sure we can come up with someplace else."

"Hopefully," I muttered as I gathered up a handful of miniature shoes. " . . . Before we get paired up for the next science project." I still couldn't believe that asshat actually had the gall to waltz into class pretending to be a student. "Did you see how mesmerized everyone was with that creep? Even Mr. Meyer was captivated."

"No, Evie . . . somehow I missed that."

I resumed my cleaning, desperately trying to avoid the incredulous look that shrouded Antonio's face; of course he would have seen that.

"Look," I tossed the little shoes into a small basket. "There's no reason for us to turn on each other. There has to be a way we can divulge what he is." I was attempting to move the focus off me and back to the jack-munch at hand.

" . . . And risk his wrath when fully exposed? Who knows what he would do. No, we need to be smart about this. We need to be one step ahead of him. We can't risk him harming anyone."

Antonio was right of course. Nightmares was a wild card. I knew he was here for me. I knew he knew I was the key. What I didn't know was what he planned to do with that key, or what he was capable of doing if he was truly cornered.

I couldn't help the shiver that ran up my spine.

One thing was certain: "He won't be able to keep up this fake persona forever. Pinehurst is full of slayers. Eventually someone is going to figure him out." Time was not on our side.

I leaned over to gather up a heaping pile of mini coats; where the hell did Havoc get all this shit?

Antonio was pinching the bridge of his nose. Something he did on occasion when he was trying to sort out the mess that was our life.

I understood his frustration. Knowing Nightmares was cruising through campus like *Joe Cool*, completely snowballing the Mageian population—all the while planning to snuff my life out, was beyond infuriating. I mean, I got the new kid appeal, but this was different. No one showed up to a new school and was instantly crowned king—this wasn't a teen movie!

"I swear there's a popularity spell we don't know about." Oh the horror . . . "Can you just imagine if Stacy got her hands on something like that? She'd—"

"Of course, he's spelled everyone . . . or at the very least himself. It makes complete sense."

"What?" I stood up, my arms filled to overflowing.

"Think about it."

I did, for half a second. "Antonio, I was joking. No one can do that . . . well, maybe except for the gods . . . We're talking about spelling an entire classroom—maybe even the whole school. That would be a considerable amount of magic." I actually couldn't fathom it. It couldn't be done. At least I didn't think so. "He's just a freaking little demon." That is totally out to get me . . .

"Yet, not another person commented on the glacial freeze emanating from the science lab."

He was right about that. No one had noticed the polar weather.

I waved him off. "He probably can control who he inflicts that upon." He wasn't trying to snuff everyone's life out after all, just mine.

" . . . And the fact that not even Ms. Leech had the slightest inkling that he wasn't Mageian?" he countered.

Ok, that *was* weird. As far as I was concerned, Leech herself was a demon. Surely she could sense her own kind.

As much as I hated to consider it, because the reality brought a whole new meaning to the word frightening, there was no other logical way to explain why not one person, student or teacher, had sensed Nightmares was anything other than a totally normal guy. But if he could pull magic off like that . . . he was anything but normal, demon or otherwise.

"I have to tell Hades."

"What?!" Antonio spun around on his heel. He'd been peeking out the window looking for any sign of ice boy. "No!"

"Antonio . . . he needs to know that Nightmares is here. He's responsible for him roaming the Earth in the first place. If we hope to have a chance of ridding ourselves of him we need—"

"No! We are not going to be indebted to Hades any more than we already are."

I dumped the last of Havoc's clothes in a drawer—she could hang her own crap up! "You're being ridiculous."

"No, I'm not. . . . And I'm certainly not going to have him thinking that you need him to save your day. We can handle this. We already know the solution."

"Oh yeah? Well, it doesn't seem like we—" I stopped mid-sentence. "Don't even think about it." I extended my arm, halting him where he stood. "Antonio, we've already been over this."

"Evie, please." He reached as I stepped out of distance. "Evie, Nightmares is here for you. He won't be leaving without you this time."

"I know that, do you think I don't know that?!" My heart was hammering. "Antonio, nothing has changed."

"Including how much I love you and want to be with you!" He'd taken my hands in his before I had even seen him move. "If you weren't the key and we didn't have this stupid curse to deal with, we'd have already made love—many times."

I couldn't have argued with that if I wanted to. But I was the key, and we did have this 'stupid curse to deal with.'

"Antonio, we can't. If you and I are together like that—"

"The hell with the consequences!" He brought me to him. His beautiful, caring eyes were beseeching. "I'm tired of looking out a window and over our shoulders. I'm tired of my father's threats and Hades' lingering claim on you. I love you, and you were mine first. Heaven would not curse us in such a way."

That was not the romantic dialog I was expecting.

He cupped my face with his hands, capturing my stare and locking it with his. "Right here, right now, is only you and me. We love each other, Evie. There isn't anything else." He lowered his lips to mine.

I wanted nothing more than to kiss him. To let all our restraints and worries flitter away. To go back to the time before I ever set foot in the Underworld. But life was not that simple for us, and the consequences of giving into Antonio's love were detrimental. 'Heaven would not curse us in such a way . . .' was not a gamble I was willing to make.

"I'm sorry." I turned away from him and stepped out of his embrace; his frustration was palpable.

"You know that if Nightmares succeeds, he'll have the power to control all of Hell and the Outer World."

I wrapped my arms around myself. I knew the magnitude of what he spoke of all too well.

"He'll conquer Olympus, Evie, and the heavens. Your father, mine—Hades. He'll enslave us all. Mageian *and* human!"

Talk about a guilt trip. Never has there been so much riding on: should we or shouldn't we have sex?

"Evie, Zeus will not allow that to happen!"

And there it was . . . I spun around, my mouth hanging open. All his beautiful words vanishing in one poof.

"*I* will not allow that to happen," he amended quickly. As if that were any better. Clearly he and his thunderbolt wielding ass of a father were teaming up—again. He attempted to resume a shred of composure. "Evie, I can't let him have you."

I stared at Antonio in disbelief. What the hell was this . . . a disaster prevention plan? A take one for the team—on my part? And I hadn't missed the fact that I was last on his list of concerns.

"You know that's not true."

"Do I?"

"Evie don't you see—"

"Oh, I see perfectly. I thought this was settled . . . I thought you understood. Antonio, I haven't changed my mind and I'm not going to. . . . And I'm certainly not having a quickie in my dorm room all in the name of saving creation!" This sounded like something right out of Zeus' 'Get Evie in bed and steel her powers before anyone else does', book. If I didn't know Antonio as well as I did, I'd think he was after me for his own personal gain.

I knew he'd heard my inner thoughts. I felt bad for thinking them—until I realized he wasn't denying them.

I studied him with disbelief. "I can't believe you . . ."

The moment he had laid eyes on Nightmares in class, his mind had been made up. He truly saw no other way. He just didn't know how to approach it with me. I could hear it in his thoughts now. He had dragged me across campus planning to sway me into making love to him—all in the name of saving me from the big bad demon and the God of the Underworld of course. But, if in doing so he was securing the safety of his father's domain . . . bonus.

"That's not true, Evie." But his words were half-hearted.

"Your thoughts say otherwise."

"Evie . . ." Antonio suddenly looked tired. "You don't know the pressure I'm under. Worrying, trying to keep you safe, trying to appease your father and mine. There is no other way. I'm doing this for you!"

I raised a brow, daring him to go on and explain the "pressure" *he* was under; and I was extremely anxious to hear how 'this' was all for me.

"I didn't mean it like that," he sighed heavily, running a hand through his hair. "You know I love you with all my heart. I want nothing more than a life where I can love you wholly—with none of this hanging over our heads. I'm trying to protect you. I don't want you to spend the rest of your days in sorrow and misery. I don't want you to have to return to Hell and to Hades again. I don't want to worry about Nightmares capturing you, or worse—killing you. I just want to keep you safe. I want to keep all of us safe."

Such words would normally melt my heart. But these had a cost, and the price was just too high to pay. He was forgetting one thing in all of this: I loved and cared about him too.

Antonio took my hands in his once more. "Evie, you said you wanted it to be me you gave yourself to." He brought each of my wrists to his lips, kissing the tops of them softly. "I just figured if we wait, you won't have that option." He had the nerve to look contrite.

Un-believable. I yanked my hands free. I had gone from zero to livid instantaneously. He was actually still trying to guilt me into giving in.

"How can you stand there, say things to me like that, and still press this? You know how I feel!"

Apparently chivalry had just died in Antonio's book: "You know why I can't just stand by and not 'press this'!" He stood tall, facing me squarely, unashamed. "Zeus has made his position quite clear. . . . And if Nightmares takes you Evie, and by *takes*, I don't mean that he will be gentle about it, *all* will be lost. *You* will be lost. You won't recover from that. Would you rather be with me, the man you say you love, or a monster who will leave you wishing you were dead?!"

"As if Hades would let either of those scenarios happen."

"Havoc!" Antonio and I both jumped. She was standing between us, attempting to look angelic.

I clutched my chest, trying to steady my racing heart as I staggered back and took a seat on the bed. "I told you to stop popping in on us like that, you scared me half to death."

It had taken her all of a millisecond to survey the situation, and she looked more than pleased with her timing. She pretended to inspect her newly painted nails.

"You seem to forget Child of Light, that Hades has taken a personal interest in you." She sauntered over to a chair and made herself comfortable. She then locked eyes with Antonio. "Do you honestly believe he would let anything, or anyone, harm what is his?"

My breath caught. Of course—Hades! I knew Nightmares couldn't escape his wrath. I felt a smile stretch across my face. Havoc must have learned that Hades had found a way to deal with the icy prick. We were probably worrying for nothing.

Antonio's eyes had narrowed on the little pixie. "Are you implying that *I* am incapable of protecting Evie?"

"Antonio . . ." Now was not the time for posturing—who cared who destroyed him!

Havoc laughed outright. "Implying? I'm saying it! Please . . . everyone knows that the sky-gods aren't powerful enough to stop demons. If you were, they'd have been destroyed millennia ago."

Her statement only managed to piss Antonio off more.

"Besides," she went on. "We don't have that kind of time. Boyfriend number four needs eliminating and quick. Do you know who I saw flirting with him?" she huffed in mock-horror, her eyes going wide, daring me to guess.

I was too shocked to speak. Not only had Havoc referred to Nightmares as boyfriend number four—in front of Antonio—but someone amongst the living was *flirting* with the ice-jerk? I mean, I knew he visually looked cute, but was there really no instinctual self-preservation?

Havoc rolled her eyes with impatience. "Stacy Wilcox!"

"What?!" And then: "No! If she gets close to him, she could learn everything!" Nightmares would definitely be the pillow talk type. There was no doubt in my mind. A total bragger if ever there was one.

The awfulness of it all played vividly through my mind like a bad B movie. Providing Antonio with the whole frightening picture: If Stacy learned that I was betrothed to Hades, my life as a Mageian was over! I would be deemed a traitor and at best, cast into Hell by morning.

Ms. Leech would love that . . . it would validate her notion of me being nothing more than a troublemaker. I could practically hear that beast of a vulture of hers squawking in agreement. Hoping for the chance to pick my bones clean; Stacy and Chad would probably lead the lynch mob themselves.

Antonio's staff appeared in his hand.

"What are you doing?" I panicked as I looked from him to his weapon.

"I'm going to kill Nightmares before he has a chance to divulge anything."

"What? No!" I was at the door, attempting to block him.

Havoc was laughing hysterically. "You can't kill what isn't alive you moron!"

The both of us looked from each other to her, utter confusion shrouding our faces.

"What do you mean?" I asked. What did she know that we didn't?

"I've slain demons before Pixie, it's not hard. They all die just the same." Antonio's resolve was unmistakable. His whole being seethed with rage. He wanted Nightmares dead more than he had wanted gargoyle Roland's head to roll; or even his hands around Havoc's neck squeezing the little life out of her, which was currently one of the top three on his to-do list.

"Yes, yes, you've *slain* demons," Havoc taunted mockingly. "But you haven't slain one of Satan's minions. For all intents and purposes, it may just as well be Satan himself you plan to challenge." She sat up straight and pointed a finger at him. "You're not ready, *Slayer*. He'll kill you where you stand. He's been kind to let you live this long."

The blade at the end of Antonio's staff was out and aimed right at Havoc's throat. "Shall I practice on you?"

"Antonio!" I moved to pull his arm in-an-attempt to shift the weapon away, but I decided better of it. If I bumped Antonio in the slightest, Havoc was done for. And as much as Havoc drove me crazy, I didn't want her dead. "Antonio, please."

A momentary look of shock crossed Havoc's face before it was replaced with a wicked grin. Chaos had appeared at Antonio's side, and he didn't look happy.

My heart stopped. This was bad. This was very bad.

"It would seem that I have impeccable timing." Chaos's dark eyes were fixed on Antonio. He was keenly aware of the proximity of Antonio's blade to Havoc's neck. An ominous cloud of dread seemed to engulf the room. "I'd remove that weapon if I were you, *Son of Zeus*."

"Antonio . . ." I placed my hands on his shoulder.

I'd seen firsthand what Chaos could do when he was "helping" someone. He'd destroyed *The Kitchen* in-an-attempt to distract the other students from seeing my demon-red eyes the day Roland and Antonio fought over me—and I was just a *"friend."* I didn't want to see what he would do if he was protecting someone he actually cared about, and Chaos more than cared for Havoc. The fact that he was referring to Antonio as "Son of Zeus," didn't bode well.

"Antonio . . ."

He turned toward me, lowering his weapon, his thoughts flooding my head: *I will kill Nightmares or die trying!*

"No!" I gripped his arm. "If what Havoc says is true, you'll just anger him more. I don't want you to get killed!" I hated to admit it, especially to Antonio. "We need Hades."

I regretted the statement immediately. The look of pain and utter betrayal that flashed across Antonio's face would haunt me until my dying day—which incidentally may not be that far away. I'd cut him worse than any enemy could. I'd all but admitted that he could protect me, that he wasn't strong enough—and worse than that . . . I stated that only Hades could.

"Antonio, I didn't mean—"

"Have it your way, Evie." He moved past me to the door, his hand pausing on the knob momentarily, not looking back. "If you think Hades can help you, then I suggest you see him immediately. You don't have much time." He left the room, and although the two pixies stood beside me, I suddenly felt very alone.

Chapter 7

I rounded on Havoc. "Well that's just great, thanks for that!"

"What?" Havoc asked, the picture of innocence.

"You had to barge in here, uninvited, and emasculate him."

"Me? Oh no, no, no, Child of Light, you did that all by yourself; and by the look of things, my timing couldn't have been any better for you."

Damn her. As annoying as it was, she was right—on both accounts. The blame lay solely on me. Havoc had stated that Antonio wasn't strong enough to kill Nightmares . . . I was the one who told him not even to try—and if that wasn't bad enough, I ground salt in his wounds by saying Hades would handle it.

"So his pride is wounded, he'll be back. He . . . *loves* you." The very word seemed to stick in Chaos's throat. As if it were a disgusting concept.

I regarded the pixie with surprise. It wasn't like him to offer comforting words. If I didn't know any better, I might think he was growing soft.

"Men do not like to look weak," he added, ". . . especially in front of those they have sworn to protect."

I nodded in understanding, not wanting to wreck the moment with unnecessary words—very un-Evie like of me.

That was as much sympathy as I would get from the little leprechaun. I was shocked that I even got that.

Havoc leaned toward her man, offering a smile before she rested her head on his broad shoulder. "That was very sweet of you, Chaos," she whispered, earning a rosy grin from him in return. "Evie needs all the guidance we can offer."

. . . And the "nice" moment was over.

I looked at my clock. It was well into fourth period. I had hours before my scheduled visit to see Hades—not that it was my choice to go, but now I would feel extra guilty for being summoned away. Antonio would look at this as an opportune moment for me to run to his nemesis for help.

The last time I saw Hades, he'd stirred my emotions. Acting selfless and releasing me from our latest bargain: I wouldn't have to remain in the Underworld upon giving my father his cure after all. I was more than happy. But a part of me, a big part, still wondered why he'd agreed to it. He never actually said what was in it for him. As far as Zeus' involvement . . . I shuddered to think.

Havoc and Chaos were staring at me expectantly with their beady little eyes. The both, trying their best to decipher my thoughts—I knew what they wanted to know.

"I'm not asking him for help."

Havoc's mouth gaped in disbelief.

"I can't run to Hades every time I need something. He won't always be there. It's not right to rely on him. I have to stand on my own."

"You mean it would crush Antonio," Havoc scoffed.

"You're mad, Woman!" Chaos stood before me, his angry face scowling up at mine. "The demon will kill you—or make you wish that it had. Do you think the Slayer wants that? You're letting his wounded pride guide you foolishly. . . . And As for Hades . . . he will *always* be there."

I did my best to swallow the giant lump that had formed in my throat. Of course, Antonio didn't want me to face Nightmares alone. But he didn't want me to run to Hades for help either. Chaos was one hundred percent right, but what choice did I have? If I went to Hades it would not only upset Antonio, it would bind me to him even more. And with the current flood of emotions between me and him, I was pretty-positive that wasn't a good idea. As an added bonus to this whole mess, Antonio would assume that I truly did believe him to be completely incapable of protecting me. That I thought him weak. I was screwed either way.

I sighed heavily at the two pixies before bending down and taking up my book bag. Suddenly school seemed more appealing.

"I gotta hurry if I'm gonna make spells!" I turned and dashed from the room, my ears just escaping their protests. I felt defeated already. Havoc and Chaos were not about to relent, and if the shoe were on the other foot, I wouldn't either.

I'd made it halfway to class before one piercing thought struck me: Would I be walking into the same room as Nightmares?

Could my life possibly get any worse . . .? I really, *really,* had
to stop asking myself that question—of course it could get worse. It
always got worse! If worser was a word, I'd say it got worser by the
moment. And this was the worstest moment ever!

Not only was Nightmares in Spells, but so was Roland, the
creep, Vandenburg. Blasted semester changes!

Roland had even offered Nightmares, Victor's old seat. The
two were apparently *besties* now.

Victor was currently seated in the front row, left of Gillian.
Having explained to Ms. Spicer that he "couldn't hear her lessons
from the back of the room," Ms. Spicer was all too accommodating
and moved him immediately. Truthfully, Victor couldn't stand sitting
beside Roland any longer. Their friendship had taken a dramatic
nosedive when Victor slugged him for the way he'd treated me at the
spring dance. I still owed Victor, a big thank you.

Gillian leaned to her right, her mouth nearly touching my ear.
"Who's the hottie?" She jerked her head toward the back of the room.

I didn't really have to look, but curiosity had gotten the best of
me.

Nightmares actually had the moxie to wink my way. As for
Roland, I swear he looked love-struck when our eyes met—gag!

I turned back around in my seat, facing forward, but not before
Roland's notebook spontaneously took on a mind of its own and
began whacking him upside the head for being the ass that he is.

"Hey . . . what the hell!?" The class broke out into hysterics as
Roland jumped out of his chair, shrieking while trying to bat away the
offending object.

I couldn't help the chuckle that escaped me as Ms. Spicer cast
a spell that didn't entirely halt the attack. It more like provided the
finale I couldn't have planned any better myself: Roland's notebook

exploded into a billion pieces right in his face, leaving a black tinge to his perfect complexion, and a plume of smoke that coated his newly bleached blond hair.

"Oh man," Victor cracked up, not even bothering to hide his delight. "That's classic!"

Gillian raised her eyebrows at me but said nothing. She knew as well as I did, Roland had it coming. I also knew she was planning to pick up where we'd left off in our conversation as soon as class was over. The possible thought of her announcing that Nightmares was the new *ten* on the hot-o-meter, was more than I could handle.

Ms. Spicer stood before the class frowning. Her eyes, quickly scanning over each-and-every one of us. Clearly searching for the culprit, but to no avail.

Roland slumped back into his seat, whimpering softly and nursing a bloody lip.

"I'm trusting that there won't be any more books springing to life?" Her eyes darted from student to student, silently conveying her warning. "Now then," she dusted her hands together, casting away the unpleasant memory. "I hope you all had a wonderful Spring Break. While most of you were relaxing somewhere splendid, I was here . . . planning a most exciting surprise!"

Uh oh. I sat straight up in my chair. The last time Ms. Spicer had an "exciting surprise," we'd spent the class period practicing defensive spells on a Ragno. Half of the junior class had spent the weekend sick-to-death from the experience—me included. This couldn't be good.

". . . But unfortunately, that surprise will have to wait until tomorrow," she added solemnly, feigning disappointment. "Today," she nearly squealed, " . . . we've got something better!" She could hardly contain herself. "Vipers!"

"Are you crazy!?" I was clambering to get out of my desk. There was no way I was reliving any part of my journey through the Underworld . . . especially the Viper part. "You can't bring Vipers into class!" I knew I sounded more than insolent, but good hell, what was she thinking?

"Yeah, isn't that illegal?" Someone panicked from the back.

Ms. Spicer rolled her eyes as if we were being ridiculous. "Sit down, Miss Hollyander. Of course, I would never think of bringing anything to class that would pose any danger . . . and no *Haven*, it is *not* illegal.”

I let out a sigh of relief, echoing my classmates. I knew I wasn't the only one afraid of Vipers—or Ms. Spicer's surprises. I moved to take my seat again.

“Mr. Epiales,’ Viper is completely harmless.”

“What!?” My butt hadn't even hit the chair.

Ms. Spicer was grinning at Nightmares as if he was holding the teacher of the year award and was approaching her with it.

“No way!” Victor had risen too, and in three quick strides, was already to the door. “I'm not spending another weekend in the infirmary puking my guts out; or dead. I'll take the detention.” He left the room amidst the chatter of agreement from the other students who were all shuffling around collecting their belongings.

I was about to do the very same when—

“Sit down!” For the first time since I'd come to Pinehurst, Ms. Spicer looked mad. *Really* mad. “Honestly, the fuss you're all making. Mr. Epiales has assured me that no harm shall befall any of you students. *Balisha* is a personal pet.”

I crossed my arms over my chest, scowling—completely unsurprised. Of course, he had a pet viper.

“Well, “pet” might be a stretch of the word,” Nightmares spoke up, having the nerve to look sheepish. “One doesn't *truly* own a wild animal after all. She's my father's. He's using her for a research project he's conducting on what effects the venom can have during prolonged exposure.”

I couldn't hide my scoff if I wanted to. “And who's your father . . . Satan?”

“Miss Hollyander! That will be quite enough young lady. I will not tolerate such rudeness. Apologize to Mr. Epiales this instant.”

“Seriously? You've got to be kidding!” I turned on my heel, glaring at the creep from Hell. “ . . . And just who or what poor animal, is he conducting these ‘prolonged’ venom exposures on?”

“Miss Hollyander!”

I looked at Ms. Spicer in disbelief. “Oh come on . . . What kind of idiot or sadistic demon would need to test or even question, what prolonged Viper venom exposure would do? It's not freaking rocket science! Doesn't anyone else sense the evil here? He's a demon! A demon!" I'd totally lost it. Couldn't anyone else see him for what he was?

Ms. Spicer was standing before me, absolutely seething. She leaned dangerously close. "Apologize now or be expelled."

My mouth dropped open. My dad would freak if I got kicked out of Pinehurst, especially now! This was so unfair.

Nightmares smiled expectantly. His grin rolling outward like the *"Grinch who stole Christmas."* He was loving this. He hadn't the slightest concern that I'd just called him out."

I glowered at him all-the-more.

"Now, Miss Hollyander."

I really, really, *really* hated this guy.

"Fine! Sorry," I gritted grudgingly, as I took my seat in a dramatic huff, trying to ignore the gasps from the other students at my apparent "rudeness"—if only they knew.

"Apology accepted," Nightmares winked playfully at me once again. "It's ok Ms. Spicer, it's normal for girls to be squeamish around such things."

Chauvinistic ass. I fumed in my chair. I couldn't imagine hating anyone more than I hated ice-boy at this very moment. Not only was he a demon that was totally out to kill me, but he was a suck-up to boot!

"That is very gracious of you, Mr. Epiales. It's a pity more students aren't as understanding and well mannered."

I slumped further in my chair. I knew that last remark was directed my way. If I had to listen to Ms. Spicer gushing over this jack munch for the rest of the school year, I was going to get my own "pet" Viper and happily put an end to my misery.

"Now then," Ms. Spicer clasped her hands together, smiling bright—attempting to lighten the mood. ". . . Isn't this exciting? And how fortunate for us all to have the opportunity to see one of these unique creatures up close."

Ms. Spicer was an utter fool if she found anything remotely "fortunate" about being in the same vicinity as one of these monsters.

"Remember," she went on, eyes twinkling. "Most Mageians never experience this part of the Slayer world;

and most Slayers themselves thankfully never have to encounter such things. To see an actual *tame* viper, without worry or risk, will allow us to become more familiar with a creature we may one day be forced to confront." Her expression turned serious. "The Underworld is a dark place, my young friends. Learn of its demons and you *will* survive its dangers."

It was painfully obvious to me that Ms. Spicer had no clue as to what she was talking about. Clearly, she had never set foot in the Underworld or she wouldn't be pushing these up close and personal encounters with these spawns from Hell.

I glanced around at the cringing students. Some, to their credit, had the good sense to look petrified.

Didn't anyone else find it odd that a new kid shows up to school and just happens to have a "pet viper" for show-and-tell in their bag? I mean, who in the hell has a pet viper? And as far as it being his father's research project   . . . I'll bet! Satan probably used these snakes to torment anything he could get his claws on. For all I knew, I was his next research project!

Nightmares was walking up to the front of the room now with a large sack gingerly slung over his shoulder. "This one's an infant," he boasted as he set the bag down on Ms. Spicer's desk and began loosening the ties.

I could feel the color drain from my face as his eyes locked with mine. His hand reached in, unafraid."

And then came the screaming . . .

He'd pulled out the two-headed beast.

Students were out of their seats, fleeing in all directions. They pushed and jumped over desks and tables, slamming them into disarray as they tried to scramble frantically for the door, all the while Nightmare's hellish laugh echoed around us.

Gillian, attempting to escape, had backed into me and knocked us both to the ground, a desk toppled over, hitting her in the head.

"Gillian!" I reached for her, pushing the desk away and taking her limp body into my arms. I could just feel her breath against my cheek—she'd just been knocked out.

The strangled cry that met my ears next, was piercing. My attention snapped to the front of the room.

"No!" I released Gillian, letting her slip to the floor. I was on my feet, propelling forward. "*Floga!*" My hands burned as flames shot from them, striking the Viper.

The monster's ear splitting screech shattered glass from the windows, casting shards into the air. I watched while it thrashed violently about, catching everything near it on fire as it withered; it was being incinerated alive.

My mind screamed in horror as Ms. Spicer crumpled to the ground. It protested what I already knew to be true: she was dead. The two-headed snake had closed both of its mouths around her neck, sinking venom deep into her bloodstream, and I had been too slow to stop it.

I crawled beneath a table to reach her, pulling her away from the flames. Tears filled my eyes as I stared into hers—they were still open, fixed with the terror she'd experienced.

Nightmares strode toward me, shoving desks from his path—completely unaffected by the fire that nipped at him; his black irises had turned red.

I held Ms. Spicer close to me, wanting to protect her body from any more harm.

"You didn't have to hurt anyone!" I cried. "You didn't have to kill her!"

Nightmares was grinning at the mayhem he'd caused. "I didn't. You did."

"No." I shook my head, not wanting to hear the hissed lies.

"How does it *feel* . . ." he inched closer, his icy breath assaulting my skin as he neared. ". . . Knowing that you couldn't save her?" He yanked Ms. Spicer from my grasp, discarding her body across the floor as if she were nothing more than a piece of laundry. " . . . Knowing that you will be helpless to save any of them?"

I subconsciously began scooting back, attempting to put even the smallest bit of distance between us.

" . . . Knowing that I will continue to kill all those around you—from your foolhardy teacher to your cherished friends . . .?" He motioned to Gillian, who still lay unconscious on the floor a few feet away.

"No." Each word he spoke was like a knife plunging into me. Twisting into my grieving heart.

"How does it feel, Child of Light, knowing that *you* can never escape?" He lunged forward, knocking me back to the floor. His icy hands wrapped around my neck like a noose as he pressed my head hard against the tile.

" . . . Knowing that one by one, I will take them from you."

"I won't let you hurt anyone else," I gritted out. My fingers were desperately trying to pry his hands from me as I thrashed beneath his hold.

He leaned closer, his lips brushing my ear. "You are powerless to stop me."

I could feel my cheekbone bruising against the floor from the pressure. I gripped at his wrists, futilely attempting to push him away, but his hold only tightened. I gasped and wheezed. Tears leaked from my eyes as his hand clenched—he was crushing my throat.

"You *will* aid me, or they will all die."

Ms. Spicer's body lay to the side. Her lifeless eyes stared back into mine, cementing the knowledge that I could not fight this beast alone. That I was incapable of stopping him. I had been a fool. Havoc and Chaos were right. I needed Hades.

I struggled my last against Nightmares hold. My breathing gurgled. I attempted to cry out Hades' name in a strangled breath . . . praying he would hear me.

The ground rumbled, reverberating through my body, and through the hands that held my throat.

My eyes shot wide-open as Nightmares released me abruptly, spinning around, creating as much distance as possible for himself in the little room.

I gasped for air, choking on the smoke from the fire that had rapidly spread around us. It had ignited everything it touched upon contact—as if the entire room was made of paper—there was no escape.

The center of the room exploded with sparks; Hades stepped from the flames—setting everything that wasn't already on fire, a blaze. His black eyes found me quickly before they landed on Nightmares, not ten feet away, smirking in delight at the sight of him.

Hades roared out, his body nearly doubling in size with each ragged breath he took in. "You will die." He descended upon Nightmares.

I couldn't think to watch. My vision was hazy. I rolled over, still wheezing as I struggled to reach Gillian's blurred frame. I pulled myself over to her limp body dragging her away from the inferno, doing my best to shield her from the fire.

I flinched as part of the far-away corner of the room caved in. I quickly searched for Hades. Had I not been there to see it with my own eyes, I never would have believed it: Nightmares charged him, completely unafraid! His body, wraith-like, was mist through Hades' fingers . . . and from the expression on Hades' face . . . that had never happened before.

Blood streaks from slash wounds suddenly appeared on Hades' arms and chest—gushing blood. He snarled in anger, roaring, unable to stop his attacker while being struck from every side.

"Child of Light!" Havoc and Chaos were beside me. "Come, we have to get you out of here!"

"I can't," I rasped. I could hardly speak. Nightmares fingers had nearly crushed my windpipe. I pointed toward the doorway that was blocked with flames; and I couldn't reach a window without Gillian and me enduring third-degree burns. We were trapped. There was no way out.

"Evie!" Antonio was shouting from the doorway. His voice called to me, but he was out of reach, I couldn't even see him.

The ceiling on the far side of the room was completely engulfed, collapsing entirely and bringing a rush of heat and air, providing more life to the already angry inferno.

Havoc and Chaos looked at one another, steeling themselves as if they were about to do something costly. Then each of them grabbed one of Gillian's hands and the three of them disappeared.

Before I could react, Hades knelt in front of me and scooped me up off the floor. His face was just as cut and bloodied as the rest of his body, and I could see that it took all his strength to hold me. He ran forward, jumping into the fire, not looking back toward a pursuing Nightmares, as the both of us disappeared within the heart of the flames; Nightmares' angry screams thundered after us.

Chapter 8

Hades staggered across his bedroom floor with me still in his arms, collapsing just before he reached the bed. His once strong body collided hard with the stone floor, turning at the last moment so that he would take the full brunt of the fall.

"Hades!" I scrambled out from his embrace.

His eyes opened. A flash of relief crossed his face at the sight of me before his eyes fell shut again. "You're safe."

I was surprised at how much effort it took for him to speak, at how ragged his breathing was, and how completely helpless he looked laying there—bloodied and limp—slashed repeatedly from too many claw marks to count. I watched as his chest rose up and down, slowly; and slower still. As sure as I was kneeling beside him, Hades was dying . . .

"No." I patted his face gently, my voice a strangled whisper. "Hades, open your eyes. Please open your eyes." But he couldn't.

His head lolled to the side. Small beads of sweat had formed on his forehead, glistening down his face to the deep gash along his jaw. I turned away from the dark crimson that leaked out onto the floor; it was my fault he suffered these wounds.

I got up, ran to the door, and flung it open. Creatures that were so distorted and grotesque . . . creatures that would haunt my dreams forever more, stood outside it, lurking in the shadows like predators waiting for their master to allow them to feed on me—this would not be that day.

"Hades need water!" I demanded. Where I got the voice I didn't know. "Bring it to me now!" I didn't bother being nice. Something told me that they wouldn't have responded to "*nice*." If I was going to survive in this place, I needed to appear strong. I could never let them know that I was afraid. I could never let them know that Hades' life was hanging by a thread . . . that he has been weakened. If they did, we were both as good as dead.

The demons slunk back, ignoring my request and withdrawing even further into the recesses of darkness, but they did not completely disappear. Some gnashed their sharp teeth together as they watched me hungrily and others slurped and sucked thick saliva in anticipation, licking their scaled and peeling lips as if they'd already had a taste of me; they obviously smelled the fresh blood, my clothes were drenched in it.

A low growl escaped one that I realized had *not* drawn back. His eyes dilated as it sniffed in my direction. Its forked tongue licked at the air. I swear it could taste the blood from a distance.

"Your master needs water!" I demanded from the creature. If it was going to openly gawk at me, the least it could do was to bring what I asked for. I locked eyes with it . . . I couldn't back down. "Water," I gritted out.

I could see out my peripheral . . . demons were looking from one to the other. What was wrong with them? They acted as if they didn't understand a word I was saying. Their large fathomless eyes stared blankly. Even the one that had inadvertently challenged me to what I would forever more refer to as: the longest stare down of my life, had turned away to look stonily at another. This was just my luck . . . non-English-speaking demons!

"Errr!" I growled in frustration as I stepped back into the room and slammed the door on them. "Stupid demons!"

I had to think. I rubbed my hands up and down my arms, for some reason needing to warm them, who knew Hell could feel so cold . . . I watched Hades lay there, still unmoving.

"I'll just have to make my own water." I knew this would cost me. Casting a spell in the Underworld was debilitating, but Hades needed help and fast. I had no choice. I looked around the room and found a small basin atop a table. I took it up and breathed into it: "*Acqua.*"

Water began to fill the bowl as a searing pain rose in my stomach and into my chest. I pushed all thoughts of my own discomfort aside and rushed back to Hades.

"Here, drink this." I tipped the bowl slightly, allowing water to drizzle into his mouth.

He drank very little before his eyes flickered open, his brow furrowing as he did so. "Where did you get that?"

"Shhh . . ." I shook my head. "It doesn't matter." I lightly brushed his damp hair from his forehead. "Do you need more?"

Realization had taken hold of him. "Evie, you can't cast spells here."

I forced a smile. "You didn't used to complain. Besides, I'm fine. Now let's get you cleaned up. You'll be alright in no time." I wouldn't have it any other way. He'd risked his life to save me from Nightmares and burning to death. I owed Hades a debt once again, but this time he wasn't asking for payment, and that scared me.

I ripped off a piece of fabric from my tattered shirt and dunked it into the water. He watched me as I lightly dabbed at a cut on his face, doing my best to clean it.

Hades closed his eyes in pain.

"I'm sorry." I paused, that shouldn't have hurt him. "I'll try to be softer."

"No, I can stand it." But he couldn't. The anguish that hung in his eyes was real.

I had to busy myself. I couldn't see him this way. Hades was supposed to be stronger than life—a tower of strength! The man beside me was anything but. *This* man was almost human.

"You're still bleeding." The wound that I had just cleaned hadn't clotted and was leaking fresh blood. His face was paler with each passing moment. "Hades . . ."

He reached up with a shaky hand and touched my neck; the burns that Nightmares had left around my throat still ached.

"No!" I moved his hand away. I couldn't believe him! "You are *not* healing me."

"I cannot stand to see you harmed. Please Evie, let me do this . . . one last time."

I wasn't sure when the tears had begun to fall from my eyes. I wiped at them futilely.

"You are not dying, do you hear me?" I plunged the rag back into the water and blotted his cheek once more, wiping off the dark soot that clung to him. "You're fine," I assured. "It's just a little cut. I must not have wiped it properly, that's all." My tears came heavier, free-falling down my face and onto his shoulder. "See . . . it's almost stopped bleeding."

"Evie . . . stop."

I looked at him through blurred eyes. "I won't let you die . . . I can't. Besides," I cleared my throat, ". . . you promised to protect me."

He reached up and cupped his hand behind my neck. And although he didn't have the strength, I let him pull me closer to him. His lips met mine. His kiss, soft and feather-like. It was a kiss goodbye.

"Forgive me, for I cannot fulfill that promise."

My heart was breaking.

"Evie . . . you should go. I do not wish for you to see me like this. Our bargain is—"

"No!" I cried, stopping him mid-sentence. I held onto him, sobbing. I would not let him release me from our bargain or let him give up. Not this way. My resolve was strong. Something inside of me had broken free . . . a truth I had been denying, though I didn't know how deep it ran. As sure as I needed air to breathe, I needed Hades alive—I needed *him*! "You're Hades, dammit! *King* of the Underworld! You can't die!"

"Evie . . ."

I turned away from him. I couldn't concentrate while looking at his defeated expression. He may be ready to give up, but I wasn't! There had to be a way.

"All things must end my love, even me. It is the way of it."

"No." I wouldn't hear it. I held him tighter to me. Think Evie, think! You're the damn Child of Light, for craps sake—George Hollyander's daughter! You're supposed to be gifted! If only I was gifted like Antonio . . . he could heal Hades with his light. He—

"That's it!" I jumped, causing Hades to flinch and wince at the same time. "Sorry." I placed a hand on his forehead, stilling him. His skin was hot, burning to the touch. He didn't have much time.

"Evie . . ."

"You're going to be alright," I promised, offering him a sincere smile this time. "Everything will be alright." I leaned over and pressed my lips to his. This had to work. "It's my turn to save you now." I wasn't even sure I knew the words. I closed my eyes and took in a deep breath as I let the spell come to me: "*Elafry.*"

A bright, pulsating light, lit from within my body, moving down my arms and through my hands and fingertips; it reached Hades, moving through him like wildfire. Illuminating his entire being like sunlight bouncing off a pile of gold ingots—I could hardly stand to look at him.

His wounds began to heal as I felt myself begin to weaken. I bit the inside of my cheek, holding back the urge to cry out in pain. I felt as though I was withering like a dry leaf before winter. I couldn't release the charm until he was healed . . . I couldn't release the charm until he was saved. Just a little longer . . .

"Evie!" Hades' voice rang out strong, bringing a smile to my face. He jerked away from me, but it was too late. "What have you done?"

I grinned, and I could feel it touch my eyes. He was beautiful . . . "I saved you."

"NO!"

Never in all of Hades' time had anyone bestowed such a gift— and a curse. Evie had literally given part of her soul to save him, and she now faded before his eyes; her life force blinking like the light of a firefly. She had crumpled into his arms, and he now held her gently while water spilled from his eyes. He was crying. Actually-crying!

"My love, can you hear me?"

Evie's eyes fluttered open. A smile rested on her lips. "If I say yes, does that mean I'm still alive?"

Hades couldn't help but laugh a little. That was Evie's doing. She had brought joy into his wretched life—yet another reason he could not let her go. Even now she tried to lift his spirits.

"You're crying. Are you still in pain?"

He shook his head. Even now her concern was for him. If he lived until the end of time, he would never understand how this girl could care so much for him—when he had brought so much pain and suffering into her life. But she did care, deeply, and he marveled at it.

"I know what you're thinking," Evie breathed, her voice sounding more tired with each passing breath. "I used to wonder that myself."

Hades stared at her in disbelief. How could she know his thoughts? "And now?" he asked, curious as to her answer. Curious to see if she actually *did* know his thoughts.

Evie opened her eyes again, staring long into his. What she searched for he didn't know, but she seemed to have found it, her smile widened. "I stopped wondering. You have taken from me . . . but you have also given. You are not as bad as you see yourself. You are not as bad as I once believed. You are capable of loving, and being loved."

For the first time in Hades' miserable existence, he felt real shame. He did not deserve any love she offered him.

"I cannot let you suffer any longer."

Evie's eyes grew wide, their color darkening to a deep red. He could sense the demon in her, strengthening her resolve—yet she was weaker than any newborn. "You will not heal me, do you understand? You will not give back what I've given to you."

Hades shook his head, his eyes still wet from tears that now blinded him. He could not hurt her by dispensing away her gift so easily. But he could not deny her life either.

She turned her head to his chest, taking in a sharp ragged breath, a peaceful calm seemed to settle on her face.

"You cannot ask me to let you die." He lowered his lips to her forehead, letting his kiss linger, taking in the scent of her, and burning it into his memory. "I *won't* let you die." Hades rose from the floor, cradling Evie in his arms. "If you will not let me help you myself, I will bring you to someone that can."

"You can't be here." I couldn't believe it. I was coherent enough to know that Hades was carrying me across Ms. Leech's common area in broad daylight. Luckily, no one seemed to be around. "Hades . . ."

"Fear not my love. Not a soul shall see us, or harm you in any way."

Like I hadn't heard that before. The last time Hades said no one would see us, Havoc caught him kissing me—in this very garden in fact! Then she opened a giant hole that led straight to Hell in the hopes that I'd fall in. As for no one harming me . . . well, Nightmares was proof that that statement was null and void.

I took in a ragged breath. "Where are you taking me?" My strength was fading fast. Even my ability to keep my eyes open for any length of time was failing.

"To the angel."

I looked up into Hades' face, stunned.

His expression was hard, and his voice was like steel. If Hades was taking me to Antonio, I truly had to be dying, and this . . . seeking help from an angel—from another man, had to be killing *him*.

"Hades, you don't have to take me to Antonio. Set me down here, he'll find me."

Hades stopped mid-step, his stare dropping to mine. "Do you think I fear being in his presence?"

I shook my head. "No, I just—"

"Do you believe that I would just set you down on the ground . . . that I could leave you here . . . wounded and unprotected?" His voice rose louder with each question. "Is that the man you think I am?"

"No!" I spent the remainder of my strength on that one word. Giving into exhaustion I let my eyes fall shut. I had to focus to draw in the next breath of air. "I only . . . meant . . . that I understand . . . how hard . . . this is for you."

Hades was already walking again, quickening his step.

"There is no suffering for which I could endure greater than losing you."

In my heart I was smiling, though I couldn't muster the strength to physically do so any longer.

My eyes were opened to mere slits when we'd reached the center of the garden, directly beside the large willow that grew there. I had barely been able to make out Havoc and Chaos who were sitting on a low branch, looking anxious as they spied me in Hades arms; they lowered their heads immediately to their master.

"You will find the angel for me," Hades instructed the two pixies. "You will tell him that Evie is in great peril. You will tell him that it is *I* that summons him."

"Yes, My Lord," the pixies answered in unison before disappearing.

I forced my eyes to stay open as best I could, watching Hades' face as his hard expression fell, fresh tears began to fall.

"Don't cry." I reached up with my fingertips, shakily brushing the moisture from his cheek. I didn't know why, but for some reason I didn't want Antonio to see him this way. Weak.

Hades was looking down on me, forcing a smile, and somehow I found the strength to grin back.

"I told you, you're not as bad as you think."

He lowered his lips to my forehead, pressing the softest of kisses. "We shall see."

"Evie!"

I looked to where Antonio shouted from. He was running across the grass, his eyes searching—he couldn't see us yet.

Then Hades dropped the cloak.

Antonio halted abruptly, not ten feet away. His face went pale at the sight of me; then his expression hardened toward his uncle. "What have you done to her?"

My hand gripped Hades' arm, silently pleading that he remain calm.

"He didn't hurt me." I could tell Antonio was surprised by the defensive tone in my voice. He shot me a quizzical look.

"She speaks the truth," Hades addressed Antonio. "I did not harm her . . . intentionally.

"Give her to me." Antonio stepped bravely forward, his arms out, ready to accept me.

This was it. The true test of Hades' love. If he gave me to Antonio, to an *angel*, so that I could be healed by another . . . there were no words . . .

"You will heal her," Hades ordered. "And you will guard her until I come for her."

My mouth dropped open. Hades was actually trusting Antonio to protect me?

Antonio looked momentarily stunned. He hadn't expected Hades to ask this of him, that much was evident. He took the final step forward, closing the gap between us.

"I will heal Evie—not because you ordered it, but because *I* love her too."

Without a doubt, Antonio now knew Hades true feelings for me—or he wouldn't have confessed his own love for me to the god. He kept his thoughts closed, but I could see the turmoil in his eyes. He hadn't dreamed Hades capable of love any more than I had. This was an unexpected turn of events—a twist in the tangled mess that was our life.

He lifted me gently from Hades arms and held me to him, all the while keeping his eyes fixed on the Dark King.

"I *will* protect Evie," he added. " . . . From *any* who wish to harm her." The warning was clear: '*any,*' included Hades, and Hades knew it.

I half expected Hades to crush Antonio then and there, for not only declaring his love for me, but for threatening him outright. The fact that he didn't, spoke volumes. Hades must have felt desperate and Antonio had to be his only hope toward my survival; and at that moment . . . I knew that my survival meant everything to him.

Then, Hades did something I never thought he'd do: he nodded in understanding to Antonio, conceding to his terms.

I couldn't have been any more surprised if I were suddenly smashed in the face with a brick.

Hades looked upon me, his expression softening. He leaned in and placed a kiss against my forehead once more, lingering long as he breathed in, taking in my scent for what I knew he hoped would not be the last time.

"I will come for you, soon," he whispered.

Antonio's arms tightened around me at that, before turning us away.

I watched over his shoulder as he headed toward my dorm, Hades posture remaining strong and sure—watching us I knew until we were long out of sight.

What thoughts brewed in his mind I didn't know, but one thing was perfectly clear: Hades loved me. And as sure as he loved me, I knew with every bit of my being, he would not be parting with me—not ever.

Chapter 9

Antonio grumbled under his breath as he hurried along with me, staying hidden in the foliage as much as possible. He made his way into my dorm and up the stairs without notice—Ms. Spencer had been nowhere in sight.

Aperto. He'd magicked the door open. "My God Evie, what has he done to you?" He laid me on the bed before placing a soothing hand to my forehead.

I could literally feel the depleted cells of my body weaving back together. My fleeting heartbeat, gaining speed until resembling the steady rhythm I'd come to know. My soul would never be whole again, but this was as close as it would get. I sighed in relief.

"Hades didn't do this to me."

I took hold of Antonio's hand and let him see into my thoughts . . . Somehow, I managed to play back the horror of Ms. Spicer being killed by the viper. Nightmares attacking me, and Hades coming to my rescue. I let him witness Hades' fruitless battle with Nightmares for himself. Lastly, I let him see Hades' bloodied body carrying me from the flames and collapsing.

"You healed him?!"

How he'd come to that conclusion from the memories I'd shown him, I didn't know. I'd been careful to keep that particular part sealed tight—or so I'd thought.

He was staring at me in disbelief. "You gave your life to save the God of the Underworld? Have you completely lost your mind?! He's a monster!"

"No, he's not! He isn't evil like everyone believes."

"Evie, he is—he's worse."

"No!" I sat up, my strength returned. I wouldn't listen to any more of this. "There's good in him Antonio, I've seen it—you saw it—just now!"

"Oh, please . . ." Antonio was shaking his head before I'd even finished my sentence. "You can't be serious."

"How can you deny it?! No matter what you think he is, he risked his life to save me—and *you* for that matter—or have you forgotten? I wasn't going to let him suffer or worse, die when I was able to help him. I'd have done the same for you!"

"I know you would have . . . don't think for one minute I don't know that Evie, but you're deluding yourself if you think you won't be paying a price for Hades' so-called gracious gesture in saving my life in Megera's lair. He didn't do it out of the kindness of his heart—he has no heart! He hasn't forgotten. He'll collect. Hades *always* collects, and he'll collect on this too."

"You're wrong."

"I'm not. . . . And the fact that you valued his life above your own . . . *his life* Evie . . ." he was shaking his head as though he thought I'd gone absolutely mad. ". . . You can't think that way, especially about a demon."

"He isn't a—" I stopped. There was no point in arguing. Antonio would never see Hades any other way than pure evil. He would never see him or know him the way I did: kind and giving.

I searched his eyes for a shred of understanding. "Would you expect anything less of me?" My words mirrored ones he once uttered to me before we descended into the tunnels of Hell. I knew the moment I'd said them they'd struck a chord.

He took in a deep steading breath. "No. I would not expect anything less of you." He stepped toward me, taking my hands in his. "That's the frustrating part."

I knew I'd scared him. I knew he was furious that I'd put Hades' life before my own. But I also knew that he'd already forgiven me—he loved me that much. He didn't need to say the words. I could hear it in his thoughts and in his fears. Antonio prayed my love for *him* outweighed my love for Hades. For when I let him into my mind, I'd exposed a small piece of my heart he'd feared existed . . . a piece I'd been trying to deny—even to myself: the piece that belonged to Hades. There was no hiding that now.

He brought me to him, hugging me softly. "Thank the heavens you're alright."

"Oh goodie, Evie's all better."

Antonio and I sprang apart, his staff was out and pointing right at the intruder's throat. "Damn it Havoc, don't you ever knock?"

She looked at him pointedly. "No, why should I? This is *my* room last I checked." Her beady little eyes narrowed. "But, I don't remember it being *yours*."

"Havoc!" Her rudeness had no boundaries, and apparently neither did her outfit. "Don't you think you're a bit under dressed for school?" I motioned to the form-fitting red number she was sporting. "You look like you're going clubbing for craps' sake."

She frowned. "*I was*. Until Nightmares offed your Spells teacher and Hades decided to make me errand girl."

"What?"

"There you are my dear." Chaos had "popped" in beside Havoc, decked out in a pin-striped suit. "How do I look?"

I laughed outright. The first real laugh in I don't know how long, completely sidetracking myself. "Please don't tell me she's got you wearing *Ken's* clothes now?"

Antonio was laughing too. "You *are* wearing *Ken's* clothes!"

Iris's Barbie doll collection was more extensive than anyone could fathom. Not only had I never seen Havoc wear the same outfit twice, but now she was dressing Chaos?"

"You two would be wise to keep a civil tone. This fellow, *Ken,* has excellent style."

I could hear the warning in Chaos's words, but I couldn't help it. I laughed harder. He looked utterly ridiculous. His usual wild and untamed mane was slicked back and styled like a nineteen twenties gangster; except for one stray red curl at the front of his head that had managed to break free from the confines of the hair gel attempting to hold it in place—it sprang with each movement he made.

"Oh, shut it, Evie."

That caught my attention. I stopped laughing. Havoc only truly grouched at me when she either A: was mad at *me* for somehow making her feel sorry for me, because I was about to get screwed over, or B: was about to screw me over herself in the most dastardly way—usually resulting in me having to fork over something from my jewelry collection as a means to escape her sporadic psychotic episodes. Either way, this couldn't be good.

By the look on Antonio's face, he'd picked up on it too. "Havoc?"

She attempted to appear bored, suddenly scrutinizing the dainty golden bracelet she wore, but I knew better. I braced for the fallout.

"Hades has asked me to pay Ice-Boy a little visit on your behalf."

"He what?" I practically choked on the question.

"Well, *asked* might not be the right word," she considered briefly, tapping a finger to her chin. "More like demanded." Her eyes flickered to Chaos who visibly cringed at the memory. "He wants him back in the Underworld—pronto."

"And, I'm going with her." Chaos tugged on each one of his shirt cuffs, straightening his sleeves.

"As what," I mocked, ". . . the heavy? You two have got to be kidding."

Chaos cracked his knuckles like a wise guy about to snuff someone's life out. "I can be *very* intimidating, if I wish to be."

I didn't doubt that. In fact, there was no denying it. But something had me growing more nervous by the moment, and it wasn't the deadly look on Chaos' face—daring us to laugh at him once more.

Havoc was hiding something, something big. The two of them were no match for Nightmares. I knew it, they knew it, hell—Hades knew it—he was no fool. So why would he send these two little pixies to do what he couldn't? It made absolutely no sense. And why did Havoc look as if this task was a mere inconvenience—an annoying disruption that *I* was causing to her personal life—hence the reason for her sour mood? More importantly, why didn't she look worried about going head-to-head with Nightmares? Why did it seem as if this was going to be as easy for her as decorating the gym pink?

"What does Hades expect the two of you to do?" Antonio had asked the million-dollar question.

Havoc's face flushed three shades of guilty. "Well now," she half-laughed, ". . . that's an interesting question I must say . . ."

"And we're waiting for the answer." Or more like for the bomb to go off if I knew Havoc. I was not about to let her slither out of this one. I folded my arms expectantly. She was up to something, and she knew I knew it.

"It's no big deal," she assured, waving us off, though I felt anything but comforted. " . . . More of a bother than anything really. We're simply to inform Mr. Freeze that he's needed back in the Underworld tout de suite."

I stared at her blankly.

"That means right away."

My eyes narrowed. "I know what it means." I also knew there was more to it than a 'come home we miss you' message being delivered here. How?"

"How? Well . . . uh . . . oh . . ." she stammered. Then stomped her foot, the carpet absorbing her dramatics. "Must I spell *everything* out, Child of Light? Can you at least pretend to keep up?"

Keep up? Was she kidding? Could anyone keep up?

"Nightmares is obviously not going to return to Hell on his own. And, since he's hell-bent on killing you, his capture has become priority one for anyone who apparently wants to continue breathing." She moved toward Chaos and linked her little arm with his. "In other words, my social life will be non-existent until Hades has his hands around that icy neck."

I must have still worn the look of confusion because Chaos interjected: "We're to deliver him back to the Underworld by any means necessary."

"What?!" And she thought I was the idiot. "That's ridiculous. It's suicide! Not to mention he'll never go with you."

"Oh, please. He won't even realize what's happening until it's too late." A far off look touched her eyes. "We'll be like his very own little personal escorts, guiding him home."

I actually had to take a bracing moment in order to respond. Poor Antonio was scrubbing a hand down his face in mental pain.

"Do you two honestly believe that? Do you think Nightmares is going to follow you both across the Underworld, overlook the giant troll and viper infested waters of his homeland, and blissfully descend into a fiery cavern—totally oblivious that he's heading back to Hell? Back to Hades?"

Havoc shrugged her dainty shoulder. "Yes?"

"No! How stupid do you think he is?!" Antonio took the words right out of my mouth.

This was completely absurd. What the hell was she thinking— and Chaos . . .? He was usually a bit more on the ball.

"Nightmares is not going to follow you anywhere Havoc— especially anywhere near the vicinity of Hell. He doesn't need a tour guide. He hasn't lost his way. He knows where he's going. And P.S., he knows you're both bound to Hades. He'll never buy what you're selling. You'll both be dead before you embark on this hairbrained journey."

"Your faith is overwhelming," Chaos chided.

"I'm being realistic."

This was unbelievable! I could practically see their travel brochures now . . . giant pink letters over a tropical background reading: *'Havoc and Chaos's Guided Vacation Tours—to anywhere but Hell—really!'* And Nightmares of course first in line for the grand opening because he's suddenly decided to take a well-deserved respite for some much-needed R&R—with Pixies as guides!

"Please, you guys can't be serious?" I looked between the both of them, sincerely hoping they'd crack up and admit this was just a joke. A bad, bad, joke.

It was times like these that I wanted to rap my head on a wall, repeatedly. I couldn't conceive that either of them would even entertain this idea for a moment as a possibility. It was too dangerous, not to mention stupid.

There was no way, *no way*, Hades endorsed this level of idiocy. No, Havoc was working solo on this one and somehow roped in her trusty sidekick. No wonder she had that: I just got caught with my hand in the cookie jar expression plastered all over her face. She apparently hadn't expected me to be smart enough to question any of this. She assumed that if I thought Hades was on board with this plan, I'd never argue it—especially if it got Nightmares out of my hair; but that didn't explain why she still looked as if this task was smooth sailing.

"I honestly don't see what all the fuss is about." She genuinely looked confused. This plan was solid in her book. "You want him gone don't you?"

"Yes, I want him gone." But I didn't want anyone else to get hurt because of me either—including the "*dynamic duo*" here.

"Well, then?"

"Look," I tried to take a calmer approach. "Short of opening a giant vortex smack in the middle of Pinehurst—literally beneath Nightmares' feet—you will never, I repeat, *never,* get him back in the Underworld." Of this I was sure.

"With you as bait, I beg to differ."

I turned to Chaos in utter shock. There it was, in a nutshell: her game plan. Her slam dunk. The hammer I'd been waiting for to drop. The nail in my coffin; and every other idiom you could think of.

Havoc stood there, all smiles—and why shouldn't she? This task was pure child's play. As easy for her as *"Bedazzling"* Gunny's uniform with him standing in it. Her plan didn't involve her breaking a nail or her untimely demise. It was my skin on the line, *all mine.*

Antonio snapped. "Hades said to use Evie as bait?!"

"Of course not!" Havoc exclaimed, feigning complete shock at Antonio's outlandish assumption. "But, what Hades doesn't know can't hurt *me. And* if the-end-result is Nightmares back in Hell, who cares how it's done? All will be forgiven."

"Who cares?" I could barely blurt out the question. I was so pissed. My life was completely expendable to her—collateral damage at best. This was a perfect storm and she knew it.

"You're both worrying for nothing." Havoc looked confident as ever. "Hades will be happy his rogue demon is under house arrest, Evie won't have to fret about the Hellhound anymore, and I, and Chaos," she swooned, ". . . will have saved the day yet again. We'll all be dancing by midnight. All the Child of Light has to do is—"

"It's out of the question!" Antonio had had enough. "Evie's not going anywhere near Nightmares or this insane plan."

"Oh . . . you sky gods always have to butt in and be difficult." Havoc stomped her foot angrily once more. Pouting over Antonio putting the kibosh on her untapped genius.

" . . . And I won't have to worry about the 'Hellhound,'" I added sarcastically, " . . . because I'll be dead!"

"You know good and well that Hades wouldn't approve of this Havoc." Antonio went on with renewed pisstivity. "He'd punish you for even considering putting Evie in such a position, not to mention what her father would do."

George! I hadn't even thought about what he'd say about any of this. I hadn't even had the chance to tell him that Nightmares was here.

"That's only because they haven't the foresight to know that this is foolproof," she argued smugly. "Put Evie out in the open and Nightmares will flock to her like peanut butter to jelly. She'll only be in danger for a moment or two, probably," she considered briefly then shook her head, casting the unpleasant thought away. "We'll have Ice Boy surrounded and back in Hell before sixth period ends—problem solved!"

I was dumbfounded. She had this entire scenario planned and already wrapped up. Damn, Nightmares may as well be roasting on a spit somewhere in Hell over Satan's hearth this very minute as far as she was concerned.

"Minimal damage," she mumbled to herself. "Maybe just a tree or two—and few   flowers . . .?"

A vision of Ms. Leech's common area becoming a blazing inferno once more, flashed through my mind. Complete with hordes of pixies, fire balls, and volcanic eruptions that sputtered hot ash and molten rock incinerating her perfectly manicured world.

"Havoc?" I could feel the color drain from my face, my stomach knotted. I was being facetious before. I hadn't thought I was actually laying out her plan of attack, minus the troll and viper infested water, I prayed. "Please don't tell me that you're going to 'escort' Nightmares to the Underworld by actually opening the gates of Hell in the middle of the school yard again?"

She scoffed as if the conversation had suddenly become ridiculous. But she couldn't keep the sly smile from creeping across her face.

This was the *something big* I'd feared, and I wouldn't put it past Hades to embrace it—omitting me as the target of course; that part I was sure he knew nothing about. He'd deal with the aftermath of the mythologically-rocked community of Pinehurst later—if that was even a word? Capturing Nightmares as Havoc put it was priority one.

She knew that I'd connected the pieces together. "Now, Child of Light . . . as if I go around doing that kind of thing, much." She winked and disappeared.

"Chaos—!" I turned to the pixie, but he'd already gone.

"Antonio, they can't!"

"They're going to." Antonio looked as green as I felt. "Hades must have figured it out."

"Figured what out?"

"He can't touch Nightmares in the Outer World. *Here* he is unstoppable. But down there . . . down there is Hades' domain. He won't stand a chance if they get him back into the Underworld. He won't be able to slip through Hades fingers. He won't be able to touch you again."

Of course! It was so obvious now that Antonio said it . . . I thought back to Hades' fight with Nightmares. How Nightmares had moved through him in his wraith-like state as though Hades were nothing but air. I recalled the surprised look on Hades' face before utter fury claimed him—knowing that he was being physically attacked by a ghost and could do nothing about it. It had been one thing for Nightmares to elude him, but once in his presence, Hades should have been powerful enough to crush the dark spirit—even one that didn't answer to him directly.

I didn't want to consider it: not only was Nightmares obviously more than just an ordinary demon, but he had to be something, or someone, more powerful than Hades himself to conceal that kind of information from him; not to mention battle him and win. I couldn't suppress the shudder that ran through me. This demon wielded a power unlike any I'd ever known—not that I was all that experienced, but I didn't think anything could be that powerful, other than the one true deity himself, and I knew there was nothing heavenly about this being. The very thought of what Nightmares could possibly do to the Outer World, or me—with no one to keep him in check—had my stomach twisting into a knot.

I was such a colossal ass. "He *was* tricked!"

"Who?"

"Hades!" I rushed to my door and flung it open, heading down the hall. I hadn't believed him before, thinking he was careless and a total idiot for releasing a demon he had no control over, but I believed him now. "Of course he never would have released Nightmares if he knew he wouldn't be able to control him—what would be the point?" Hades had told me that he was repaying a debt by releasing the creep, and in doing so 'would gain an advantage.' What debt, he never said, but it had to be a doozy if Satan was involved. For all we knew, Nightmares was his number two guy.

Antonio was close behind me. He took my hand, cloaking us as we descended the stairs into the common area, the room was still empty. We'd reached the front doors, Antonio removing our cloak as we burst out into the sun.

Hades had absolutely no idea what this bastard had planned. I'd bet my life on it. Especially since his plans now seemed to include me.

It was clear that Nightmares' had his own ambitions. What exactly they were, I still didn't know for sure, but I could feel it in bones that they were laced with an evil that would render the Outer World helpless. An evil that I feared would rival the One True Deity himself. An evil I recognized, because I too had the ability to possess it—not fully, but the darker I got, the more I realized that there was indeed a difference between the Underworld and Hell. Nightmares oozed the latter.

"This changes nothing Evie." Antonio quickened our pace as we cleared the dorm buildings. "Hades is still responsible for Nightmares being free. He's still the bad guy."

I rolled my eyes. "Yes, he is technically responsible for Nightmares being free, but *he* is not the bad guy, Antonio."

"Evie . . ."

"If you want to point blame, blame me. I'm the one who actually opened the damn gate."

"Upon his orders!"

I ran on. Bickering about it wasn't going to do us any good.

"We have to help Havoc and Chaos get that monster back to the Underworld, no matter the method! They can paint a freaking bull's-eye on me for all I care." Locking Nightmares' sorry ass back up would be the highlight of my gate-keeper responsibilities!

"You will not be the target, Evie."

We could argue this later. Right now: "We have to hurry." I gripped onto Antonio's hand firmly as we broke into a full run. A foreboding feeling had come over me. I couldn't explain why, but it was as if I could feel the dark shadow of Satan himself looming over us. Thank the deity *he* wasn't here—that's all we needed; but he wasn't far away either . . . I began to slow.

"What's wrong?" Antonio slowed with me.

My head was swimming. "I can't believe I didn't put it together before . . ."

"Put what together?"

I stopped dead in my tracks, facing Antonio squarely. "Nightmares demanded that I '*aid him*' . . . but I didn't understand what he meant." For some unexplainable reason, Nightmares' words had just abruptly made sense as if he'd spelled them out in precise detail. In fact, all the things he'd ever said to me had just clicked into place like some ominous cryptic puzzle. "Keys don't just open things, they lock them too."

"What?"

"He wants to use me to control the gates of Hell, but not just to open them like Hades wishes. He wants the ability to lock them too."

Antonio's eyes widened in realization. " . . . Shutting in all who would oppose him."

"Exactly."

Then: "The Olympians—good hell!"

"Your dad is going to be *pissed*!" I couldn't help the slight grin. Finally, Nightmares was doing something I could get on board with. Personally, I could care less if Zeus was thrown in on his ear. It would serve him right to spend a few hundred years in Hell for being the conniving arrogant bastard that he was. I could easily ignore his pitiful pleas for release.

"Evie, you don't understand." Antonio gripped onto my shoulders suddenly, he could barely contain himself. "This is bad. Very bad. Nightmares isn't just going to lock Zeus away . . . we're talking about *all* the Olympians—Hera, Poseidon, Athena, Ares . . ..

Where the hell were all these gods hiding?

"They'll be thrown in with the Titans."

"The Titans . . .? Aren't they like, a sports team? Why would they be in Hell?"

Antonio seemed to go rigid, staring at me, blinking. "They're the original Gods Evie, before the Olympians. How do you not know this?" He stared at me like a parent who had realized the educational system had failed their child horribly. "They were tricked by the Olympians and overthrown millennia ago," he went on, explaining quickly. "They were cast into Tartarus."

"Tartarus . . . ?"

Antonio released his hold. Looking upon me in utter disbelief. "A prison in the deepest region of the underworld; a fiery abyss of constant pain and torment for which there is no escape."

Holy shit. "Why am I just now hearing about this place? Hades never said anything about a secret prison." Was I the freaking key to that establishment too?

"Evie," Antonio took my hands in his. "If the Titans and the Olympians are thrust together and war—which they will because the Titans are no doubt furious for having been deceived and tortured for all time, the entire world as we know it will be destroyed; it could not sustain such a battle."

And I thought my head was spinning before.

"Evie . . ." Antonio's tone grew more serious. "It won't be just the Olympians cast into Tartarus . . ."

My eyebrows furrowed in confusion.

"The angels, your father, me. We'd be banished too."

"But, the angels, my father, you, you're not Olympians."

"Yes, I am. I'm Zeus's son. And as for your father and the angels . . . they fight for the One True Deity. Nightmares will need to eliminate *all* who would oppose him if he is to assume total control."

The plan was brilliant. What better way for him to escape the confines of his own personal hell and ensure absolute power and control for himself, than to imprison all threats. Locking a door to the Outer World that Satan doesn't even realize he could possibly have access to while supposedly doing his bidding—whatever that unknown assignment was couldn't be good either. This was Nightmares ticket to freedom.

Figures, it was just my luck that Zeus might actually be needed in the Outer World. That *he* was the lesser of two evils; I was never going to be rid of that guy.

This was certainly an interesting turn of events . . . Hellish plans had not changed, only the Grand Marshall. Satan only ever wanted one thing: control of the Outer World and everything in it— revenge against the One True Deity, and Nightmares was paving his way—so he thought—courtesy of Hades' brilliant plan to distract his brother Zeus long enough so that he could claim Mount Olympus for himself—idiot! Now we were all going to pay the price for his visions of grandeur. How Hades had been so stupid to have trusted Satan, I'll never know. And Satan was more of a stupid ass than Hades! His go-to guy was duping him right under his gnarly nose.

"Greed and desperation blinds even the gods," Antonio offered.

I rolled my eyes. Immortal Men were impossible.

"Not all," he defended.

"Yeah, well, that remains to be seen." My eyes were *wide-open*. All gods, demi-gods, demons, magical beings of any kind, assholes, and anyone with a remotely diabolical sounding plan, was officially on my radar.

"Come on," Antonio motioned toward the path. "We better find Havoc, quick."

"Agreed."

We had to make up time. We descended down the hill at warp speed. Operation: open the gates of Hell in the middle of the school yard, was the best plan we had. Havoc's brilliant idea to let the earth swallow Nightmares whole had my official endorsement; and after the conversation I'd just had with Antonio, it had his too.

We sprinted, cutting through the newly planted "Community Gardens." Leech was so going to have our asses!

"Not if we save the world," Antonio exclaimed.

"I'll settle for saving Pinehurst for now. Though, if Satan finds out that his boy has gone rogue, the entire world will indeed need saving." I'd let Hades deliver that bit of cheery news!

We slowed a little as we ran past my old Spells classroom. Yellow caution tape crossed the charred door, warning all to keep out.

"I wonder how Gillian is?" I was ashamed that her well-being had just come to mind.

"She's fine," Antonio promised. "She's in the Infirmary. She has smoke inhalation, but she'll heal."

I sighed in relief. Thank goodness she was rescued. Though I'd have to remember to ask Havoc how she and Chaos were able to "pop" out of the classroom with Gillian as they did—considering she never once did it to help Antonio and me when we were suffering in the depths of Hell, *or* dangling to our doom in Megera's lair!

"I'd like the answer to that myself," Antonio grouched.

We rounded the corner heading straight toward the gym. Havoc was nowhere to be seen; and neither were any other students. "Where is everyone?" The campus was completely empty, not a soul in sight.

"They're attending the memorial."

"The memorial?" My heart sank. The memory of Ms. Spicer dead in my arms was still fresh. "How did they organize that so fast?"

"Ms. Leech has gathered everyone into the gym to pay their respects, and to relay a temporary schedule until a new spells teacher can be found."

I couldn't imagine anyone but Ms. Spicer teaching spells.

"Did they punish Nightmares?"

Antonio shook his head. His eyes were still focused on the path in front of us, but I knew he was searching the minds of the other students, seeking the answers we needed. "He claims it was an accident. He pretends to grieve with the others."

This was more than I could stand. "He isn't even being held responsible?!"

We reached the gym doors, panting excessively, my heart about to explode. If Nightmares was in there, maybe Havoc was too.

I put my hand on the handle, steeling myself. Preparing for what I might find on the other side.

This was it. Nightmares was going down—literally. Which reminded me . . . "Antonio. . . how did you know Hades needed to get Nightmares back into the Underworld if he has any hope in defeating him?"

"Oh Dylan, you poor thing!" The doors to the gym had flung open that very moment, full force, knocking me aside and sending me onto my butt. Stacy strode out, arm and arm with, '*Dylan*?'

Antonio helped me up from the ground as other students filed out. Ms. Spicer's memorial must have ended. Great. How were we going to cast Nightmares into Hell with the entire student body present?

"Will you look at that, see, I told you she'd turn up." Stacy gestured my way, looking crestfallen at the sight of me. She cuddled against the strong arm hers was linked with. "I'd hoped she'd met some untimely demise, yet here she stands. I swear I'm cursed."

My mouth gaped open. What a—

"Your concern is touching, Stacy, but as you can see," Antonio motioned my way, " . . . Evie is perfectly fine. No harm has come to her, or will." He'd taken a towering step toward them. He was addressing Dylan, I mean Nightmares, the two of them practically toe to toe; he had purposefully blocked him from my view.

Stacy snorted in disgust. "Put your hackles down, Antonio. As if Dylan's interested in Evie. He's *my* boyfriend." She ran her hand up Nightmares arm seductively, giving his bicep a slight squeeze before returning her attention back to us.

I could just gag at the love-struck glance she'd given him.

"What would he want with your red-headed twit anyway? She's not even pretty."

Oh that was it! "At least *my* hair color is real," I defended as I moved past Antonio, wanting to knock Stacy on her ever-growing ass! "And at least my *'boyfriend' . . ."* I made air quotes, ". . . isn't a murdering demon from Hell!"

Antonio yanked me behind him as a slight growl escaped Nightmares.

Stacy's mouth opened wide enough to consume the Grand Canyon if she so wished. "How dare you," she gasped. "Dylan is grieving. . . .And to think, I offered Ms. Leech a deal on a casket if we found your charred body decomposing somewhere so that you wouldn't have to be embarrassed looking all dead and burnt." She folded her arms in a huff. "My father's in the funeral business you know."

I was totally dumbfounded. I had no idea if I should feel insulted or touched.

A few stragglers exited the gym, Iris being one of them. "Evie!" She rushed over and threw her arms around me, saving me from being incinerated by Stacy's death-like stare. "Thank God you're alright!"

Nightmares blanched.

"Yes. Thank *God*," I repeated her, ignoring the buckling pain of the word to myself. But by the looks of it, it bothered Nightmares much more; though it hadn't escaped his notice that it had taken a toll on me as well. He glared at me with utter loathing.

"Isn't it awful," Iris began as she pulled out what looked to be a well-used tissue. "Ms. Spicer was so nice. I can't imagine the pain she must have endured." Iris started to cry all over again. "She must have been terrified."

The last images of Ms. Spicer, would never leave me.

"Yes, Iris," I patted her back, trying to talk through the lump that had formed in my throat. "It was awful."

Stacy snapped. "Well that's real nice you two, make Dylan feel worse than he already does. It was his pet after all!"

I looked over at the demon, stunned at his mock-sorrow. He'd hung his head down, pretending to grieve once more, and Stacy was buying every bit of it.

"I'm sure *Dylan* will survive," Antonio jabbed. "I can't say the same for Ms. Spicer."

"How rude! Come on Dylan, you won't get any sympathy from *these* idiots." Stacy linked her arm dramatically with Nightmare's and yanked him away, outraged at our ". . . lack of compassion . . ." She mumbled angrily as they went. Like a murderer *needed* compassion!

'Dylan' looked back over his shoulder as he let Stacy lead him away, his "tear-filled" eyes meeting mine, and winked.

I stood there, too surprised to move.

He'll pay for that. Antonio warned mentally. And somehow, I believed him.

Chapter 10

"How am I supposed to eat with Stacy practically devouring what's his name's face over there?" Aubree set her fork down with a loud clatter. "I'm pretty sure that's illegal PDA. I mean, look at them!"

"I'd rather not." I'd already caught more than one glimpse of the twosome kissing like it was going out-of-style—and my back was to them.

"Who is he anyway?"

Oh no. Under her expressed disgust, I could sense Aubree's peaked interest. I couldn't even blame her. Every other girl in *The Kitchen* had their eyes on the bad boy from Hoffmyer too. They were intrigued, not to mention practically drooling.

"The creep's name is Dylan." I groaned. Even his name implied that he was a bad-boy trouble maker—and not the troublemaking go nowhere scum of society one naturally avoids . . . but the tall, mysterious, and unknown hunky-hottie that shows up unexpectedly from the land of elsewhere. The guy that probably sports a leather jacket and rides a motorcycle without a helmet and still, his hair manages to look good. The guy that walks with a certain swagger of confidence, smiles like he's the poster-boy for a toothpaste ad, and dresses like high-end designers tailor their clothing line solely with him in mind. The guy that you know for a fact your parents would ground you into your next lifetime for even contemplating as a possibility; but the guy you'd secretly trade your soul in a heartbeat for the chance to walk arm and arm through campus and publicly announce on every form of social media that he was yours.

"Dylan, huh?" Aubree hadn't taken her eyes off him.

What the heck were we going to do now? With a name like that, accompanied by his outer-worldly looks, Dylan would surely lure every girl in a twenty mile radius. We needed to keep people away from him, not draw them in!

How the student body was buying his devastated victim's act was beyond me. I'd heard through the grapevine: AKA Iris, who apparently had weekly sessions with the school counselor due to the fact that her parents left her here to basically rot, that 'Dylan' would undergo daily visits of his own to the school shrink; to help him cope with the 'unfortunate accident' as it was coming to be known. If that hadn't been enough to turn my stomach inside out and thoroughly piss me off, he was also being excused from classes for the rest of the week.

"You know, that asshole doesn't even have to make-up work. It's totally not fair. I was practically blown up and no one has approached me about taking a week off for a mental rest."

"Yet another reason. If you would just allow me to—"

"No!" I cut Havoc off mid-sentence. I knew where she was going with this. "You can't just . . . you know . . . right here. In the middle of dinner." What was she thinking? Not only would it raise questions that I didn't want revolving around *me*, but we'd be sure to acquire a casualty list, something I refused to be a part of.

We'd been going over this for the past hour. We could not afford to expose what we were to the rest of the Mageian population. We all had powers, sure, but the level in which Antonio and I possessed would definitely raise fear. If there was one thing I'd learned in history, it was that a feared person or object was always obliterated—that was not going to be us.

"You're so difficult."

I would not give in to Havoc's tantrum. I agreed one hundred percent with any method she deemed acceptable for Nightmares' capture—so long as it had that jerk-wads demise written all over it, I didn't care. But we would do it with little to no exposure upon ourselves, and absolutely none of the students were to be hurt.

"No witnesses," I reiterated. "We have to wait until he's alone."

"Fine, but it's your head," Havoc added in a sing-song voice. "You can tell Big H that you delayed his plans. He'll *love* that!"

She was right. Hades was going to be pissed. When he wanted something, he wanted it last week. Patience was not his virtue. And after what Nightmares did to him—to me—he had to want his hands around the demon's throat as much as he wanted me in the Underworld forever.

"What are the two of you even talking about? Big H?" Aubree was looking from Havoc to me.

I'd completely forgotten we weren't alone.

Iris had been sitting quietly. I could tell she was silently trying to piece our conversation together, her eyes were filled with a million questions.

"Never mind," Aubree blurted, "I can't be bothered to find out. I've entirely lost my appetite."

"That makes two of us." Iris had risen from the table with Aubree, her hand to the side of her head, attempting to block the overexaggerated make-out session we were all being exposed to. "Come on, Aubree, I'll walk back to the dorm with you." She gave me a knowing look before they left. Iris would be expecting answers, and soon.

I grudgingly cut off a piece of ham and had just dipped it into the mustard sauce when—

"Well, well, well . . . this *is* my lucky day!"

Would the misery ever end? I gave Havoc a dry look before looking up into Roland's face.

"Now I've lost *my* appetite," Havoc complained as she tossed her little napkin aside. "Is it too much to ask that they keep the undesirables out?" She looked around as if *The Kitchen* had bouncers for this sort of thing.

"Shut your mouth, Demon!"

"Roland!" I placed a hand on his arm, holding him back. He looked as if he were about to lunge forward and strangle her.

"Why don't you run along before Antonio spots you harassing his girlfriend," Havoc warned cheerfully. She was intentionally egging him on.

I groaned. Havoc was pushing all of Roland's buttons and enjoying it! This could only end badly. "What do you want, Roland?"

He looked back to me, his eyes traveling down to my hand that was still firmly gripping his bicep—I slowly released him. "I wanted to talk to you. *Alone.*"

Havoc snorted. "As if that's going to happen. The last time you '*talked*,'" she made little air quotes, " . . . you attacked her. Pervert!"

"I am not!" Roland barked. "We were just kissing! Besides, Evie knows I'm not going to hurt her . . . don't you, Evie?" He took hold of my hand, squeezing slightly.

That uneasy feeling . . . the one that creeps up slowly and then screams: *warning*, had taken hold. I felt cornered, like Roland had me once again pressed up against the railing of the balcony at the Spring Dance. When he'd implied to everyone that we wanted some 'alone time,' so that he could take advantage of me. Only this time I felt as if I wouldn't be getting away.

"Roland, I don't think that's a very good idea," my voice cracked. "Besides, there isn't anything for us to talk about."

"*Understatement.*" Havoc rolled her eyes, still craning her neck—scanning the joint for muscled assistance. She turned her face to find Roland's dangerously close to hers.

His expression tightened. "This *doesn't* concern you, pixie-trash."

"But it concerns me." Antonio stepped into view. "Would you like to remove your hand, or shall I remove it for you?"

Roland still had a firm grip on me. Crap. This had gone from bad to worse. Now all I needed was for Nightmares to—

"Is this a private fight, or can anyone join in?"

Un . . . freaking . . . believable! 'Dylan' had taken a stand beside Roland, his arm casually draped over one of his shoulders like they were BFF's.

Antonio grinned. "The more the merrier."

Oh, hell no! He did not just say that?!

Roland's fist flew past my face and met with Antonio's jaw in the next instant.

Screams broke out all around us—one of them mine. Chairs skidded as students cleared the way, scattering from the tables. With the destruction of Ms. Spicer's classroom still fresh in everyone's mind, no one wanted to stick around and be collateral damage—including me.

"You're mine." Nightmares grabbed my arm and yanked me across the table, squishing Havoc and knocking her to the floor.

"Havoc!" She wasn't moving. "Let go of me!"

My free hand came up and slugged him across the face, burning my knuckles on contact, but that wasn't all: Nightmares' head had whipped back—I'd struck him! And if I could strike him . . .

His eyes flashed red. "You'll suffer for that!" He gripped my arm all the tighter, burning his fingerprints into my skin.

I screamed out in pain. Self-preservation mode took over. My knee came up, meeting him square between the legs.

The unholy scream that accompanies one's balls being kicked in, reverberated off the walls. Nightmares was doubled over, clutching his family jewels.

Roland's body hurtled past me just then, colliding into Nightmares and knocking them both into a set of table and chairs.

Nightmares was up before I had a chance to move; Roland still lay dazed on the ground.

Antonio jumped in front of me, shielding my body. "Evie, get out of here!"

There was nowhere to go. My arms came up over my head instinctively as furniture began exploding around us, sending splinters of wood into the air. I crouched to the floor, ducking.

Chaos had found Havoc. He knelt over her. One of his tiny hands touched her delicate face while the other was smoothing back her limp hair. She had not yet woken, and Chaos was raging. Chunks of ceiling began to fall like rain.

"Havoc!" I rushed over and knelt down beside her, studying her unconscious body. She didn't look good. "Please be okay."

Chaos's lips pressed against hers for the barest of moments.

She looked so frail . . . for as much trouble as this little menace was, I couldn't stand to see her like this.

"Havoc," I poked at her shoulder.

Her eyes fluttered open, she groaned at the sight of me. "Did you have to land on me with your big, fat, body, Child of Light?"

"It was Nightmares' fault!" I defended happily. "And I am *not* fat!" I was so glad the little brat was alright.

"You are so fat," she gave me a pained smile.

"He will pay dearly for this," Chaos rounded on the demon. The little pixie brought new meaning to the word: demolition. Not to mention a flash back to our time in Hell when the pixies attacked us en masse while trying to rescue Roland—who incidentally should have been left there to rot. *Chaos* was everywhere!

Antonio was at the center of the fray, his foot connected with Nightmares' chest a moment later. With *The Kitchen* full of spectators, Nightmares didn't have a chance to go "stealth" on him;

but that didn't stop Chaos from sending every glass, every utensil, every piece of furniture that wasn't nailed down, hurtling his way.

An arm snaked around me from behind just them, capturing my waist, as a hand muffled my scream. I was being dragged out the door, kicking.

Antonio!

Antonio turned in time to see me slip from the room.

"Quit fighting me!"

Roland! I fought harder, trying to break away, but he was much stronger. He was pulling me into the wooded area of the campus, away from buildings and watchful eyes.

"I told you, we need to talk!"

"The hell we do," I snapped. My mouth had finally broken free. "Let go of me!"

He spun me around, my back slamming into the trunk of a tree as he did so. "Evie, stop!"

I thrashed against him, trying to twist my way loose, but he held strong.

"What's wrong with your eyes . . .?"

"There's nothing wrong with my eyes!" I obverted them as I struggled to free myself. I could feel my anger rising and that only brought forth one thing: my demon side. There was no way I wanted Roland to know that bit of information. If anyone thought I was a demon, or even part demon, I'd become a live target for Gunny's Slayers faster than Stacy switched boyfriends. Hell, Chad would probably lead the damn crusade.

"What's happening to you . . .? And don't tell me I'm imagining things, this happened before."

Roland's grip loosened and I jerked away from him. I was seething.

He'd seen my eyes turn red in the Underworld—a detail I thought he'd forgotten, or that he thought he'd imagined. Why he'd kept his mouth shut about it was anyone's guess.

I looked right at him. There was no avoiding it now.

"You're turning into one of *them*, aren't you?"

What my response was going to be, I would never know. Roland flew at me, tackling me to the ground as he slammed me into the hard dirt.

I couldn't help but cry out as the back of my head hit a tree root.

He grabbed me by the shoulders and began slamming me over and over into the unforgiving earth—as if the action alone would somehow stop whatever was happening to me.

"I'm not going to let you become one of them."

My vision blurred. "Roland, stop!"

Before my head had a chance to hit the ground once more, Roland was suddenly ripped away.

My heartbeat echoed in the immediate stillness. It was as if all manner of life became afraid to exist, myself included.

"It has been quite some time since I've had to kill a mortal."

"Hades?" I let out the breath of air I'd been holding.

Hades stood before me, his entire body raging with fury.

My voice alone snapped his attention away from an unconscious Roland laying several yards away—totally oblivious that the Lord of the Underworld meant to destroy him.

Hades hardened features turned worried. "My Love, are you alright?" He knelt down and gently lifted me from the ground, careful to support my weight.

I was safe. There, sheltered amongst the shadows of the pine trees, I leaned against his frame, hugging him tightly, thankful he'd come. Already feeling my demon side calming and slinking back to the darkened corners of my soul.

"How did you find me?" But I already knew the answer before he spoke.

"The pixie came to me."

I smiled inwardly. I owed Havoc one, again. "I'm alright now."

I looked over toward Roland, still unconscious—I hoped—under a tree. Even though he was a world-class ass and a definite candidate for Chad's jerk-squad, I didn't want him dead—at least I didn't think so. Although, if he wasn't dead I was surely going to kill him later myself. I had a goose egg on the back of my head that was going to throb for weeks.

"I will never be so foolish to entrust another with your safety again." Hades somehow managed to draw me closer. He lowered his face to my neck, nuzzling it, taking in a deep breath of me. "I told the angel to protect you . . ."

The angel: Antonio! I couldn't believe I'd forgotten.

"Hades! The angel is fighting Nightmares right now. Come, we have to hurry!" I gripped his arm, attempting to tug him with what little strength I had, but he wouldn't budge. "You have to help him!"

Hades stood tall, his feet firmly planted where he was. "I cannot fight the demon in Zeus' realm."

"Yes, you can! His body just has to be in a solid form. As long as others are around he won't transform. I don't know why, but he won't. If we hurry—"

"No." His voice was softer now, yet none the less firm. "You do not understand."

I stood there, staring at him in disbelief. "I understand that if we don't hurry, Antonio could get hurt, or killed! Hades, please."

He shook his head, unwavering. "The angel has a greater chance in defeating the demon than I."

"What?!" I released my grip on his arm. "How can that be?" I'd never heard him say anything so ridiculous. Antonio was a good fighter and yes, a demi-god, but compared to the strength and power of a higher god like Hades . . . there was no comparison.

"Unless I am of *this world* . . . I cannot physically touch the demon. I am powerless to stop him here, *regardless* of his form."

My eyebrows furrowed in confusion. "But—"

"*Nightmares* is not who he appears to be my love. *Satan* has been very cunning in his exit."

"Satan? What does he—" Then: *Oh . . . my . . . God . . .* I staggered back. I could feel my blood actually still while all color drained from my face at his horrific revelation. Antonio was battling Satan . . .? I looked toward the direction of *The Kitchen,* my throat tightened—I couldn't formulate a word; and if my body was crippling at the utterance of the deity's name I couldn't feel it. I was in total shock.

Hades cursed himself aloud, snapping me to attention. "There is no excuse for the danger I have placed you in." He had his fists clenched tight, pressing them hard into his forehead, blocking me from his view.

"No," I shook my head in disbelief. This couldn't be happening. This wasn't real. There was no way Nightmares was—I couldn't even freaking think it let alone say it!

I could feel a full-blown panic attack coming on. I regarded the man who was, to my way of thinking: an impenetrable tower of strength. A man who had inadvertently become my safety net in nearly all things. A man who had just told me that I'm basically on my own here. There was nothing he could do . . .? Bullshit! I wouldn't accept his words. I couldn't!

"I need you!" I could hear the fear and desperation in my own voice. Hell, it could probably be heard from across campus. "You *have* to stop him." I reached out and pulled his hands away from his face, forcing him to look at me. "He's here because of you. You can't abandon me!"

"I *have not* abandoned you!" Hades thundered as quickly as I had accused him. "Nor will I." His steely gaze narrowed on me. His eyes, undisputedly darker than any storm I had ever seen, made my entire being flinch. "I will do whatever I must to protect you from him Evie, but I *cannot* do it here." The ground rumbled beneath my feet. " . . . And . . . I *vowed* I would not keep you in the Underworld, yet." That last sentence pulled at my heart somehow. The way he said it, as if the very words cut him deep, torturing him in the most unimaginable ways. There was so much Hades wasn't telling me, but now was not the time.

"There must be a way." I stared up into his eyes, beseeching him. My fate was literally teetering—again. If we couldn't manage to drag Nightmares back into the Underworld, then we had no chance in stopping him. If Hades couldn't do it, no one could. The success of

Havoc's plan, as crazy as it was, was more necessary than ever; if Satan could be so easily tricked that is?

"If only—" I paused mid-thought. Realization taking hold of me like a slap in the face. I regarded Hades, incredulous. "The gates. That's it, isn't it?" It was the reason I was in this mess in the first place. It was what Hades first sought from me. It was what I was determined to keep Antonio from suffering. And it was the one thing I had total control over. The one thing everybody wanted, but me. "For you to be of *this* world, for you to stop Nightmares *here* . . . you need my powers."

Hades didn't answer, he didn't have to, I saw it in his eyes, and damn if he didn't look tortured. Hadn't this been what he'd been after all along . . . my powers . . . Olympus . . . *me*? So why did he look as if that was the last thing he wanted right now?

"Evie . . ." I don't think anyone had ever looked more sorry for me than Hades did at this very moment. He'd hoped I wouldn't piece that together, I could hear it in his thoughts. "We will find another way."

But there wasn't.

How in the hell had it come to this again? Would I never free myself from this 'blessing,' as my father so delicately referred to it? If I gave Hades my powers, he'd control the gates of Hell too. He would be able to deal with Nightmares, but he would also wage war on Zeus in a heartbeat. The ramifications of that were unfathomable, but it was a much easier outcome to swallow opposed to Satan taking the helm. Hades would be able to cast the bastard back into the dark, the world would still be intact, and everyone I loved would be safe—I'd see to that. But, most importantly . . . the heavens would not suffer, unless Hades decided to claim that for himself too . . .

I also couldn't help but consider the *personal* ramifications of such a decision. In the grand scheme of things I was one person— taking one for the team so to speak. I shouldn't be selfish to think of myself when the entire world was at stake. But I was a person, and this wouldn't be as easy as handing over an actual key and saying: 'here you go.' This would be me handing over my virtue. This would be me giving the most intimate part of myself to Hades. This would be me tying myself to him forever; a detail I didn't believe he was actually aware of. I didn't even know if he was on board with forever.

My heart sank even further. Why did everything have to be so difficult? Until the end of time, I'd blame Zeus for this mess. If he hadn't have been such a controlling ass from the get-go, putting unnecessary restrictions on Hades—just because he could—cursing him to a life of misery and preventing him from freely moving between worlds, he'd easily be able to—

I paused mid-thought, my eyes drifting to Hades, before widening.

He raised a brow.

I looked him over, pondering. Was it even possible? Yes. It was. It hadn't even entered my mind as a possibility, but it was so obvious. I don't know why I hadn't thought of it before, but it made perfect sense. The most sense!

"I can let *you* through the gates!"

I smiled excitedly. This would actually work. Hades wouldn't gain my powers, but he would be of this world. He would be free and able to battle Satan. Order and life as we knew it would still remain. Zeus could keep his precious Mount Olympus because Hades' army couldn't follow him to take it.

Hades' expression fell.

"No, no," I exclaimed quickly, sensing his reluctance. "This will work!" I clasped my hands excitedly.

This was by far the best plan. All would be saved   . . . well, save one. My smile faltered. In this, I would lose all that was left of my soul. For each time I released a demon, I lost more and more of it. Releasing someone as powerful and as undoubtedly dark as Satan had nearly consumed me completely. Releasing Hades after someone like that, well, that would be the end of me. There was no way my soul would survive this.

I held my head up, resolved. "This will work."

But Hades had already puzzled this one out. He'd known this was an option, and he'd deemed it unallowable. I could tell by the look on his face that he hadn't dreamt I'd come to this conclusion. Not ever.

He stepped closer, taking my hands in his. He had never looked more serious. "This is not the solution, Evie. I will not let you forfeit your life, your soul, or your body, in any of this. You will not take my place."

His words would have been laughable to anyone else that had been following my pathetically sad life from the moment I'd set foot in Hades lair—Hades had wanted nothing else, especially in the beginning. But here, now, to me . . . there were no words I could gather to express how treasured I suddenly felt.

. . . And although this was ultimately my decision, and Hades had expressed his unwavering command, I really had no choice. I could not obey. The odds of Nightmares tripping into a gaping hole leading to the Underworld were slim; and if that didn't happen, releasing Hades through the gates would be our best hope. It was the only way to maintain the balance. Satan was not meant to roam the Outer World, the heavens would crumble to the ground, and Mount Olympus and all who dwelt there would be a distant memory whispered across the wind—like legends long forgotten. My father's army would perish by Satan's will and humanity would be lost.

Shame for having a hand at his release gripped me as I imagined the angels crying at his feet. There would be no mercy. And the One True Deity . . . our beloved creator of all . . . would be no more.

I turned away slightly, wiping quickly at my face. I wouldn't let Hades see me cry. I had to be strong, for all of us. The decision was clear. I knew I would lose both Antonio and Hades forever. I would lose myself—my penance—but our world and all that I loved would be saved. That's what truly mattered; and Hades . . . Hades would be free. . .

"Zeus!" I shouted as if he had just appeared in front of me in all his shining glory—my saving grace, and he suddenly was. "I can ask Zeus to help us!" Where had Antonio been on that suggestion? This was even better!

"NO!"

"But there isn't any other way!" I pleaded. At least one that didn't involve my soul shriveling up and dying, and me living in the dark like a troll. "Zeus is of this realm Hades. I'm sorry, but if what you say is true, he is more powerful than you here."

I tried my best to ignore the dangerous waters I'd just tread in. Proclaiming Zeus superior to Hades was not the smartest thing I'd said; and I knew without question had anyone else dared to say it, they'd be dead before the last syllable left their mouth. But it was the truth—in this case. And I knew he knew it. This was Zeus' turf and we needed him—quickly. Who knew how Antonio was faring. The only reason I hadn't ran back in there by now to help him myself was the small comfort that Chaos was at his side; that and I knew Hades would never let me.

I tried to make him see reason. "Whatever your personal feelings about him may be, you know he can stop Nightmares. He can save us all."

It made perfect sense and it was the easiest solution—other than the fact that I had to get face-to-face with him to ask. But I would do it and with a smile if it meant avoiding plan A or B—both ending badly for me. Besides, Antonio was Zeus' son, he would want to help; and even if he didn't, I couldn't imagine any debt that Zeus would hold over me to be any worse than what I was facing now. It certainly couldn't be any worse than what Nightmares had in store.

Hades stepped closer, closing all distance between us. His body towered over me. The sympathetic look he wore moments ago was gone, and the monster I once feared shimmered through him, threatening to break free. He gripped at my arms. "You will not seek Zeus's help, do you understand? I will not have you indebted to him—not ever. I will not let him take pleasure in protecting what is mine!"

"But—"

His hands had moved up to either side of my face, holding it firmly as his fingers splayed back into my hair. I couldn't have looked away if I'd wanted to. My heart was beating out of my chest. His eyes churned with love and utter possession, it literally took my breath away.

"You are mine to look after, and *I* will be the one to secure your safety. *I* will save your world."

With that, his mouth claimed mine. Stealing whatever words I might have said and devouring all thoughts. All I could do was hold onto him the best I could and have faith that he wouldn't let me fall when my knees gave out—and they were damn close.

He pulled back slowly, one hand still held my face, while the other had wrapped around my waist, his arm, holding me to him, supporting my weakened state.

Just then he looked more beautiful than anything or anyone I had ever seen, and he was completely enamored of me. My heartbeat quickened.

"I will never tire of seeing you like this," he leaned in close to my ear. "*Flushed* from my touch."

A smile had swept across his face, reaching his eyes. He looked so young and carefree that I nearly forgot who he was and that life as we knew it was hanging by a thread. Hell, I could hardly remember who *I* was at the moment, I tried to focus.

Hades' reaction to me seeking Zeus' help made sense. When I'd challenged him, claiming that if he didn't protect me from Nightmares I wouldn't think him "manly" enough to be worthy of me, it had not been easy for him to swallow. Being helpless against the soulless wraith didn't help his ego either. How would Hades be expected to fight what he couldn't touch? Not even I would have held him to that. But just now, stating that Zeus of all beings would be the one to save our day . . . that had to be the equivalent of kicking him in the balls while wearing stilettos.

I'd only challenged him in the first place to buy me time to thwart the deal I'd made with him, hoping that he'd be so busy chasing after Nightmares that in the meantime I'd be able to find a way out of the bargain we'd made. The bargain that would bind me to the Underworld for the rest of my life; not to mention giving Hades the freedom to claim Mount Olympus and turn the world upside down. I would have never been so childish as to make him prove himself if so much had not been at stake. His manhood had never been in question.

"Hades," I'd finally found my voice. "We can't lose sight of what matters most. This isn't about your pride. It isn't even about *my* safety anymore, or the preservation of Mount Olympus for that matter."

He looked taken aback. As if the 'preservation of Olympus' had not occurred to him—which of course it wouldn't.

"The safety of the Outer World and the Heavens are at stake. Even what the human world believes to be true, teeters in the balance. We need your brother's help."

Hades' resolve was stronger than ever. "You are asking too much of me. I cannot simply step back and let Zeus battle for me. It is not in my nature. Especially when the battle is for the woman I love."

I would forever marvel at those words. The fact that he meant them, that *I* had captured the Lord of the Underworld's heart . . . There would be no arguing this. Hades saw this as a battle for my life and hand, and he was going to be the one to win it.

"Evie." He'd captured my chin with his fingers, turning my head to face him fully. "Trust when I say that I will find a way to protect you, and your human world. Even if I have to remain in the underworld, I will find a way."

I sighed, could anyone be more stubborn? He would never ask Zeus for help, and Hell would have to freeze over twice before he'd let me do it. But Antonio on the other hand . . .

"What plot runs through your mind?"

For not being able to read minds, Hades was pretty good at reading *my* thoughts. I shook my head, offering him a small smile, doing my best to conceal my worry. He'd been trying to reassure me. I didn't doubt the sincerity of his words, but I knew they held no weight unless he was set free. I hated to mislead him, again.

"I trust you to do what you can. I won't ask Zeus for help." *But if Antonio managed to survive this night, he'd be on Zeus' doorstep by morning.*

Hades nodded in understanding, accepting my promise. Relieved I was no longer pressing the matter. "I will not fail you."

I reached up, my fingers gently grazing the silhouette of his face. There was no denying that I had gone soft when it came to him.

The way I saw it, I had two choices now and none of them included giving Hades free reign to wage war on Mount Olympus. Who knew what kind of catastrophe that would provoke? What would that truly mean for the Outer World if Hades were to *actually overthrow Zeus*? I tried to envision the unholy mess of it all. . . . And what would the God of the Sea do if Hades were to attempt to take the throne?

I had no idea where that thought had just come from. Though it had been a whisper of a consideration, it nagged at me none-the-less. . . . And with my luck as of late, I honestly half-expected Poseidon to emerge from Ms. Leech's koi pond on the spot and growl his intentions of grandeur himself. The world did not need a battle between these three brothers—*this much* I knew.

Roland let out a soft moan. His body still lay limp on the ground. He must be coming to . . .

Hades turned his attention fully to the creep that had nearly split my head open.

"Now . . ." he pondered.

"Hades, no." I stepped in between them.

"Why would you protect him? Why should I spare his life?" he asked out of what appeared to be genuine curiosity.

They were good questions, and I knew the answers. "Because he is young and afraid. Because he doesn't understand what it means to really care for someone." I threw my arms around Hades' shoulders, hugging him to me. Letting him feel my heartbeat against his. "Because no matter how hard he tries he will never have me, and *that* seems a fitting punishment does it not?"

I smiled at him, wrinkling my nose a little. I knew the last part sounded a bit conceited. Okay, it was totally conceited. But I also knew Hades' mind. He would agree. The thought of not having me would be the worst pain of all in his mind, and I knew Hades was the kind of man that would enjoy nothing more than to rub it in that I was his—for whatever that was worth.

I found myself suddenly wrapped in a kiss; Roland's life for the moment was safe.

The deep seeded affection I felt for Hades had surfaced once more. I kissed him back, and I found myself wishing he could whisk me to his made up world and keep me blessedly oblivious. But I knew that could never happen. We couldn't run away. And when the time came for me to let him pass through the gates . . . I would have to let him go.

"Evelyn!" My dad's voice hollered from a distance.

"You have to go." I stepped away, moving toward Roland. I couldn't let anyone find me with Hades, especially my father.

"I cannot leave you," he warned.

"Please . . ." I looked back in the direction from where my father called out. There were other voices with him. They were getting louder, closer.

"I'm not afraid of your father, Evie." Hades was standing his ground.

"Evelyn!"

We so did not have the time for Hades and my dad to have a face to face.

I was desperate. "I'll come to you later, I swear it." And then I did the only thing I could think of to assure him I spoke the truth: I rushed back to him. Like a cheesy love story, I found myself jumping up and throwing my arms around him. Our bodies colliding perfectly; and our lips meeting with an intensity and passion I didn't know either of us possessed.

His fingers, gripping my shoulders while his heart pounded against mine. His thoughts promising we'd finish this later, and the images that flooded his mind of he and I together, made my face flush crimson.

He reluctantly broke our kiss. "If you should need me . . ."

" . . . I'll call for you," I finished for him. "I promise."

He nodded reluctantly and disappeared.

Chapter 11

"This isn't the first time your daughter and her *friends* destroyed school property." Ms. Leech leveled her stare, causing me to sink further into my chair.

I'd been whisked into her office *tout de suite*, when her goons found me standing next to an unconscious Roland; whom I was still pissed at for manhandling me the way he did.

"The hell with school property, I want that boy's ass! Just look at her!" My dad reached over and plucked a twig from my hair.

I must have looked like I'd just battled a pine tree and lost. With Chaos' open-assault on *The Kitchen* and Roland slamming me repeatedly into said tree, I was covered in all manner of debris from plaster to pine needles.

"Mr. Hollyander! I cannot simply *give* you Mr. Vandenberg on a silver platter. This isn't the *Wild West*. I can assure you, however, that his parents have been telephoned. And as ill-behaved as he may have been, there isn't a *law* against kissing!" The old bat pursed her lips.

What did she know about kissing? I was willing to bet all that is holy, that no one had kissed her puckered lips in the last billion years—which incidentally was the speculated date of her birth by many whispered classmates.

Herman squawked beside her, bobbing his ruffled body up and down, eyeing me; I leaned away.

"Kissing?" I could actually see the anger coat my father's face. "*He* attacked her! I want that boy not only expelled, but charged!"

"Now, Mr. Hollyander, I think that's a bit rash, don't you?" The smug look on Ms. Leech's face made me want to scrub my body with a wire brush. The old expression: 'made my skin crawl,' had never been clearer. " . . . After all, your daughter wasn't the one found unconscious . . . and Mr. Vandenberg certainly isn't the only boy having been led astray by her wiles."

My mouth dropped open, aghast.

"Mr. Epiales himself only just confessed moments ago, that he and Mr. Vasques' dispute erupted from the emotional tug-a-way your daughter has inflicted upon their tender youth." Ms. Leech managed to look appalled that anyone could behave in such a way.

"And just what are you implying?" my father raged.

"That according to Mr. Vandenberg, your daughter, well, let's just say . . . was perfectly fine with kissing him back."

"I was not—Daddy!"

George slammed his hands onto Ms. Leech's desk, causing her belongings to jump. "Don't you dare try to pin this on Evelyn! I don't want that boy so much as breathing the same air as my daughter!"

The old witch looked visibly shaken.

"I donate more financial support than any other board member. With my government pull, I can have this school shut down before morning, and you out of a job within the hour!" The threat was loud and clear. My dad seemed to grow before me, towering over the hag with all the strength of a Divine Guardian. He was power incarnate, and Ms. Leech knew it. She sat upright.

"Very well, Mr. Hollyander. I will see to it that the boy is at the very least suspended, pending further investigation. As for the charges you speak of . . . you'll have to pursue that matter privately. I won't have the other students disrupted and the school's good name tarnished over this ugly affair. As I said, Mr. Vandenberg claims that he and Miss Hollyander—"

"For God's sake woman, look at her arms! The evidence is practically burned into her skin!"

I looked to where my father pointed. Nightmares' fingerprints still glowed red from where he'd had a hold of me.

"Daddy, that wasn't Roland." I clambered to get out of my chair to give him a better look. "Dylan, I mean Nightmares, did that to me before Roland took me into the woods. The demon goes to our school now."

"Really, Miss Hollyander. There is no need to name call. Mr. Epiales may have come from Hoffmyer, but to refer to him as a demon . . ."

My dad looked torn between slapping Ms. Leech and tearing out the door—he now had two targets. "You have a *demon* on campus and you didn't even know it?"

Ms. Leech sat tall in her chair. Her patience looked spent. She pursed her lips once more, resembling the appearance of having just sucked on a lemon. "According to your daughter."

George leaned over the old bat's desk, his face, dangerously close to hers. "For your sake, let's hope she's mistaken."

He strode from the office leaving me behind. The long black dress coat he wore fooled no one. The inner pocket that was meant to conceal his staff, visibly outlined it. My dad was going to war.

"Dad!" I ran across the common area, heading for the kitchen.

Ms. Leech had taken full advantage of my father's abrupt absence and ragged on me for ten painful minutes. She was convinced that *I* misled Roland—*as if!* And, that this whole "ugly affair" was somehow *my fault*—Witch!

Meanwhile, my dad was nowhere to be seen . . . the kitchen looked to be in shambles. There would be no repairing this time, we'd be looking at a total rebuild.

It had to be approaching midnight. The sun had gone down ages ago and I hadn't seen a single student or skulking school guard since I'd been forced to enter Ms. Leech's torture chamber. If I didn't find him soon, I'd be whisked off to Hell while he and Nightmares went at it; and considering the damage Nightmares inflicted on Hades—an all-powerful God—I didn't want to think about what he could do to my father if given the chance.

Where could he be . . .? And where in the hell was Antonio? I rounded the corner of building B heading for the gym. *Maybe George decided to enlist Gunny's help . . .?*

"Watch it, you big stupid Mageian!"

I yelped, tripping over my feet, and skidding to a halt—barely dodging a pixie as a tree came crashing down beside me, its branches clipping my shoulder and knocking me to the ground; the giant spruce collided with the earth, sending tree bits and plumes of dirt into the air.

There were no audible words . . . I scrambled to get up, wiping dust futility from my eyes as I climbed over the enormous trunk. The grounds that led from me to the gym had become an impenetrable battlefield. Pixies, thousands upon thousands of them, were fighting other small pixie-like creatures whose bright clothing gleamed iridescent in the moonlight.

One of the strange beings wore a white dress resembling a daisy. She ran past me, howling a rebel yell as she threw . . . *tomatoes*?

"What the—"

"Child of Light!"

I turned my head, cowering as a flash of fire shot up from behind me, then another. The rumbling ground under my feet began to split and the flashes of fire became spurting geysers of volcanic liquid, rising up from the depths; the tree beside me caught fire. I ran forward, shrieking as another flame burst, singing my shoes while I danced from spot to spot avoiding the blasts.

More pixies were emerging from underground to join the fray.

"Child of Light!" Havoc's shrill voice called out to me once more. "You taking up fire walking . . . get out of there!"

As if I wasn't trying.

"Hurry!" She'd pushed through a nearby bush, waving me over. She looked like a mad woman with black smudges smeared across her cheeks and wildly spiked hair going in every direction.

I hobbled her way, already feeling that the soles of my shoes had been melted off.

"Evie duck!"

Something juicy smashed into my face.

"You're gonna pay for that Isabella," Havoc shook her tiny fist. "You almost ruined my dress, you shrew!"

Angelic giggles filled the air. "Since when do *pixies* care about their looks?"

I spat tomato from my mouth—the only thing that saved Havoc from receiving a landslide of obscenities. It was just like her to be thinking of her stupid dress when it was *my face* that had just been assaulted—not to mention our whole world was exploding to bits around us.

"Havoc!" I wiped at my eyes, still sputtering; I'd swear that tomato had been stewed. "What in the hell is going on? What are those things?"

"Wood sprites!" she screamed out as she lobbed a rock in retaliation toward the tomato thrower.

"Ow!"

"Hahaha." Havoc jumped up and down, laughing wickedly while clapping like a loon. "That's right, you goodie-goodie sky skum . . . run home to your big sister. And tell *Shimmer, red* is *not* her color. It's *mine!*"

"Havoc!?"

"We're at war, what do you think?" she exclaimed. exasperated that it wasn't blatantly obvious. "Zeus has sent his wood sprites, and a few other horrid sky-creatures," she growled in disgust, " . . . to plague our world."

The utter loathing and contempt she held for these beings was unsurpassed. Not even the initial hatred she'd shown to Mageians compared to the rage she was exhibiting for the creatures of Olympus. She scooped up a few chunks of tomato from the ground in each of her little hands and was winding up to throw them.

"Wood sprites . . .?" I looked back to the pandemonium, leaning toward Havoc as another blast of fire shot into the air—as if she were big enough to shield me. We were standing at the threshold of Hell once again. "Wait. How did you know that sprite's name?"

Havoc's beady eyes flickered my way. "Long story." She chucked her missiles, nailing the sprite wearing the daisy dress in the side of the face as she tried to run past us in hot pursuit of a pixie holding a slingshot. "Take that you dirty sky-witch! . . . And next time Sue, pick your tomatoes before they turn to mush!"

I couldn't help the incredulous look I shot her. How in the world did Havoc know these guys? And when had she become a gardener? And why wasn't the whole freaking school here by now? The seismic disturbance alone of the Underworld opening up, magma illuminating the night sky, and the ten thousand or so mythological creatures sparring and caterwauling in the middle of campus, should have at least caught the attention of a few people. How could anyone miss this—especially the grownups?

"Where is everyone?"

As if on cue, screams from the distance, reminiscent of the frightened students during gargoyle Roland's attempt to kill me in the gym—yet another cozy Pinehurst memory for the yearbook—rang out.

"Head's up!"

I heeded Havoc's warning just in time, ducking as a potato came hurling my way.

"Little monsters." I searched the ground, looking for ammo of my own.

Havoc threw the offending potato back toward a particularly ornery looking sprite with pink hair.

"You missed me, Havocca! Looks like fraternizing with the undesirables has made you just a wee bit more Pixie," she mocked. "Your aim stinks!" The sprite's laughter was booming. "Your mother must be proud!"

"She is," Havoc hollered back. "She's grateful every day that she never gave birth to an oversized ogre like yours did; and you still look horrible in pink!" Havoc blurted over the slew of obscenities the sprite was screaming back at her.

"*Havocca* . . . your names Havocca?" That was actually pretty. I hadn't imagined *Havoc,* had been short for anything, especially something cute. Would the day's shocks ever end? Then: " . . .wait, you have a mother?" I looked at Havoc expectantly. I would give almost anything to hear about the woman Havoc referred to as mom—even while standing in the middle of a blazing war zone.

"Of course I have a mother!" she snapped. Then she hurled a rock at the pink haired sprite with lightning speed, knocking her right off the branch she'd been about to ambush us in. "Just never you mind about that. And for all that's evil, don't just crawl around the ground like a turtle, lob some of those carrots over there. We're under attack, you know!"

"I wasn't crawling. And where are all these vegetables coming from? Holy crap!" I scurried backward. "Are those *centaurs*?"

"Yes, the bastards," Chaos had joined us, slightly out of breath. "One nearly stepped on me. Are you alright my sweet?" He held Havoc's troubled face in his hands for a moment, taking her in and assessing she was well. She softened under his stare. "You look magnificent."

"Those are real centaurs," I stammered in awe, pointing, looking from the love-struck pixies to the half human half horse-like creatures that had just descended from the sky. "Centaurs are real?!"

"Yes, yes, centaurs are real." As if this was yesterday's news. Havoc leaned Chaos's way. "Evie's still catching up."

"Ahaa," he nodded as if her words explained away my apparent idiocy to this whole shittery.

A sudden explosion of fire and Earth sent us into the air, landing several yards away, eating dirt.

I moaned, too sore to move, straining to see through the debris. My ears were ringing. The west side of the gym was gone, replaced by a fiery geyser.

Student's screams were coming louder, closer, as school alarms began to sound.

"Die demon . . . in the name of Olympus!" A centaur charged our way, sending a spear past my head at warp speed, harpooning what looked to be a giant boar—with fangs!

The beast squealed as its back end flopped against my leg; I hadn't even known he was beside me.

"Oh hell no!" My strength recovered. I dove for the bush we'd been ambushed in, hiding like the coward I suddenly was. Nobody said anything about there being vampire pigs on the loose.

"Move over!" Havoc crammed her way in beside me, pulling Chaos along too. "Those things eat Pixies, you know."

"Why is this happening," I cried out, wide-eyed at the horrific sight before me. Pinehurst was being destroyed. "Why would Zeus attack us with an army?"

Havoc looked momentarily reluctant. She looked briefly to Chaos. "I saw Nightmares running this way and—"

"You started this?"

"No!" she defended. "It was totally under control. Chaos and I were leading the pixies in OSH. Operation seek and herd . . ." she shouted out over the growing noise; her eyes rolling at the obvious abbreviation she sensed I was struggling with. "I opened up the portal to the Underworld at the precise moment the pixies chased

Nightmares through the commons—it was completely foolproof." She furrowed her brow in reminiscence. "By estimation, we should have had him . . . and we *would have* had him if those sky-twits hadn't *butt in*!" she yelled upward.

"You tried to capture Nightmares yourself?" I rounded on her in disbelief.

"Of course not. Chaos was there too."

Of all the stupid—

"Ahahhh . . ." A pixie wearing green catapulted past us.

I stared at Havoc in disbelief. Was she totally out of her mind? When I told her we'd help her get Nightmares back into the Underworld no matter the method, I had thought there'd be an organized yet covert plan of attack. One that would actually work the first time so that we wouldn't be standing around afterward wondering what to do next, having given the whole thing away. Not sending an army of pixies to round him up and chase him all the way home—now he was onto us!

"Don't you dare look at me like that, Child of Light, this was well thought out. I mean, it's not like I acted on a whim."

My eyes had to be bugging out of my head. Was that a rhetorical comment?

"I did not act on a whim!" she reiterated, stomping her foot as if that was the end of it. "Hades ordered us to retrieve Nightmares by any means possible and that is exactly what we're doing."

"We're not doing anything Havoc, we're hiding behind a bush!"

The chaos was all-encompassing. There wasn't a safe place in sight. I hadn't caught a glimpse of my dad, a slayer, or any Mageian for that matter. I wasn't sure what to do. Part of me wanted to scream out for Hades help right now.

I couldn't believe he would endorse all-out war in a school zone. No way. This was the result of Havoc's crazy plan. No wonder Zeus sent down an army. By the look of things, the Underworld had staged a small-scale invasion and this was ground zero. He probably thought Hades was behind the whole mess. He had no idea that Satan had escaped and was running around freely right under his nose.

"Evie!" Antonio rushed over to me, narrowly dodging fire blasts and zinging arrows. "There you are, I've been looking all over for you, this is madness! You're hurt!" He put his arms around me, barely sheltering me from a vicious zucchini attack from behind.

"Ow! *I'm fine*," I gritted as I picked up the offending vegetable that had just pelted me right in the ear. I chucked it back in the direction it came from. "It's tomato juice." My whole arm was covered in it.

Antonio turned just in time to see the culprit. "Sue!" he scolded the sprite dressed like a daisy. She was armed with another zucchini and a tomato, this one looked extra juicy.

I scooted back.

She bared her teeth. "Don't you 'Sue' me. I'm still not convinced you're a prince." She chucked the tomato for good measure, this time hitting Antonio in the leg before she ran off, zucchini in hand.

"Come on." He pulled me toward thicker shrubbery on the outskirts of the field, Havoc and Chaos were close behind.

"You've been looking for me?" I started in on him, " . . . I've been looking for you. Where have you been? We need to find Zeus, quick." I hadn't even given Antonio time to answer. "We need to tell him Nightmares isn't Nightmares."

"What?!" Havoc and Chaos blurted in unison, turning and completely dismissing the mythological warfare surrounding us.

"Nightmares isn't just a demon," I announced. "He's Satan."

Havoc's little mouth gaped open.

"That's not possible," Chaos declared. "Satan can't just freely roam the Outer World. He would have had to be—" The pixie stopped mid-sentence, his eyes drifting to Havoc, disbelieving what he already knew to be true.

"*You* released Satan through the Gates?!"

I frowned at her. "It's not like I meant to. I didn't know it was him—not even Hades did!"

I turned to Antonio, fully expecting him to freak out, or at the very least look mildly astonished, but he didn't. He didn't look surprised at all. In fact, he looked as if this was old news.

"You knew?!" I stated, too dumbfounded to say anything else.

"Only just," he admitted. "Zeus informed me when I went to see him."

"What? When?" When had he had time for a visit to Mount Olympus . . . when my head was being bashed in by Roland? And how in the literal Hell did Zeus know Nightmares was Satan?

"Right after *The kitchen* blew up and Nightmares escaped me," Antonio began, answering my unspoken questions. "I couldn't find you so I went to Zeus for help. He told me who the demon really is. He's known for some time Satan has been afoot."

If I looked shocked before, I had to look appalled now.

"Zeus knew this whole time?" Oh I couldn't wait to tell Hades this. "He knew that monster has been tormenting us and he's done nothing? You're his son! How could he put you in danger like that?"

"Zeus is loyal to no one," Havoc remarked. She looked just as disgusted by Antonio's revelation as I was.

"He had his reasons," Antonio defended.

I didn't even want to hear it. There was no way on what would be left of this Earth, that Antonio would be able to justify Zeus' "reasons," in my book.

"He is willing to intervene when the time is right."

Students' screams were all around.

"Are you kidding?" I motioned to the interdimensional war at our feet. "'When the time is right' . . . and just when is that blessed moment? I was going to go to Zeus for help myself, Antonio, or rather have you go to him."

Now it was Antonio's turn to look surprised.

"We don't *have* any more time. You were right. Hades can't fight the demon in the Outer World, but Zeus can! We need him to defeat Nightmares and cast him back into Hell."

Antonio shook his head. "We'll have to find another way."

"There is no other way!"

"Just a minute." Havoc interrupted. "How did *you* know Hades couldn't fight Nightmares in the Outer World?"

"I was wondering that myself."

Havoc's question was laced with suspicion. Chaos stood beside her, arms crossed, the both of them accusing; they were nothing if not loyal to their master.

I looked to Antonio. I too had wondered that very question when he'd first made the connection, though he'd never got the chance to answer when I'd asked.

"It wasn't hard to figure out," he defended. "Hades had been mortally wounded and Nightmares didn't have a scratch on him. It was the only explanation. I just didn't understand why."

The two pixies narrowed their eyes. They weren't buying it, and something deep down tugged at my suspicions too. There was more to this story and now was not the time to launch a full-scale investigation; except it was.

"Evie . . ."

I shook my head at him. "If Zeus knows that Nightmares is Satan, that would mean that he knew I released him from the Underworld; and he isn't *ready* to intervene yet?"

"As if Zeus would turn his cheek to that!" Havoc spat. "He knows Olympus is the last stand before the Heavens."

I locked eyes with Antonio. A cool sweat had formed over my body. She was right.

Antonio closed his eyes in dread as I gasped in realization. The both of us knowing I'd hit the nail on the head: "He knows Satan could use me to release the Titans." *Who would be all too eager to wipe out the Olympians for him before he locks them up again.*

Antonio didn't say anything, he didn't have to.

Havoc and Chaos were stunned to silence. But I knew they knew the ramifications of this.

The only thing that troubled me more than the total universal destruction that appeared imminent, was what Zeus could possibly have asked of Antonio in exchange for not killing me outright?

It is not for you to worry about. Antonio's words invaded my mind. But it was not the words that worried me, it was the solemn tone in them. He was resolved to do whatever his father had asked of him in return for my life; and the price had been hefty.

Hades had been right. I knew then and there that I did not want Antonio indebted to Zeus any more than I wanted to be. Whatever bargain he made on my behalf, I would undo. Somehow I would shoulder that burden too. I had to. Antonio would not suffer because of me.

"Evelyn!" Antonio gripped my arm as I moved to leave, his fingers nearly cutting the circulation off—I had never seen him look more serious. "You are to go nowhere near my father without me, do you understand?"

I shook my head no. I was not going to promise him that, and I was not going to lie. Why bother, he could read my thoughts anyway. I yanked my arm free.

"The only way out of this mess is to capture Nightmares myself."

"Evie, no!"

I started backing away. "Zeus can't hold you to your bargain if he doesn't come through now, can he?" Before Antonio could utter a word I turned and ran—right into the living Hell Havoc, had provided.

Chapter 12

Evie! I could hear Antonio screaming my name mentally.

I didn't stop. I had to find Nightmares, and quick. By the look of things, he hadn't been captured yet. Then again, who could tell?

A flash of purple entered my peripheral before slamming into my face. I cried out as I tried to pull it free. The little menace was yanking at my hair with everything it had.

"I saw the young Prince holding you!" she growled through gnashed teeth. "He's too good for you, Demon!" She kicked me in the nose.

I spun around, trying to break free of her and tripped, tumbling down a small hill and rolling right into Ms. Leech's coy pond. I yanked the creature from my hair, gripping her tightly around the waist with one hand and holding her at arm's length; I wiped at my nose with the other, I knew it was bleeding profusely.

It was a wood sprite dressed in purple, and she was . . . beautiful. Even her dark-violet eyes that screamed she'd kill me the moment I let go, were captivating.

"I know I'm beautiful . . . you don't have to gawk!"

Conceded little . . . I narrowed my eyes at what could be none other than evil incarnate. I understood why Havoc hated these little beasts.

"Aren't you a bit . . . *small* to be crushing on Antonio?"

She opened her mouth and gasped. "I am more than enough woman for him." She tossed her wet hair aside, pond weed and all. "Besides, he likes me better than you." She bit my finger.

"Ouch!" I tossed the little menace aside, throwing her just to the pond's edge; she landed with a hard splash.

I clambered out of the water alongside her, dripping wet, picking debris from my hair.

The sprite snorted at the sight of me.

"Oh shut up! Like you look any better." I didn't have time for this.

I stood up as wild screams came from behind. I whirled around, my eyes just focusing on Stacy and her witches in training as they ran my way in feather clad pajamas, a giant troll with salivating teeth at their heels.

"Move!" Stacey's hands came out, shoving me from her way and sending me right back into the pond.

I came up this time sputtering and spewing water from my mouth; the little sprite's laughter rang in my ears.

My hands frantically wiped at my eyes in time to see her wiggling her little fingers at me before fleeing into the bushes.

"Tell the young Prince, *Elise* says helloooo."

I slapped at the water angrily.

"You alright there, Evie?"

I looked up to see Victor smiling down at me, a staff in one hand, the other extended to help me up.

I nodded, accepting his offer. "Thank you."

This wasn't the first time Victor had come to my aid. He'd socked Roland on my behalf and shunned him socially for being a presuming ass. He was a good friend.

"No problem. You see Iris in this mess?"

I looked over his shoulder toward the ongoing battle. Fiery explosions and mythological creatures of all shapes and sizes ran this way and that, wielding weapons of steel and . . . fruit.

Havoc was so going to get it for this. There was no way Ms. Leech would be blaming *me* for 'destroying school property' this time.

I pushed my wet hair aside. "Sorry, I haven't."

"Chambers!"

Victor and I both winced. How Gunny's voice managed to carry over the noise, I'll never know.

"Stop playing around in the water with Hollyander, boy! I've got a dozen trolls invading the girl's dorms and six angry centaurs tearing up Leech's botanical garden."

We'd managed to climb back out of the water in time to see a pair of said trolls chasing a screaming Stacey and her gaggle of hags in the opposite direction.

"Hollyander, I suggest you get yourself a weapon! Chambers—Anderson!" Gunny jerked his head toward the fleeing girls. "The rest of you, follow me!"

And just like that I was left alone. Now . . . where would that creep be hiding . . .?

Poseidon sat back on his throne of gold, stroking his chin, staring long at the watery image before him. The girl was brave, he'd give her that. Foolhardy to be sure, but without question, brave. She had so much of her father in her that it troubled the Sea King, but he could also see the leery nature of her mother in her too. The untrusting part of her heart that thankfully held her back from committing wholly to Hades, for the time being; and that was the only thing that saved the bastard from eradication.

Poseidon had not spoken to Hades in over a millennia, and that had felt as though it were yesterday to him. To consider a meeting between the two would evoke questions. Questions that Poseidon would rather not answer. But if Hades were to force his hand . . . if he were to move toward a more intimate relationship with the girl, Poseidon would have no choice but to intervene. He could not allow Hades to become keeper of both worlds. He could not allow the demons of the Underworld to claim Mount Olympus. . . . And he could not allow Evie to be condemned to darkness; he would never be able to look her mother in the eyes again—a fate he could not bear.

Gwendolyn had come to him mere days ago. An event so monumental in itself that Poseidon was still at a loss for words at it. She stood before him. Right here in this very throne room—at the center of Atlantis! Her eyes were filled with determination, but he could see the awe in them too. She was beholden to stand before him. The man who once held her heart and foolishly toyed with it; one of the very few regrets he had in his much too long life.

Gwendolyn Hollyander was a rare beauty. Her dark lush hair and piercing stare to this day, bore into his very existence. Her skin— flawless. Hydrated with youth that would always be hers—a gift from the fairy's. She was a true marvel—a fairy-goddess—worshiped by all who knew her. Much older than most would conceive, though not quite as old as he. She had gone by many names through the ages, forever masking her identity; though she could not hide from him. She would always be his Áine, his Lady of the Lake.

That she came to him at all, could only mean she was desperate. It could only mean that she believed the world as she knew it would crumble without his aid. That her husband, the Guardian of the Divine Army himself, was helpless. It could only mean that she believed that the Heavens would soon fall, and that all she had natured and provided for would be lost, and she was right.

Poseidon had been watching Zeus for some time . . . catching glimpses of him through fountains and ponds scattered throughout Olympus. Hearing whispers of conversations Zeus thought private. Gwendolyn's fears had long been confirmed.

Zeus had put a magical ward around Mount Olympus the day he had cast Poseidon and Hades away. A protective shield that neither could break. Poseidon, with his ability to control the water, had spent all of time since trying to break through that barrier, and as luck would have it, at long last did. The watery ornamental pieces Zeus decorated his gardens and halls with, provided a window into Olympus for him. A window that Poseidon alone controlled.

Talk of mal intent soon touched his ears. There were plans of such treachery, such utter blasphemy, that Poseidon could not believe his brother would be so ambitious—though he knew Zeus' thirst for domination. History had proven that Zeus was capable of every despicable crime Poseidon believed he intended to commit. Crimes Zeus himself resolved would be so.

It was through his spying that he learned of Evie in the first place, and her connection to the Underworld. It was through that spying that he learned Zeus himself had grand plans for the girl, long before Hades had staked his claim on her—two details that had the Sea King furious!

Had fate not played him such a cruel hand, Evie would have been his daughter. His everlasting love for Áine compelled him to treat her as such; and as such, no daughter of his would be in league with the King of the Underworld. No daughter of *his* would be at the mercy of Zeus. Not now— not ever!

The very thought had angered Poseidon so much that the sea had felt it and responded. Hurricanes were decimating coastal villages at this very moment, and ships passing through were sinking to a watery grave. There had been earthquakes . . . too numerous to count, that the merfolk had taken to the mountainous caves in the deepest depths below to "wait out the storm." Never had his wrath driven his people away into hiding, but he had not had such cause for anger since Zeus sent him to command the sea. Legends of a peaceable agreement between the brothers, a draw of who would get what world, were greatly sweetened in Zeus's favor—the only point Hades and Poseidon shared a common view on. That and Medusa.

Had it not been for Hades desire to woo the girl with an ocean paradise smack in the middle of the Underworld, Poseidon would not have been able to watch them at all when she was forcibly whisked away at every midnight. That had been Hades' mistake . . . a mistake he still did not know he'd made. For up until the moment the watery world was created, Poseidon had not been able to see into the Underworld—Hell hath no living water.

He regarded young Evelyn Hollyander through the pond-water's reflection with renewed interest. He would uphold the vow he made to her mother: so long as he drew breath, no harm shall befall this girl. She had the protection of the Sea King, and all of Atlantis. Evie, would never become a pawn in Zeus's scheme. And she would never become a victim to Hades' Curse.

Evie! Antonio's voice entered my head again. He was frantic.

It took all that I had, but somehow I managed to block him out—I had to. I had to find Nightmares before Zeus did. It was the only way to save Antonio from the foolish bargain he'd made with his dad on my behalf.

If there was a foolish bargain to be made, it'd be by me; I was a dead-girl walking anyway. I was not about to have whatever "deal"

Zeus concocted, put Antonio in the same position I was in. What would be the point? Antonio was not going to suffer because of me, and no one was going to use me as leverage against him. As sure as I was running right into hell's path, I knew Antonio's fate hung in the balance, and the clock was ticking.

I hurried toward the far end of the campus . . . away from the fight and the fiery explosions of the Underworld; I wasn't going to find Nightmares there. No, he'd be as far away from any of that as possible. He was probably lurking in some dark, quiet hole somewhere on the outskirts of Pinehurst. Skulking, like the village rat that he was; and I was running right to him.

This was such a bad idea. A bad, bad, idea. Top, of my ever-growing list of bad ideas. Why in the freaking hell would I be running to Nightmares? Sure I knew I had to protect Antonio from the deal he'd made with his dad, but what was I going to do once I found him? If Hades couldn't touch him, I didn't have a chance!

The further away from the sounds of war I got, the closer to my demise I was. I needed help, now; and there was only one bastard who wielded the power.

I was breaking my promise to Hades by even considering this. There would be no words to express his impending fury; but this was for him too!

Whatever deal Zeus made with Antonio I would gladly match it and sweeten the offer. I'd keep the Titans locked up for all of time if that was what he wanted. So much for not being leverage . . . there was no other option.

"Zeus!" I yelled out his name. If he was watching me as closely as I believed he was, he'd heard my cry.

"Well that was unexpected?"

"Shit!" I skidded to a halt, toppling forward and right into Nightmares' arms.

"Did I startle you?" He had the nerve to look apologetic. He'd casually leapt from a tree, purposefully landing just in front of me. "He won't come, you know."

Before I could think to answer, a blanket of ice constricted around me, gripping my bones and crystallizing through my veins—freezing me where I stood—I couldn't move.

"And here I thought I'd have to actually put forth effort in trying to find you."

His warm carefree smile didn't fool me. Nor did the sexy heart-throb look he was still trying to sport. This was not some random cute guy. Hell, this wasn't even the deranged serial killer guy women feared lurking in the bushes somewhere, waiting to grab them unawares and drag them off—never to be heard from again. This was the king of all demons. The root and creator of *all* evil; and we were nose to nose. I was so dead . . .

Nightmares leaned in slowly toward my ear, his warm breath bringing even more of a chill to my frostbitten skin. His voice, just above a whisper: "You needn't worry, Child of Light. If I wanted you *dead*, you'd be dead."

Oh God . . . My body tightened with unimaginable anguish at the mention of the deity's name. If I wasn't frozen in place, I would surely be on the ground withering. But that wasn't what was tormenting me: he'd *heard* my fears . . .

Nightmares chuckled with mild amusement as he stepped back a little, opening his arms wide and giving me full view of his smiling face. "It's what I do."

I stared at him uncomprehending, unable to form even the simplest plan of escape. If he could hear my thoughts, I was totally exposed. Every spell I had in my arsenal would be useless. Not to mention that my lips were too frozen to say the words; I wasn't entirely sure they'd even work on him.

"Calling out to Zeus . . ." he began, shaking a finger at me. " . . . Now *that* would have provided you with a formidable ally. Had he not been restricted to the confines of his own ambitions, he may just have answered your call. That, and of course had Antonio not agreed to the . . . *arrangement,* between he and his father . . ."

Our eyes locked.

"Oh yes," He grinned. "I know that Antonio is Zeus' son."

I could feel my heart pounding out of my chest, panic gripping me. How did he know that?

"I'll admit," he explained as he began to circle me, ready to pounce at any moment should I attempt to move—as if that were even a possibility. "He deceived me for quite some time. Had we not engaged in battle, he may have eluded me longer. Only a god of the Outer World would possess enough strength to combat me," he finally answered my unspoken question. "Only one who's blood is connected to Zeus, would have been able to withstand to fight; though only one as powerful as Zeus himself, would truly be my equal—theoretically," he winked, catching me by surprise. "I'm not saying he would win," he added almost playfully.

Who was this guy? I was face to face with Satan. I knew that. Yet he looked and acted like any old stereotypical male who was full of himself.

His smile broadened. "You really don't want me to turn beast do you?"

No! I mentally remarked. We could forgo that pleasure.

He laughed outright. "You see, I knew you and I would get along. All this playful banter between us . . . it's like we were destined to be . . ."

If this guy said we were soul mates, I was going to scream. Mentally.

"Comrades. No, no!" He jumped back, dramatically lifting his hands to the sky as if to offer the full picture. "*Soul . . . friends*."

That did it. I was mentally screaming. There was no way I was going to be soul *anything* with this guy. I didn't care who or what he was!

He stood beside me now, casually propping an elbow on my shoulder, leaning in. "This isn't because I'm not an Olympian is it?"

If my mouth could gape, it would be. Was he kidding?!

"Don't act like that's a stretch . . . not that I can't see why you would set your heights so high; given the current selection of potential suitors that dwell here." He jerked his head toward the direction of the school. "But I would have never fathomed you would be so bold as to toy with the affections of *two* Olympians—especially the Lord of the Underworld! You do like to play with fire don't you?"

If I could have kicked him in the balls I would have.

He leaned in once again, his lips just grazing my ear. "Then it's a good thing you're frozen where you stand."

I hated him. With every fiber of my being, I hated him. He'd frozen my mouth so I couldn't even verbally kick him in the balls.

He was laughing. Actually laughing. I didn't find any of this the least bit funny. Nor the fact that he seemed to know more about Antonio than I did!

"Oh you mustn't be angry with your Antonio," he toyed with me all the more, pretending to sound concerned. "After all, he did bargain on your behalf."

The bastard had my full attention and he was relishing in it.

"Had he not sworn to take your place as the Key, Zeus would have done the honors himself. That's the reason he hasn't answered your call by the way; that and some nonsense about you residing permanently in Olympus and your father becoming Zeus' slave."

All life drained from my body.

"Now," Nightmares mused. "As I understand it, and please, correct me if I'm wrong, but there seems to be only one way that you may transfer your . . . *ability*, shall we say, onto another? It seems wrong to me that Antonio wouldn't even consider your opinion on this matter."

I was seething. Within my frozen body, my blood boiled. Antonio had bargained with Zeus on who was to be the key? Knowing full well what that meant? I was so enraged that I couldn't even consider what Zeus' twisted plan for my dad was. Someone would die this night, and at the moment I wasn't sure Nightmares was number one on my hit list.

"Of course I'm not number one on your 'hit list,'" he exclaimed, feigning offense as though the idea were inconceivable. "I'm the one kindly informing you of the brutish Olympian mentality you are to be subjected to. I myself have no desire to take such advantage of you. *I* will leave you as you are: completely intact and *untouched*."

If he didn't have my interest before, he had it now.

"It's not that I don't find you attractive," he offered quickly, " . . . it's simply a matter of not clouding the lines between us. I can't afford the unnecessary physical distractions."

He needn't justify his reasoning on that to me. I was fully on board with not having the "unnecessary physical distractions," as he put it, between us.

Strangely, all I could think of at this very moment was Stacey, and how she had unknowingly fallen under Nightmares' spell. She had no idea who he really was. I actually felt sorry for her.

"Ahahh," Nightmares smiled in remembrance, hearing my inner thoughts. "Between you and I," he winked again, "I will miss her fiery heat."

I didn't even want to think about what he meant by that. There wasn't enough therapy in the world to get even the suggestion of his implication out of my mind.

"You might feel differently about that one day," he remarked.

If looks could kill I would have incinerated him on the spot.

"Okay," he threw his hands up in playful surrender. "That day is clearly not today."

And it wouldn't be tomorrow either.

"Very well. Let us speak plainly," he changed gears. " . . . And freely."

I was suddenly mobile. I collapsed to my knees as blood began to circulate through my veins once again. I looked up into Nightmares' face, only an inch from mine, my heartbeat quickened.

I could see it in his eyes as his pupils grew smaller. I could see it in his shoulders as his muscles flexed. I wasn't kidding myself. Just then, he looked very much the predator that I knew he was, and I had never been more the prey.

"Make no mistake, that there is something I want from you. Something I *will* get." He moved a fraction closer and suddenly all the air between us was gone; my breath hitched. There was no play in his tone. "The terms of our agreement, are completely up to you."

Antonio shoved his staff through the mountain troll with renewed vigor and pushed onward before the beast fell dead. He'd fought off countless creatures from both the Underworld and Olympus, and had long since stopped caring what his father would think about him killing the very beings that would one day look up at him upon the high throne; for now, it was kill or be killed.

Neither side knew he had struck a bargain with Zeus that would land him in a most powerful position. A position that would save his Evie; and as chaotic as it was . . . he couldn't imagine they'd care. If a weapon so much as graced one's presence, the challenge was accepted and swiftly settled. Thus far, he had been the victor each time.

Much blood had been spilt this night, and so far as he could tell, it looked as if only the Underworld and Olympus had suffered losses. Antonio prayed that none of the students had been slain. It was going to be hard enough to explain what had transpired here this night, without having to add a student death toll to the mix.

The Mageian world, although aware of the existence of demons and angels, was not privy to the existence of the Olympians; damage control would be needed and fast.

Zeus had screwed up in his opinion. Sending in his army of mythological creatures had only caused Hades to respond in turn. The two Gods had in one swift move, compromised secrets that had been kept in place for thousands of years. Secrets that were necessary for the human survival. Nothing would ever again be the same.

Evie had successfully blocked Antonio from her mind some time ago, and he was growing frantic in the silence. She was on a path in which she believed would free him from a bargain poorly made. Though she could not possibly understand the vastness of it. This bargain was to secure her future. It was necessary to her survival!

Zeus' ambitions left Antonio little room to discuss terms and conditions. Though he had accomplished the most important contingency: *He* would become the key to the Underworld, and thereby giving Zeus control over two realms.

Antonio knew what this meant. He knew that he would be taking Evie's virtue and with it, her heart—forever; something she may not so willingly allow, but he hoped in time would understand. He would not let Zeus take this from either of them.

The Olympian had conceded that if he allowed Antonio this favor, he must agree to Evie residing in Olympus. Only then would her father offer the Heavens to get her back; and that was what Zeus was counting on. With the Divine Army at his disposal, and the Under World at his beck and call . . . Zeus would be unstoppable.

"EVIE!" Antonio screamed her name mentally, as well as physically out into the night. It was all he could do.

Chapter 13

If I didn't have chills running down my spine before, I did now. I stared up into Nightmares face. 'The terms of our agreement' as he so delicately put it, was code for 'I would be making a deal with the devil.'

"You needn't phrase it like that," he scolded. "There is no reason that you should see me any other way than I am here before you." He stood up and stepped back, giving me full view of him. "You don't even know what it is that I am asking."

I regarded him skeptically. Alright. I'd bite: "What do you want from me?" It was the first time I'd actually spoken since he'd turned me into an ice cube, my voice surprising me, sounding hoarse.

He extended his hand, offering me assistance to stand.

I took it cautiously, afraid of what might happen if I refused.

"You see," he began excitedly. "We are already working together."

I stared at him expectantly, he was stalling.

"Very well. Let us not pretend with one another. We no longer have the time for it."

I was about to ask, when:

"EVIE!" Antonio screamed out my name; he was close.

I looked from his direction back to Nightmares.

"We'll have to do something about that," he warned as he moved to leave.

"Don't you dare!" If anyone was going to kill Antonio it was going to be me. Right after I asked him what in the literal hell was he thinking?!

"As you wish," Nightmares tipped his head slightly. "Come."

I wasn't sure where I was agreeing to go, but something told me that if I didn't take his offered hand once more, the demon behind the façade would be exposed; and as much as I knew I was talking with Satan, I knew that I was not prepared to truly meet him face to face.

"You mean to tell me, Commander, that my daughter is still unaccounted for?"

"Yes, General," the Archangel Commander Samuel bowed his head solemnly. "I regret to inform you that she is not in the Outer World, or the Heavens."

A light breeze drifted through the temple, whispering a melodic chorus as it embraced all that crossed its path with a breath of hyacinth—not a soul flinched. The assembly of twenty-eight, remained quiet and still.

"And Olympus?"

Antonio's head snapped from the Commander to George and back. Surely he had heard the question wrong. There was no way George Hollyander would send his Archangels to Olympus—not even to look for his daughter, Zeus would never stand for it. The act alone would invoke all-out war!

"No, General." The Commander's eyes were downcast. "She is not on Olympus either."

Murmurs broke out.

"How do you know this?" Antonio spoke up for the first time and out of turn since this meeting began, quieting the room.

The Council of Angels had convened over a day ago in the Celestial Chamber upon discovery that Satan had not only been unleashed into the Outer World, but had managed to escape capture. The whereabouts of Evelyn Hollyander had become priority one, due to the fact that Evie held the power to open the gates of Hell for Satan's demons to wage war alongside their master.

The disastrous revealing of the Olympians to the Mageians, took a close second. The *worlds* as he knew them, had collided.

The Archangel Commander looked up to his General, awaiting permission to answer the Son of Zeus . . . and yes, there were no secrets about Antonio's parentage any longer; as well as Evie's importance to all of creation.

Her father had opened up this meeting divulging all—and who could blame him. He wanted his daughter found and protected by the Angel Hierarchy. If he hadn't explained her "unique situation" to the council, they would have dismissed her absence as an unfortunate affair. After all, what could possibly take presentence over Satan's release?

George nodded from his seat at the head of the table for Samuel to continue.

"We . . ." the Commander's cheeks flushed, ". . . have so been informed."

"Informed? By whom?" George demanded. "You did not come by this information on your own?"

The Commander looked more uncomfortable than before. "No, General. We received word from a Wood Sprite and a rather . . . unsavory looking Pixie."

Gasps echoed around them.

"We do not consort with such creatures!" One of the three Seraphim present declared; and the entire council bowed their heads to him in immediate agreement.

The Commander respectfully lowered his head even more. He did not look at the Seraphim who spoke—none of the assembly did. It was out of the utmost respect that one simply bow and comply with anything the highest power of angel stated. For they were the most glorious and most beloved protector to the Deity . . . and if *he* trusted their council, there was no disputing their word.

Antonio closed his eyes and took in a shaky breath. He could not sit here for much longer when Evie was God knows where— which incidentally he probably *did* know where she was.

Why no one had consulted the Deity on the matter of her location was beyond him. Especially if he alone had "gifted" her with this great responsibility. Wouldn't it stand to reason that he would want Evie safe too? Why hadn't he just swooped down to wherever she was and brought her back to the Heavens with him? Wouldn't his *"key"* be safer by his side?

It would have surely made Antonio's task of delivering Evie to Olympus all the harder however if she had been brought to Heaven.

Zeus could not just enter Heaven's realm and take her . . . and Antonio wasn't sure anymore if he would have that ability to either. By the look on the faces around him, he was no longer entrusted in the fold. He had deceived them. He was here for one reason and one reason only: he was George Hollyander's guest; and that was the one thing that kept him from their damnation.

"Forgive me, High Council," The Archangel Commander replied humbly to the Seraphim. "I only reported what was asked of me. I would not have consorted with the creatures had there been another way."

Antonio watched as George took a moment to gaze over the room, pondering. He seemed undistracted by the grandeur of it. As if he sat amongst this splendor daily and it was as ordinary as gazing at a field of cows; though the room was anything but ordinary.

The floating crystals of light overhead, were tethered to an endless sky of orange and yellow. It brought a warmth and comfort that was unsurpassed by anything Antonio had ever felt. Its beauty paled in comparison however to the golden decorations of Angels praised for their benevolent acts upon humanity. To stare at the statues for any real length of time, brought tears of beauty, joy, and peace to one's soul.

But the most glorious and most wondrous object in the entire room, would be the table at which they sat at. It was made of pure gold and angel's tears. When asked, the tabletop would reveal whatever information was sought after—like a crystal ball. In the wrong hands . . . the Table of Truth could become a tool for great evil; and Antonio hadn't missed that it was one of the items high on Zeus' list to possess.

George had been noting each of the orders one by one— acknowledging the three representatives from all nine levels. Antonio knew that he understood their minds intimately—as he did; and he suddenly did not like where this meeting was about to turn.

"Where are we?" I asked. I literally had no idea where on the freaking planet I was.

When I had taken Nightmare's hand, I wasn't exactly sure what would happen to me— teleporting hadn't been a consideration.

"We're almost there," he called back over his shoulder.

Wherever 'there' may be . . . I mentally rolled my eyes. " . . . Way to not answer the question." I mumbled under my breath.

We'd been walking down a long dark corridor—a tunnel really, made completely of some sort of stone or rock. The only sounds besides our feet shuffling along, was the occasional drip, drip, dripping, of water that echoed with every splatter.

I couldn't stop all the creepy visions that began to run wildly through my head. If a rat so much as squeaked by my foot or a freaky clown popped his head through some grate on the wall, I was going to scream big time.

Nightmares stopped and turned to look at me. "Those are your fears?" he asked, sounding surprised.

I'd just barely missed colliding into him. I was not about to be shamed by a demon. "Everyone hates clowns!" I defended.

"No, I agree about the clowns, it's the rat that surprised me. With all the creatures you've faced from the underworld, you fear rats?"

I stared at him in disbelief. "You hate clowns?"

"As you said, 'everyone hates clowns.' They're unnatural," he turned and began to walk on, leaving me stunned in his wake.

"I never understood the human obsession with them," he spoke over his shoulder as I hurried to catch up; I wasn't about to be left wherever we were, alone. "No demon would ever mimic such an oddity."

Well now I had without a doubt, officially heard absolutely everything there would ever be to hear: Satan hated clowns too . . .

"Ahh, here we are, through here."

I stopped just before the open door he held for me. The dimly lit room on the other side screamed vampire horror film—it looked like a dungeon; if not for the small fire in the hearth and the few pieces of furniture. Nope. There was no way, *no way*, I was setting a foot in that room. For all I knew I was walking right into a torture chamber!

A rat squeaked as it ran across the top of my foot.

I screamed and practically scaled the wall, somehow managing to shove past Nightmares and make my way not only into the room, but atop a chair in the far corner.

Nightmares leaned heavily against the door, using it for support; I'd practically knocked him over.

"You know," he commented dryly as he righted himself. "There are no vampires."

I frowned. With all the creatures I'd seen as of late, vampires he tells me are myth?

He chuckled lightly. "Sorry to disappoint. The female population I think would crumble in devastation at the knowledge of that information. They so hope for a dark prince to swoop in and give them immortality." He shut the door. "To keep the rats out," he explained.

I double checked the floor before stepping off the chair. Not all the rats were out, I thought as I glared his way.

" . . . And not all girls want that," I corrected. "I don't."

Nightmares laughed outright. "Oh no, not you. You just want a dark *king*!" He laughed all the harder. " . . . And not just any king, but the *King* of the Underworld!"

"Hades is not dark!" I defended. " . . . And what do you know about what I want?" I was mad. *I* didn't even know what I wanted half the time myself. I was not about to have Nightmares acting all knowing—especially about me!

"I know that you are torn between two loves," he began in all seriousness, his laughter subsiding. "I know that you do not know how you will confront Antonio who has betrayed you so entirely, and I know that you do not want this life-burden that has been saddled onto you."

Ok, so maybe he did know me. Now I was really mad. "You stay out of my head!　　　. . . And what are we doing here, what is this place?" There was something unsettlingly familiar, an energy that I recognized. I knew I'd never been in this room before, but still . . . I couldn't quite put my finger on it. " . . . And what time is it?"

"It's nearly midnight."

At last . . . luck was finally on my side! I'd be whisked to Hades any minute and Nightmares would have to manage his own dastardly plans, solo.

"You will not be going to Hades."

Wait. "What?" I couldn't compute what he was saying. "Not go to Hades . . . that's not possible." I didn't know that I physically had a choice. I actually didn't know what would happen to me if I attempted to fight the pull.

"That would have proved to be slightly troublesome," he agreed, " . . . had we not entered Megaera's lair."

Her name alone brought an instantaneous panic and sweat to my body. I took in the room fully: This was not Megaera's lair . . . at least not as I remembered it.

"Do not tell me that you have forgotten me already?"

"There must be another way!" One of the three Powers interjected amidst an eruption of divergence. "We have had many wars over the age of time, all of them without Mageian involvement."

"We agree," The Dominions concurred. "The Mageians play a very small role in demon control."

"They simply are not equipped to battle at this level, General," a Virtue squeaked out, their voice sounding like a distant song. "The

Deity would not wish for his 'gifted warriors' to be decimated like this."

Antonio couldn't have agreed more. The bulk of the Mageians that would play a role in George's proposed plan, were either too young, too inexperienced, or too ignorant to survive this. There were literally a handful of Mageian men, Antonio would consider suitable for such an assault—Gunny being one of them. The simple facts were that Slayers primarily fought 5-1 odds—demons didn't have a chance.

But this . . . this was undoubtedly turning the tables by double at best. Most Slayers were not in the frame of mind or body for such an undertaking—they'd never been trained for it—there had been no reason to! A war involving Heaven and Hell would be no place for Mageian or Man to tread . . . the loss would be catastrophic!

No. George was clearly reacting on impulse here. He wanted Evie back, and he was apparently willing to sacrifice everyone to see that that happened. This was a mistake.

"This is not up for discussion!" George rose to his feet and slammed his fist onto the table, silencing the room instantly. His red hair seemed to glow like flames with his rising anger. Even the piercing blue of his eyes had churned black; and they bore down on each soul before him. "Satan is gathering his army as you debate. Can you not feel it in the wind . . . ? Can you not sense the evil growing? Do you not hear the heavenly song stilling . . .? They will move upon us quickly—and before the next full moon—the table has shown us this. We have no choice! We must all defend what is ours! We must call upon all who have trained to fight—there are no exceptions!"

Antonio hadn't realized he'd leaned back in his chair, cowering almost, away from the Commander of God's Army—as the entire assembly was doing. There was a power that radiated from George that rivaled the Seraphim; and Antonio was witnessing it for the first time.

In all of Antonio's teachings, the Seraphim were the closest beings to the Deity. They were so powerful and so full of light and energy from his love, that it was impossible to look at them. But in this room, at this very moment, George Hollyander wielded a power more concentrated than any Antonio had ever seen. He was stronger than all these angels combined—himself included.

Antonio was suddenly afraid of what George might do to him if he ever found out his plans for his beloved daughter. If George ever found out that at this moment, Evie was supposed to be safely tucked away on Olympus—insight he was expecting to receive from Zeus very soon. Not even the One True Deity himself could save him from *this* father's wrath.

"Commander." George turned his attention once again to the Archangel, Samuel. The force of his words made the entire room

afraid to breathe: "You will gather a few warriors and descend upon the Underworld. I want you on Hades' doorstep before nightfall."

The Commander paled, then quickly bowed his head humbly—as the other two Archangels beside him did. They would not shirk their duty, but what George was asking of them was beyond dangerous. Angels did not tread in the Underworld and return unscathed; if at all. "Yes, General," he replied before they each backed away into the mist that surrounded the room.

This doesn't make any sense . . . Antonio pondered. *Why would George send only a few soldiers to the Underworld . . . he would need every angel he has to get Evie, if she were there, and these men back out. Where was he planning on sending the rest?*

"Dominic."

The Dominion Commander rose from the table. Although he remained tall, he by no means looked confident. "Yes, General?"

George had his hands on the table, leaning heavily on them. His eyes scanned over the images before him, taking in one horrific scene after another.

Antonio looked closer at the table. . . these images were different than the ones they'd viewed earlier . . . It was as if George had asked the table to show him a possibility of what *could* happen if certain events were to take place. In these images, the gates had been opened. Demons poured out from the Underworld like a raging river of overflowing sludge to aid those already fighting with Satan. The demons and the Angelic Army were brutally slaying one another— blood and body matter soaked the ground; but it was not just Heaven and Hell that fought . . .

Antonio could feel his mouth hanging open. He could not believe what the table foretold: Olympus was there too among the bloodshed, and their numbers were nowhere near enough to turn this war in the heavenly favor.

Antonio let his head fall in defeat. By this reflection, the Mageians would be suited for battle before sunset, and there would be no survivors.

George's eyes met the Dominion Commander's. "I believe it is time we called in that favor."

My entire body was petrified in fear.

That voice . . . I would never in all my days forget the hissed voice of Megaera—it would haunt me into the afterlife.

I somehow had managed to regain movement and bolted behind Nightmares—my new best friend! I was gripping his shoulders for support. If I had to choose between him and Megaera, I'd choose him, hands down.

"I never thought I would witness a being fear *me* over Satan," she made a sound that I could only fathom was laughter.

I didn't care. She could mock me all she wanted. I didn't want her within a mile of me, let alone 6 feet.

I leaned in toward Nightmares' ear and whispered: "What is she doing here?" More importantly: what were we doing here—with her?!

Nightmares turned toward me and I suddenly felt a bit too close for comfort. Our bubble was nearly non-existent.

"I needed to bring you to somewhere that Hades pull cannot reach," he explained. "Somewhere he would not go—beyond the Angel's grasp. Somewhere that only the darkest of magic and the darkest of beings can exist."

"Megaera's lair?"

"Indeed," Nightmares stepped back a little, giving space between us.

I was totally confused. The place was creepy, I'd give him that, but it didn't have the all-encompassing dark vibe he was claiming it had. Aside from the unnaturally freaky energy that was Megaera, there was nothing striking or familiar about this place. This was not the dilapidated prison we'd trespassed through nearly a

month ago on our way to find the cure for my father. No, we were somewhere else entirely. The question was: where?

My eyes quickly darted around the room, all the while keeping vampire girl in my peripheral—she was leering at me. I didn't care what Nightmares said about them being myth. I hadn't forgotten her sharp teeth or wickedly long nails. If anyone screamed vampire, it was her.

I stated the obvious: "This is not Megaera's lair."

"Allow me to regale you," Nightmares began theatrically. "I'll set the scene, shall I?" He took up a spot by the fire, allowing the flames to dance behind him, casting shadows over his performance. "As you undoubtedly recall, Hades had rushed to your aid in the nick of time; when you had so foolishly attempted to protect the Angel from Megaera's rightful claim—saving you from yet another fatal blow!"

I frowned. I recalled the occasion clearly. I did not need a play by play.

"Ahhh, but you do," Nightmares rebutted, stepping closer. "You see, this is where it gets interesting. *This* is where the rest of the pieces come together."

I nodded, prompting him to go on.

He smiled in delight. "Now, where was I . . . oh yes! When you were no longer in peril," he continued,   " . . . and the angel had so valiantly taken you to safety . . ."

'The angel . . .?' This was the third time Nightmares mentioned an angel. Realization took hold of me. He had no idea who the angel was!

" . . . Hades came to me with the request of imprisoning Megaera for her crimes against his betrothed; that would be you," he paused his theatrics to reiterate the obvious—as if I needed the clarification. He was so caught up in his performance that he'd missed my mental reverie. "You see," he explained, " . . . Hades deemed her punishment: the remainder of time in the lower levels of Hell. And while Hades commands the Underworld, he cannot imprison a being to my domain without my allowance of passage."

"An unjust fate caused by you and your angel!" Megaera spat.

She moved toward me and I instinctively dove behind Nightmares once again.

"I didn't know he would do that!" I defended. I didn't like Megaera, but 'the remainder of time in the lower levels of Hell' seemed a bit harsh. Killing her outright would have been kinder. Though knowing Hades' fury, mercy would not have been on his mind.

"*The agreement*," Nightmares went on, his voice warning Megaera to keep her distance—which she instantly obeyed—"would indebt Hades to me and provide me with an opportunity I would not have foreseen. You see Child of Light, you set this all into motion."

"Me?" It took all of a millisecond to catch up. "That's the favor Hades owed you?!" I exclaimed. "For you to imprison Megaera, he had to agree to let you out?"

Nightmares grinned. "Not *me* by name exactly. I would never have been so foolish as to suggest that . . . he would never have agreed. I presented him with my terms: in exchange for imprisoning Megaera, he must agree to release a demon of my choosing into the Outer World; and that demon I swore would wage war on Zeus and do whatever necessary to eliminate him from Olympus."

My mouth gaped.

"I had to sweeten the deal a little," Nightmares explained. " . . . And I knew that appealing to Hades' eternal war against his brother would cement the bargain."

I was absolutely stunned. Could Hades have been anymore stupid? Not only had he made a deal with the devil, but he had agreed to release any demon Satan chose—so long as that demon eliminated Zeus for him, he hadn't bothered to care who it was. He hadn't considered for one minute that Satan would choose himself.

"Tis the trouble with the male mind," Megaera grumbled from her corner. "They think only of their advancement."

Nightmares actually had the nerve to look offended.

To her credit, among these men, she wasn't wrong.

"I'll try not to take further offense to that thinking, Child of Light." He glared Megaera's way, as if she had provoked some new nonsensical view of shaming the male population.

"Are you kidding?" I had to be in an alternate universe. "I wouldn't be here if it weren't for your plans of advancement—and speaking of, what exactly are they? Why am I here?"

It was well after midnight, Hades would be freaking the hell out, Pinehurst was probably in ruins by now, Antonio and Zeus were plotting who knows what, and my father would be gathering his army the moment he realized I was missing and making a beeline straight for the Underworld—with Hades as his target.

"And *that* Child of Light, is what I am counting on."

Chapter 14

It only took a moment for the entire assembly's minds to sync with George's—and it had nothing to do with telepathy.

"Poseidon has had much time to himself . . . do we not all agree?"

Antonio, couldn't have been more surprised. Even with all that he had just witnessed through the table's showings, he would never have dreamed George would choose this path. There was not an angel or Olympian that wanted to involve Poseidon—not even if he were the last wave of defense—which apparently was the case.

If there had been controversy before about the Mageians joining the fray, it was nothing compared to the outburst of protests now.

"We *cannot* call upon the Sea King!" The Principalities pled as they tried to beseech all at the table that might hear them—the General especially. "Man cannot handle his wrath!"

"Remember Atlantis . . .? It's why the Deity made the bargain with Poseidon in the first place. He's too unpredictable," The Powers cried. "His every mood is tied to the sea."

"He'll destroy everything in his path!" One of the Cherubim shouted out.

"He'll unleash the Kraken—"

"Enough!" George slammed his fist onto the table once more, causing the very air around it to ripple, silencing the panicked crowd.

"Commander!" The Seraphim who had spoken earlier had risen from his chair abruptly, the brilliant light that radiated from him glowed amber. "You cannot make this decision on your own accord—there is protocol to respect, and there is the bargain made with the Deity to uphold."

The room was still for a fraction of a breath. Each soul praying as one that this new strategy would be dismissed as quickly as it had been suggested, and that another option would present itself—fast.

"*I* am the Commander of the Divine Army . . . the highest ranking *power* in this room!" George's controlled façade had broken. He looked directly at the Seraphim, unbothered by the brilliance of his light. "Do you believe that I would not have already consulted with the Deity regarding this matter . . . having his full support?! Do you believe that I would wake this sleeping giant if there were another way? *I know* the consequence of this. I know that invoking Poseidon will pit all three brothers against one another. We *have no* choice!"

The entire assembly lowered their heads in what was none other than shame—Antonio included. Although he did not agree with this decision, he did not doubt that George would never have made it without the blessing of the Deity.

"He will not be put back," the Seraphim gritted out, still unwilling to accept this outcome. "We will have an Olympian war to contend with yet again."

"*That* . . . has always been inevitable."

All eyes followed the sound of the new voice.

Antonio didn't have to look to know that every being in the room was wide-eyed in awe—dumbstruck, as he was.

There, standing not twenty feet away, stood Poseidon himself—trident in hand, it could be no other. He had the look of both Zeus and Hades . . . yet the Sea King was second to none. His body mass alone rivaled Zeus' . . . and made Hades look like a beefed up runway model. There was an ancient wisdom that radiated from him—more pronounced than his brothers. Poseidon was no one to trifle with. And by the instant rise of tension in the room, Antonio knew that he was not alone in his thinking. Every single angel seated at the Table of Truth was quaking in their cloak; all except for George Hollyander, who surprisingly didn't look entirely shocked to see the third brother of Olympus.

"Such a *warm* welcome," Poseidon mocked as he took in the stunned assembly. "It reminds me of why I do not venture from my Water World."

Not a soul moved or breathed for that matter.

"Could it be that I am no longer remembered . . . or *respected*?" His voice was ten times deeper than Hades', and had more bark to it than Zeus could pull off on his best day.

"Poseidon." George was the only one in the room that seemed to recall how to speak. He bowed his head ever so slightly. "How fortuitous of you to come. We were just discussing a meeting with you."

Poseidon regarded George with mild amusement. "So I have just heard."

"You may have my chair, Sea King." The Dominion Commander who had been still standing and awaiting orders from George, stepped away from the table quickly, offering his seat with an elegant bow. "I would be honored."

Poseidon made his way across the room, seeming to absorb it's every detail in a matter of moments before taking his place. More importantly, Antonio could see that he'd also noted every angel there just as quickly—himself included; and to Antonio's surprise, when their eyes had met, he realized that Poseidon knew exactly who he was. The God of the Sea missed nothing.

"Perhaps I am not as forgotten after all?" he mused as the nearby angels were visibly shaken by his close proximity.

There were so many questions Antonio wanted to ask his uncle. Hell, they were questions the *entire world* wanted to ask him! But, this was hardly the time. To actually have *Poseidon:* the God of the Sea, at the same table as him, was surreal. Even more so than finding out that Zeus was his father.

Zeus and Hades never really hid themselves from the world. One way or another, those two had always seemed to intertwine their involvement in everything. Poseidon on the other hand, was truly a God of Myth—or so Antonio had always thought—forever remaining reclusive.

To his knowledge, the Sea God had not ventured from his "Water World," since Atlantis was lost millennia ago; and that in itself prompted a plethora of questions: why had he claimed such a treasured city and where was it now? Was it laden with gold and jewels as the stories depicted? Did it really pop up from time to time as rumored? Was Megalodon real? Were there mermaids? And what about the Bermuda triangle . . .

"So many questions, Son of Zeus." Poseidon's dark eyes met Antonio's, cutting off his mental interrogation. "Perhaps your time would be better spent pondering why it is that I am here." . . . *And who it is that I will upturn the earth to find.*

That last part had been for Antonio's ears only; and a cool sickening sweat came over him. As surely as Poseidon could hear his thoughts, Antonio knew that he was also aware of his intentions regarding Evie. The question was: how?

"This meeting is not all that 'fortuitous' General." Poseidon's abruptness distracted the council from the odd exchange between he and Antonio. "You know why I have come."

If it weren't for the sudden darkening on the image the table swiftly displayed, Antonio wouldn't have been able to divert his eyes from the tension that now loomed between the two men; a hurricane was building somewhere in the Pacific—the circumference of it alone was unprecedented.

Antonio saw George's face visibly pale at the picture—as did everyone else witnessing the geological disaster in the making. He knew as well as the rest of the Angel Hierarchy that Poseidon's temper was precarious at best. If he was agitated and appeared this calm having just orchestrated the birth of a category 6 storm, what would he do if he was really angered?

"Did you truly expect me to stay away?" Poseidon's fathomless eyes bored into George's. "Did you believe that I needed an invitation to protect what is rightfully mine?"

"Olympus is *not yours*, Poseidon! You will not use these dark times as an excuse to upturn order. You were given the sea and all that dwells there. That was the bargain!"

Poseidon laughed outright. In another setting, at a jovial occasion perhaps, Poseidon's merriment would bring delight to any ear that had the privilege of listening to it. As it was . . .

"*Do not* pretend to understand me!" Poseidon roared at the Seraphim who had inadvertently challenged him. He was on his feet now, towering where he stood. "*Do not* speak to me of bargains made . . .! Your '*order*' is failing!" His eyes were solely on George now. "Your weakness is what has set this all into motion."

Antonio was utterly shocked that Poseidon would take such a vicious stance against the Commander. He could feel the energy of the room buzzing with the instinct to defend their beloved leader, yet he could also feel the fear of all there, who were afraid to move. Afraid to breathe—for fear of simply being noticed. For all, Antonio included, looked as though they wished to evaporate so as not to witness the exchange of anger that was now suffocating the room.

"Your *pathetic attempt* to capture Satan, is a *mockery* to your commands," Poseidon left no one avoiding scrutiny.

The very air around them swirled with unrest. Even the heavenly song that was carried along the wind, had become muted. For the first time since Antonio could remember, Heaven was at a stand-still.

"Capturing Satan is no longer our focus." George spoke evenly and precisely, his eyes never obverting the Sea Kings. "Retrieving *my daughter* and securing the gates of Hell, *is*."

Low murmurs began to revolve around the table.

The image of the hurricane had doubled and turned to an unnatural shade of black. Antonio could only imagine what that meant.

All eyes were on Poseidon as he leaned heavily on the table, his threat, directed solely at George; and it was clear that only *he* understood Poseidon's warning: "I *will not* stand by while all that she loves crumbles at the demon's feet."

"She is not yours to defend," George stated firmly.

"She will *always* be mine," Poseidon growled. " . . . And when you expire, she will be again. She was not meant to cross paths with you."

Antonio was as lost as the rest of the assembly, who were collectively looking from one to the other for meaning. The private battle between the Sea King and the Commander of the Divine Army was just that, private. Though Antonio knew in that instant that their rivalry ran deeper than any ocean Poseidon controlled.

"You know my mind, Commander." Poseidon pushed away from the table and moved to leave. "I will destroy *all* that threatens the Child's return." The trident pulsed, fortifying his promise.

George nodded in understanding.

"You have the support of my domain, and the strength of all that is Poseidon."

"At what cost?" The Seraphim Commander blurted out the million dollar question. There wasn't a soul there who wasn't thinking it, but no one else had dare ask: what payment would be deemed acceptable for saving the daughter of the Commander to the Divine Army from Satan, securing all of creation, and maintaining the balance of the universe. "We will not support an uprising from the sea. We will not aid you in the fight for Mount Olympus."

A lethal smile swept across Poseidon's face, promising absolute contrition would be ours.

"What a fitting name . . . I rather like the sound of it: 'The *Fight* for Mount Olympus.' He turned as if to leave then paused, still grinning; his eyes grazing over each of them before settling on Antonio. "A *worthy* campaign to be sure."

Now it was Antonio's turn to go visibly pale. Zeus was not going to like this turn of events. If Poseidon aided the Heavens in the search for Evie—or worst case, single handedly found her and safely brought her back to her father, George would feel personally beholden to the Sea King. The Divine Army would be at Poseidon's disposal, and from what Antonio had just ascertained, certain hell would befall anyone who had taken part in her capture.

Antonio hadn't even realized that Poseidon was still staring directly at him until the piercing weight of his next words struck; and they were a burden Antonio was not sure he could shoulder.

"So it begins . . . *son* of Zeus."

Midnight had come and gone and Evie had not shown. It wasn't possible . . . she was bound to him. Bound to their oath, and it was unbreakable!

Wild scenarios ran through his head. Horrific reasons that could have prevented her from coming to him—each one worse than the last, and all resulting in her demise.

Hades roared out in frustration, knowing full well that the Earth would quake because of it. He needed Evie in his arms. He needed to know that she was alive and well. He needed to know that she was safe; and from this point onward, unless she was with him, the answer would be no.

He had last seen her before the chaos had erupted at Pinehurst. Damn the pixie for botching the simplest of plans, although it had not been entirely her fault. Zeus had responded prematurely, something he was known for. Never bothering to acquire all knowledge before literally plunging into hell's path. Zeus' actions had opened the door to the "mythological world" that would no longer be deemed as myth. He had exposed all . . .

Hades pressed his fists to his temples. He could not afford the time to think about that right now. He would leave that in the hands of the One True Deity. For a masking of knowledge at this level could be achieved by no other; and as much as Hades wished to rule Olympus, he was not so arrogant to think that he would ever have such control over all of creation.

More beast than man, he paced the confines of his throne room, his breathing labored—like the caged animal that he was. He could feel it in his very bones: the balance of power was off. He was attuned to the elements enough to know that.

He could feel a stirring in the heavens . . . an upheaval that he had not known in all of his lifetime—a movement, and then a sudden stilling—as if Heaven's song had stopped—yet another impossibility. He couldn't explain it any better than that. *Something* was coming, and if Hades were an ordinary man, he might feel very afraid.

But that wasn't the whole of it. The sea was churning with turmoil. A violent pool of rage that rose and fell with a thunderous reverberation that could be felt in the Underworld. Hades had not witnessed such wrath from Poseidon since he captured Atlantis— Zeus' treasured city—sinking it to the depths and concealing it for all of time. What could have propelled Poseidon into such a state now was anyone's guess.

Though if Hades did have to guess . . . he would lay his life down that whatever was causing his brother's blood to boil with such fury, had everything to do with what was plaguing the Heavens. The two were tied. The question was: why? What did Poseidon know that he didn't?

And then he felt it: an electric pulse broke the barriers of his realm. Punching through time and space with a boom so loud that the very air around him seemed to shimmer with movement.

Hades whirled around, facing the doors to his throne room, the approaching steps growing louder and they neared. He could think of only one that would have permission to wield such power to enter . . . only one that would have the confidence to approach, though he could not imagine any reason so dire that would give him cause to tread into the Underworld.

The doors burst open.

"I see there is no need to ask, old friend . . . the Child of Light is not here either." The Archangel Samuel had entered the room with conviction, regarding Hades with sympathy.

Hades strode forward, his eyes locked with Samuel's. Had any other dare breach his realm, storm into his personal chambers, and look upon him in this way, he would kill them where they stood.

"Why are you seeking my betrothed?" he demanded.

Samuel could not have looked any more surprised. "I was not informed you had claimed her."

The four angels flanking Samuel broke protocol, looking from one to the other, but said nothing.

"Hades . . ." Samuel spoke cautiously. "You know she cannot stay with you."

Hades wanted nothing more than to choke the life from the angel, but he would not. Samuel, as he so crudely noted, was his friend once upon a time; until he was "gifted" with the task of residing over the Underworld that is. Since his command millennia ago, the two had not met—angels do not venture into the Underworld; and here, Hades had no friends.

"Why are you seeking my betrothed?" Hades growled out the question this time, no longer able to conceal his anger. Samuel was here for Evie and he wanted to know why, now!

The Archangel stood tall. "Commander Hollyander has ordered her retrieval."

All fury seemed to have deflated from Hades in an instant. Samuel's revelation meant only one thing: that if the Commander of the Divine Army had no idea where Evie was—his own daughter—no one did.

Samuel took a step closer, placing a hand on Hades' shoulder, all seriousness in his eyes and an empathy that could exist only in Heaven. "I can see that she means a great deal to you. I'm sorry my friend, but there is nowhere else left to search. I'm afraid she is gone."

Hades' eyes grew darker than any night could conjure, his demon taking nearly full control for what was to come next. "There is but one." How Satan had managed to get Evie there was beyond his comprehension, but there was no other place she could be.

"You know we must follow," Samuel warned Hades. "To whatever level of Hell you mean to travel, you have our swords. We must retrieve the Child of Light."

Hades demon regarded Samuel for the power and strength that he was, noting the other four angels' equal resolve, and raised a brow. "You cannot follow where angels fear to tread."

A look of sheer horror struck them all.

"You do not mean to imply—" Samuel couldn't even finish the thought aloud.

Hades knew the Archangel had full understanding.

Angels did not venture lightly into the Underworld, to consider entering Hell itself would be a death sentence to them; one that Hades knew they had each accepted upon embarking on this quest. But to roam below the lowest level of Hell itself . . . no. No one could trespass upon the damned soil unless they were utterly consumed by darkness; and Hades would have to give in to his demon wholly to achieve that, something he was prepared to do.

I stood there like a statue, stunned.

Nightmares wanted the Divine Army at Hades doorstep? My mind tried to wrap around the consequences of that. What would happen when they arrived and found I wasn't there?

"I do hope that was a rhetorical question," Nightmares gave me a look of disappointment as he once again eavesdropped in on my mind. "Honestly, Child of Light, can you not consider what might happen once Hades learns that you are nowhere to be found? That the worst, and by the worst I mean *me*, has befallen you?"

I thought about that. He'd go crazy. He'd tear through every inch of everywhere until he found me, leaving utter devastation in his wake.

My eyes looked from Megaera to Nightmares. "But he won't find me because he can't come here, right?"

Nightmares gave me a sympathy smile. "I said wouldn't, not couldn't."

"But you said 'only the darkest of magic and the darkest of beings' can exist here—*which* by the way, I'm neither."

"Aren't you?" Nightmares questioned. "Do you not control the gates of Hell?"

Megaera cackled from across the room.

I frowned. "I may control the gates of Hell, but I still believe in–"

"Ah, ah, ahh!" Nightmares cut me off. "Do you not suffer intolerably simply *thinking* of him?"

I could see Megaera cringing out the corner of my eye in disgust.

"That doesn't mean I'm damned," for craps' sake. "I still have a soul!" I could feel it. It was ever so slight but it was there, and it was mine.

"Yes, you *still* have a soul." Nightmares' voice turned raspy. "For now."

I stepped back a little. I didn't know what that meant and I didn't want to—and I definitely didn't need him going all beast on me! If we were truly in the land of the 'darkest of magic and the darkest of beings', I wasn't sure how long he would hold onto his fake persona. I was getting the feeling that my comfort would not be priority for long.

"Tis the witching hour."

"What?!" I looked to Megaera. "It can't be." I glanced around the room as if I was going to find a clock on the wall . . . that . . . was no longer there.

The room we had been occupying for the past several hours was vanishing before my eyes. The "safe" façade that protected me from wherever Nightmares had brought me, was crumbling.

The hearth seemed to be the only true article in the room, and I was slowly gravitating toward it.

"You asked what it is that I want from you?"

I couldn't even tear my eyes away from the cacophony of my new surroundings to give Nightmares' question any attention. I was literally petrified. I couldn't have moved to defend myself if I'd wanted to. There wasn't a remnant of mental self-preservation that could have prepared me for what the fires' shadows allowed my eyes to take in . . . I was truly and utterly horrified.

Creatures that clung to the ground, barely able to lift their heads, had become hideous, gnarled shells of what they once were. Burnt and withered. Skin and bone. Too pained, too weak to exist; they were not allowed to die and pass on. They wailed in their own self-inflicted torturous pain—yet nothing touched them. I could see it in the dark hollow of their eyes, a beseeching that I may end their suffering—eradicate them from their plagued existence.

Tears streamed down my face as I grieved for their souls.

One by one, louder and louder, their voices invaded my head––calling out to me, screaming. It was maddening!

I put my hands to my ears, trying to muffle out the cries. They knew who I was. They knew I was the key . . . They did not plead for release, they plead for abolishment; save one.

I took a step closer to it. I don't know where I found the strength or courage to move, but something pulled me. Our eyes were locked. It's mouth opened and closed like a fish out of water. I couldn't look away. It's repulsive form should have made me shield my eyes. It should have sent me screaming, but I found myself kneeling down before it. It was physically broken and battered, but it was still alive. It clung to one thread of strength: retribution.

"I see you have met Cronus."

Chapter 15

Nightmares did not just say what I thought he'd said. I hadn't heard him correctly—because if I had, and I was indeed face to face with Cronus, I was not only kneeling before what had been one of the most powerful gods—the supreme ruler of the Titans—I was in Tartarus, and *that* could not be.

I stared into the withered face of the creature that had beckoned me. Searching for any sign of truth to Nightmares' claim. I had no idea what Cronus looked like, but I could imagine that he would bear some resemblance to Zeus or Hades; I searched for that resemblance.

"Do you think I would mislead you?"

I'd turned and gave Nightmares an incredulous look. "Did you really just ask me that? Of course you would mislead me!"

"Darling, you are Satan," Megaera slunk out from the shadows, making herself known once again. If anyone could pull off goth, with a sprinkle of creepy, it was her! "You speak half-truths, or pure lies."

Nightmares eyes narrowed ever so slightly at the witch. "I speak the truth and you know it."

She shrugged her shoulder. "Perhaps you are getting weak, having spent too much time among the mortals?" She raised a challenging brow. " . . . Or perhaps you too have fallen under the Child's spell." A wicked expression flashed across her face. "Perhaps you too seek the heaven that only she can give."

Ew! She had better not be trying to hook us up. There was no way Nightmares and I would ever be an item.

He'd squared his shoulders with hers. I could see his breathing had become deeper, heavier. He was seething.

She was pushing his buttons and I didn't like it. I'd seen this with Hades a million times. I knew how to calm *his* beast . . . but there was no way I was going to or wanted to attempt that with Nightmares; though I wanted Nightmares' beast calmed more than I'd ever needed to calm Hades'. This was a whole new level of scary, and while Hades' dark side was scary, I knew it had nothing on Satan's.

"Do not question me!" His once appealing voice became raspy and deep.

I scooched back, putting myself closer to the gruesome creature on the floor, knowing my chances were greater with it than they were if Satan did indeed show himself.

The slightest of a touch settled on top of my hand. I froze—not wanting to move and draw Nightmare's attention. But most importantly, I wasn't afraid. I knew the being beside me had used what was probably the rest of its strength to reach out, and I was suddenly engulfed with visions that only the ruler of the Titans could brandish: Olympus . . . how it once was . . . it could be no other place . . .

Bright and blue—flourishing with life and color! Vast fields of vibrant green. Trees with sweeping delicate flowered vines—I could smell the fragrance of them—and laughter—it was all around. A joyous melodic harmony with butterflies larger than I had ever seen dancing from flower to flower, teasing small elegant looking creatures that ran through the tall grass chasing after them—hand and hand, frolicking; their white hair flowing behind them, exposing their pointed ears—they were Elves! They waved their free hands excitedly toward the sky. I looked upward, and I knew my own mouth had to be gaping. Angels were flying among them, waving back, smiling and blowing kisses their way. Angels were in Olympus!

The vision shifted to a temple-like structure, reminding me of ancient Greece in its glory days. Large pillars of pristine massive stonework, reached to the sky, touching the sun's rays! What I assumed were gods meandered carelessly among the gardens and fountains, greeting one another with warm smiles and affection; I could feel I was smiling too. I couldn't help it. Never had I felt such warmth.

My eyes flickered to a young man sitting by himself on a stone slab, one leg dangling and swaying back and forth. He was reading some sort of book. There was something familiar about the way he sat, thoughtful like. The way he held the book with one hand and had the other arm resting on a propped bent knee for support. The vision let me look closer just as the boy's face looked up into the light. My breath hitched. It was Hades! Quite young and wickedly handsome, maybe 15 or 16 in my thinking of years.

The boy turned his head sharply as if called and I could see that a man approached him. An older man. He was magnificent in his own right. His tall muscled frame was very Zeus like, though this man had a majesty about him that Zeus did not. A calm and regal manor. Those passing bowed their heads ever so slightly as he greeted them in kind.

Hades was running to him, a smile bright enough to rival the sun splayed across his face as he threw his arms around the man. The man hugged him close, tussling his hair in play, and I could see that Hades didn't mind it at all. The man turned slightly, and it was then that I saw a golden medallion hanging from his neck, displaying a large golden C. Cronos!

I broke contact with the creature on the floor. I turned completely toward it, our eyes locking once again before I looked to what would be his neck. A slight gleam of a golden chain caught my eyes as the fire flickered our way. With all the courage I could muster I reached out and put a hand on what I hoped was his shoulder and ever so gently lifted him. I could see that it pained him greatly and my heart broke all the more, but I had to know. There, just below his body in the charred soil beneath, lay the rest of the medallion, a golden C still attached.

I gently set him back down. His breathing was more labored and I wasn't sure how I was going to help him, but I had decided then and there that I would find a way. This was Hades' father, and I could not imagine he would ever want him to die this way.

I nodded and I knew that the Titan King understood.

"Then fulfill our bargain!" Megaera hissed, snapping me to attention and back to their conversation—completely unafraid as she continued to challenge Nightmares. "You know he comes. You know there must be a trade. It is the only way."

"What are you talking about? Who's coming?"

Nightmares head snapped in my direction, and I couldn't help but flinch. I was not looking into the eyes I thought I knew—though he tried to mask it quickly, the damage was done. I'd already caught a glimpse of who he truly was, and it terrified me.

"Hades," Megaera spat.

"What? Why would he come here?" I was on my feet. Nightmares was right. This place was for the damned, and only the darkest of souls and the darkest of magic could possibly dwell here—and like the Titans, this place wasn't for Hades. This place would eat him alive; and that was not going to happen.

Nightmares studied me for a moment before answering: "For you. He comes . . . for you."

I shook my head, not wanting his words to be true but knowing they were. If Hades thought for a blink of a moment that I was here of all places, he'd tear through the universe to get to me and I knew it.

Nightmares stood some distance away, his hands resting on the hearth stones as he gazed heavily into the flames. "I'm afraid this is the part you won't be liking."

As opposed to what? I wanted to ask. I haven't liked any part of this. But something within his surprisingly solemn demeanor told me that this "part" he now spoke of, was different.

"For you to leave Tartarus . . . Hades must be willing to make a trade."

I stared at the back of his head, dreading the answer before the question even left my lips: "What kind of trade?"

"A life for a life," Megaera interjected cheerfully.

"What?" The question came out more of a snarled warning. I could feel my demon side ready to erupt; and it wanted nothing more than to rip her smug face right off.

"If he wishes to free you from this prison," she was more than happy to clarify, " . . . he must forfeit *his life*, for yours."

"No." The word was absolute.

"It is the law," Nightmares stated as he turned abruptly. "It is binding and unbreakable."

"Then why did you bring me here?!" Though I already knew the answer—and realization was a brutal slap in the face. He'd wanted to trap Hades and he'd used me to do it. He knew Hades would come for me and that he would do whatever necessary to keep me from harm—even if it meant harming himself.

The hellish reasoning behind Nightmares' shit plan didn't matter. I didn't care to know the details of whatever he hoped to achieve by entrapping Hades. Bottom line—it wasn't happening.

"Hades will stay here, literally, over my dead body."

"Do you think you will have a choice in the matter?" he asked, in utter disbelief. "Do you think Hades would debate it with you? If there was even a remote chance that he could save the woman he loves from eternal torture, do you think he wouldn't do it—no matter the cost? You willingly entered Tartarus Evie, you are not entirely bound to its laws. You were not condemned here therefore you may leave—but only if another willingly takes your place—and Hades, will be more than willing to take your place."

"What about you, and Megaera?" I blurted. "You both entered willingly."

Nightmares laughed without mirth. "Tartarus, Child of Light, *is* my Hell." And as if to prove it, my entire surrounding exploded into a raging fiery inferno.

The shrieking screams of agony of those littering the floor, filled my head. He was burning them alive and they were too weak to escape.

"Stop!" I rushed over to Cronus' body, the fire hadn't touched him yet.

Megaera was laughing at the chaos, and I could see by the look on Nightmares' face, I was losing him.

"What do you want from me?" I screamed out above all noise, my voice reverberating off of every wall and surface; the flames dissipated instantaneously.

I looked around the room quickly, the bodies around me smoldered, but I could see that they were still alive. I wanted to vomit from the smell alone. The torture he put them through . . . Hades would not be suffering this.

"I want you to release the Titans."

"What?" I cried, truly bewildered.

"It's what you were planning to do yourself, wasn't it?" Nightmares cocked his head to the side, daring me to say otherwise—he'd been listening to my thoughts all along.

"I don't understand," and I didn't. He was just roasting them alive and now he wanted me to free them?

"I can see this would be confusing for you." He gave me a sympathetic look as he strode toward me. He reached out and before I could think to move he had my face between his hands, his thumbs quickly wiping away tears that I didn't know had been streaming. "If circumstances could only be different," he murmured, our eyes briefly locking.

"The Titans have been imprisoned here for millennia," he revealed matter-of-factly as he stepped away from me, severing all contact and shifting cryptic gears. "They long for freedom, and revenge—we will grant them this; so long as they take Mount Olympus back and destroy the Heavens."

My mouth had to be gaping. "They'll never do it." I knew they would want their home back, and if it were me, I'd be out for Zeus' blood too, but from what I'd just seen through Cronus' vision . . . the Titans and the Angels coexisted in harmony. If that was part of the deal, they'd never take it.

"Do not underestimate the torture they have endured Child of Light. Do not so freely dismiss their resolve for vengeance. They have longed for freedom above all else, and those that have been strong enough to survive will have it."

"The angels didn't cause this!" I defended, motioning around me to the dying.

I knew Nightmares was baiting them with an impossible choice—it's what Satan does, and he was using me to pave their way to destruction.

"You may get them to take back Olympus, but they will not destroy the Heavens for you." I tried to believe my own words. I had to believe that old ties would prevail.

"They will if they do not wish to return."

And there it was: the lethal bargain to be made by all who wished to pass through the gates—a vow cemented with a ticket straight back to Tartarus if they failed—and knowing Satan, he would guarantee that they did. He would not want them roaming freely to combat him. He was using them to eliminate the Olympians. He wouldn't need their help in destroying the Heavens once that was done, his demons alone could handle that. It would be a fool's bargain. He would never truly free them . . . surely they knew that.

Nightmares stepped close once again, invading all personal space to lean in toward my ear; I held my ground. "For a taste of freedom and relief," he whispered across my skin, causing me to shiver, " . . . they will do anything." He stepped back, allowing that sober thought to resonate. "And so will you."

Hades had made his way through the trenches and bowels of Hell to the gates of Tartarus. A place he was sworn and bound by oath to never enter. He knew Zeus and Poseidon were fully aware of his whereabouts, and he knew that the moment he stepped onto the forbidden soil, they would feel it.

His inner demon didn't care about the consequences of bargains made, and that was just fine with Hades. His sole objective was to locate Evie and remove her from this prison before any irreparable damage has been done; and for the sake of all, that had better be the case.

He was no fool. He knew the laws of this place. Drafted by Zeus himself and signed with the blood of the three Olympian brothers to ensure that none of the Titans would ever escape, the moment he entered Tartarus, he would be trapped there unless someone foolishly took his place; and there wasn't a soul who would ever do that. But he was Hades, Lord of the Underworld, and it came with certain privileges. Tartarus was damned soil, and very few could trespass upon it with the assurance of leaving on their own accord.

He took in a deep breath, steeling himself. He knew that only his demon—his salvation that had allowed him to mentally and physically withstand the retched task of keeping the Underworld—would be strong enough to endure the torturous brutalities of Tartarus; and he would have to give into him fully to do it. Something he had never done, and as far as Hades knew, there would be no recovering from it. Giving into his demon would mean becoming the beast he detested most. It meant losing what was left of *him*—a necessity if he was going to free Evie. He knew his demon would recognize her, that it craved the light that only she could give. The light that even now it could feel beyond its reach. The light that it would do whatever necessary to protect; and it was this comfort alone that allowed Hades to surrender wholly.

He burst through the iron barrier, having no trouble obliterating the obstruction that blocked the path between he and his light.

He could feel her . . . the warmth of her soul beckoned him onward with the promise of stepping into glory; and he craved it as much as Hades craved her.

He knew that Hades loved this girl—as much as he had ever loved anything—a concept that was entirely foreign to him; though he tried to compare it to the adoration *he* felt, toward what was the closest thing to Heaven he had ever, or would ever, behold.

He would not hurt her. It wasn't in his nature to be gentle, but he knew that if he were anything but, he would crush her—mentally and physically.

She had not seen him in this form—a consideration he would not take in had it been any other, but that could not be helped now. Tartarus was not for the weak, and *he* was anything but. *Here* he rivaled Satan, and he knew the beast could feel his impending approach.

He rushed forward, moving quickly through the dark and vial surroundings—unafraid of what was ahead. He drew strength from the dark energy and relished in it. He did not fear this place as others did. He'd feed off of whatever he must to sustain . . . Tartarus would be his domain, and he would destroy anything that dare step in-between he and his light. *Satan,* would die this day . . .

"Never in all my days did I imagine myself once again walking these halls." Poseidon couldn't help but marvel at the ornate surroundings, though one wouldn't know it to look at him. He feigned disinterest like no other, and he detested Zeus even more. He strolled side by side down the stone corridor with his brother. "You have rotted away our heritage."

"I do not call you here to lament the Olympus of old," Zeus countered. "That time is dead. These are the glory days and Olympus stands brighter than ever!"

Poseidon scoffed as he looked to the gardens that had lost their luster in his opinion. "Not so dead, brother. Hades crosses the barrier as we speak."

Zeus looked visibly affronted. "Yes. He broke the blood oath with no regard. The foolish boy has given his demon complete control." Zeus couldn't have displayed any more disgust for Hades behavior than he did at this very moment.

"He is no fool," Poseidon countered firmly. "He is an Olympian—a high god—the Lord of the Underworld!"

"I am fully aware of *who* Hades is," Zeus dismissed.

"He has shouldered his responsibility despite his youth," Poseidon defended. "He is formidable, Zeus, though you may not wish to admit it; and perhaps more than that he is a man, and he is in love."

"That is a dangerous combination," Zeus gritted out. "A man . . . he is still but a child. A man would have embraced Persephone for the gift that she was."

Poseidon gaped at Zeus' still offended ego. "You unleashed a tigress upon a cub. Hades was not equipped for such battles of the mind. The relationship was doomed before it began."

"In love," Zeus mocked. " . . . For all the good it will do him now. He is but a prisoner of his own device."

Poseidon was more astute than Zeus. He understood why Hades had given into his demon—and although risky, it was brilliant. *Hades* was bound to the laws of Tartarus, but his demon was not. His demon could come and go as it pleased; and Poseidon knew Hades' demon would not be leaving Tartarus without the girl—not ever—and Poseidon couldn't be more happy about that. He did not relish having to explain to her mother her whereabouts, and he detested even more having to admit that *he* could not personally retrieve her. The very idea that he had limits . . . was unacceptable.

"You do realize what this means," Zeus spoke, drawing Poseidon from his reverie. "There *will be* another Olympian war; much life will be lost."

Poseidon nodded his head solemnly. He'd known from the moment he'd entered the Heavens to meet with the high council that this was coming—and if truth be known, he did not welcome it. He did not wish to see any more blood loss.

He'd known Satan's ambitions, he just hadn't puzzled in Evie's place in all of this. He hadn't dreamed she would be used as the vessel to release this chaos. He hadn't dreamed that all Satan desired would ever be in his reach.

This war would be far more dire than the last—the survival of the Heavens depended on it. . . . And if the One True Deity himself did not intervene, the universe as they knew it would collapse; for the Titans and the Olympians could not coexist. . . . And Satan . . . could never be allowed to rule supreme.

Poseidon sighed heavily. "I suggest you humble yourself and ready for battle, brother. We will need a great deal more than the sky and water if we are to defeat Satan, *and* the Titans. We will need the Angels; and we will need Hades."

Chapter 16

Nothing could have ever prepared me for the impossible choices I would have to make from the moment I was dropped off at Pinehurst. There were no self-defense classes, spells, or parental heart to hearts that could have made any of this easier for me to accept or understand.

I took stock of what I knew, and it boiled down to me: I was the Child of Light. The chosen one charged with keeping the gates of Hell. I was the only one standing in between Satan and the loss of Heaven and Earth. I was the wall that was to keep evil at bay. I was the light that the One True Deity depended on; and right now, most importantly . . . I was the only one that could free Hades from this curse.

We heard him coming long before he'd broken through the doorway. His labored breathing giving the illusion that a gigantic bull was heading our way, but it was so much worse than that . . .

The force of the barrier breaking sent me flying back—beyond Cronus and well beyond the fires light.

I could see Megaera not too far away from me, emerging from the debris. She too had been cast into the air.

Our eyes met and we both shared a moment of recognized fear—but not Nightmares. No. Nightmares held his ground; and if it weren't for the abrupt spark in the fires light, I'd have never seen the flicker of surprise that touched his face when what was left of Hades came crashing through, towering, nearly twice his size.

His eyes, having taken in his surroundings the moment he had entered the room, had zeroed in on me. He roared out in fury—the reverberation causing bits of Earth and rock to fall from above.

I crouched, attempting to cover my head as I slowly rose to my feet.

Hades, if I could even call him that anymore, had become a monstrous mass of protruding muscle, his physical form bearing an infinitesimal resemblance to who he once was. If it weren't for the violet eyes that I had looked so long into nearly every night, I would not have recognized him.

"Tread softly Child of Light. *That* is not Hades."

I looked to Megaera, surprised that she even cared to throw me a warning. But by the expression on her face, I could see that she was truly afraid; she slunk back further into the shadows.

The abrupt outburst of misplaced laughter snapped me to attention, though when I turned, Nightmares was not smiling.

"He was a *fool* to have given into you," he rasped. "She is not yours to take!" His own body seemed to grow as he stepped in between us, his fingers already elongated.

My heart pounded to the point of deafening. I was frozen where I stood. Nightmares was squared off with what I had just realized was Hades' demon; it's eyes met mine.

I knew that if it so much as made a move toward me, Satan in all his terrifying glory would materialize. I also knew that if there was even the slightest hint of Hades' left within him, there was no way he was leaving without me.

I could feel tears streaming down my face. He couldn't be gone. He just couldn't. My heart broke a hundred different ways thinking that he'd given his life to save mine.

The room suddenly became an explosive blaze, a ring of fire encircled us. Nightmares had blocked off all paths of escape.

"Hades!" I called out to the demon, desperate. Hoping that *my Hades* would somehow emerge.

The creature's eyes flickered for the barest of moments from Nightmares to me, and I knew in that instant that Hades was still in there. As small a part of him as it may be, he was there, and he would not suffer this life.

"Hades is no more," Nightmares snarled. "His *claim* is forfeit. You want her," he challenged the demon. " . . . *Come* and get her!"

There was no time . . . Hades' demon had already advanced when I dropped to my knees, channeling my strength as I drew in the darkness.

Hades tumbled along the soft grass, rolling down a small hill until landing onto his back. He looked up into a cloudless sky, feeling the bright sun kiss at his face. He bolted upright.

He did not recognize his whereabouts. The last thing he remembered was standing outside the gates of Tartarus and giving into his demon. How had he gotten here? . . . And how was he himself again?

As if an ominous premonition struck him, revealing all, Hades was suddenly engulfed with what could be none other than his demon's memories—something that had never occurred before: he charged Satan, unafraid and prepared to violently collide with the beast who had at long last shed the façade of the youthful boy he portrayed.

He leapt at him, and was instead embraced with a twisting darkness that wrapped itself around him, relentlessly pulling him deeper into an abyss.

"*Forgive me!*" Was the strangled sob that echoed through his very bones as the darkness struck light.

"No. Evie . . .!" Sheer panic gripped him as he turned and scrambled back up to the top of the hill. He stood there, frantic, looking out over a vast field of grass, the wind rustling the blades.

Hades dropped to his knees, his thoughts spinning. He screamed out into the nothingness as he let his body collapse to the Earth; the gate was gone, and there was no way back to her.

"No . . . Evie, no . . ." He cried. Grieving at the incomprehensible loss. Evie had sacrificed her *soul* for him. She had taken his place in all things so that he would be free. She had released him through the gates of Hell—forever separating his ties to the Underworld.

He could feel the freedom of it now. The weightless existence he once knew. The peace of only being Hades: Son of Cronus; and he would give it all up to spare her even one second of the torture he knew she would endure.

"Punish me!" he yelled out to the heavens, sobbing. "Not her. Me . . ."

"Master?"

Hades whirled around, scooching back in the process. His blurred eyes meeting the tiniest of faces—but a face he knew all too well.

"How did you find me?"

The pixie bravely offered him a sympathetic smile. She extended her hand, revealing a small key; the brilliant gold of it gleamed in the light.

Hades regarded her a moment before reaching out and taking it. His breath caught. There, etched in the shaft, was a trident. He looked back to Havoc, knowing now that Poseidon had sent her; he knew where this key led.

She grinned wickedly. "I've always wanted to go to the City of Gold."

Hades looked back to the key held tight in his hand. His heart was unbearably heavy. Aside from the involuntary movement of his thumb tracing over the delicate image, he could not will himself the strength to move.

The pixie placed her tiny hands atop his, the vast difference in size was startling, he looked back up. Her eyes glistened with moisture—a very un-pixieish thing.

"She was my friend too. I will help you get her back."

"We both will!"

Hades turned to see Chaos standing off to the side. His expression resolved, yet respectful, he bowed his head.

Hades knew that the pixie would not let Havoc go on this quest without him. He knew that Chaos loved Havoc, and he knew that Chaos *cared* for Evie; Havoc was beaming at the sight of him.

She turned back toward Hades with what he knew was renewed vigor. "Shall we?" she coaxed.

If there was even the slightest chance in saving Evie, this was it. She had freed him from his curse, and on his life, he would repay the favor.

"We're going to need some help." A concept entirely foreign to Hades. "Either of you know how to get to Ireland?"

Havoc clapped her hands excitedly. "I thought you'd never ask."

Pinehurst Book 4: The Fight For Mount Olympus . . .

BIOGRAPHY

Nicole Grane currently lives in Washington State with her family. As a lover of mythology and folklore, she enjoys using the Pinehurst series as a means to share her inspiration and findings with her readers; opening them up to worlds built off ancient beliefs. Creating a fanciful tale from much research and study, has been a wonderous journey that she is happy to say isn't over! Nicole is obtaining her Bachelor's degree in Ancient History and Classical Archaeology to further her knowledge and to acquire unique material that she may incorporate into her writing.